A SCHOOL FOR DRAGONS

A SCHOOL FOR DRAGONS

Amy Wolf

RED EMPRESS
PUBLISHING

A School for Dragons
Published by Red Empress Publishing
ISBN: 978-0-9977729-6-8
www.redempresspublishing.com

Copyright © Amy Wolf 2017

Cover Design by Cherith Vaughan
www.empressauthorsolutions.com

Interior Art and Map by Alex McVey

To the memories of Mark Bourne, Jay Lake, and Lucius Shepard, and to the indomitable Pat Cadigan

Special Acknowledgments
Cynthia Ward
R.E. (Rachel) Carr
Celia Whittome, for her Latin translations

Cavernis

Lumen

Jötunheim

Dentes Mtns

Mons Gelido

Lake
Detritus

Artorius
Cave

The Plat

High Desert

Ash

The Saints
Woods

Georgia

Flavius River

Cavernis

Quad

Brazzaland

The
Castle

Pau'Au

Ur-El-Dal

Mons
Influuent

"But it is one thing to read about dragons and another to meet them."
~ Ursula K. Le Guin, *A Wizard of Earthsea*

Prologue

An Unexpected Discovery

Seven years ago...

"Whoa, boy, whoa!" Mattie laughed, reining her pony to a halt.

The Griffith Park trails were pretty. It was spring, so there were rough patches of grass as opposed to the normal dirt. Once you left the dark, narrow tunnel that took you under the street, the weather was practically mild and there was even a breeze.

Mattie really loved horses, so much that her usually thrifty mom offered to pay for lessons, which was beyond awesome since Mattie got to ride Spitfire anytime she wanted. It was almost like owning her own horse.

She loved everything about riding: the sheer joy of loping, the careful setting of tack. Even the dusky smell of her pony's spotted hide. This was her greatest pleasure, and she wouldn't trade it for anything—not even her own tortoise!

From her saddle, Mattie smiled, then became serious. She was riding past Forest Lawn Cemetery, where flowers dotted some graves and scattered mourners knelt. *How horrible to be dead!* she thought. You couldn't even feel the breeze...

Spitfire's ears shot up—his senses were much sharper than hers. He gave a low whinny, then pulled back on the bit. She turned and saw what he saw: a deer—a full-grown buck—with fat eight-point antlers and a white tail tipped in black. Mattie knew, proudly, that he was a mule deer.

"Hello, Mr. Buck," she called. "Where's the rest of your family?"

The deer raised his head from grazing and stared at her with dark eyes. Being native to the park, he must have been used to people. Still, he was careful. He reluctantly gave up his feast, slipping back behind thick-grown sycamores. Before he vanished from view, he lowered his antlered head.

"Wow." Mattie was so caught up in his beauty she almost didn't notice the strange object in its place—an egg, twenty times the size of the ones in her fridge that was *blue* with light streaming through its jagged cracks!

Mattie dismounted and dropped her reins. She might have been only ten, but she knew enough to realize that deer *don't* lay eggs. She had once read in a book that ostriches lay huge ones, but what would one be doing here? Unless it had escaped from the L.A. Zoo next door...

Curious, Mattie strode forward in her black Western boots. The egg's light brightened, as if it were electric! The cracks widened with a sound like breaking glass until something alive popped out.

"Oh my gosh!" Mattie cried, falling to her knees. Spitfire snorted in fear.

She was facing a newborn *dragon.* Though covered in goo, which coated its wings, tail, and head, there was no doubt in Mattie's mind that she was looking at a dragon. She rose shakily, brushing dirt from the knees of her jeans. Approaching the hatchling slowly, she imagined it would soon be all flames and claws thanks to Hollywood movies.

"Hey there," she cooed. "Did your mom run away from the zoo?" Did the zoo even *have* dragons?

It gave a little peep, not much louder than a chick's. It was only about a foot long, its scales a dullish gray.

"You're a dragon, right? Are you a boy or a girl?"

It flapped its tiny wings, ridding them of the goo. Then it tried to stand, but fell back, peeping in anger. Mattie, knowing her lizards, looked closely at the base of its tail.

"I see that you're a boy."

The dragon flicked out its tongue—forked, of course—and started to clean himself. That's when Mattie noticed it only had two legs.

"Oh, poor thing!" she said.

The baby had front claws with black manicured pointed nails, but in back there was only his tail, swatting in tandem with Spitfire's.

Not wanting to make him feel bad, Mattie said nothing more. If the dragon was aware of his loss, he gave no obvious sign.

After his grooming was done, he lazily darted his tongue, snagging some nearby flies. Mattie saw that his teeth were grooved just like a shark's.

"So, are you a reptile or a bird? Are you cold or warm-blooded?" She stood tall, priding herself on her knowledge.

"Neecck!" said the dragon. He happily spread his batlike wings and landed on her shoulder.

"Whoa!" Mattie's whole body shook. She was grateful that he was polite, not raking her with his nails.

"What should I call you?" she asked, bundling him into the folds of her shirt.

17

"Rrrrrggh!" he answered, his response muted by cotton.

"That's a silly name."

She kissed to Spitfire and swung onto his back, surprised that he hadn't been spooked. He seemed perfectly calm around her adopted friend.

"I'm going to call you Toutles, since I once went to a place named that."

She recalled the long car trip to Washington, when Mom and Dad were still together. How they'd all laughed and joked! They'd marveled at Mount St. Helens and the felled trees around it. That had been a whole two years ago.

Mattie rode back to the barn where she removed Spitfire's tack and let him into his stall. As she fed him some carrots, she was careful with her precious cargo.

"Bye, pony!"

Mattie walked the short distance home as Toutles cuddled into her chest. The dragon was a good traveler and hummed softly to himself.

"I hope my mom lets me keep you."

Toutles let out a sharp whistle. He seemed confident that she would.

Mattie ran into her apartment. It was Sunday, and Mom was sprawled on the couch, trying to relax. As always, she looked tired.

"Mom! Mom!" Mattie shouted. "Look what I found!"

She unveiled the tiny dragon, his wings now folded neatly.

"Oh, honey, not another stray."

Mom closed her eyes. Mattie had so far brought home a bird, three cats, and a puppy. Their home was starting to look like Dr. Doolittle's parlor.

"What is it this time?" Mom buried her head into a flowery cushion.

"It's a dragon!"

Mom smiled. She opened one eye to examine Toutles.

"Oh, one of those Komodo things." She turned back into the couch, then wheeled around. "Wait a minute! Aren't they deadly? Like, one tried to take off Sharon Stone's ex-husband's foot?"

Mattie shrugged. She didn't know who Sharon Stone was.

Mom sighed. "It better not bite! Where did you find it?"

"In the park. It hatched from a ginormous blue egg!"

Toutles lifted his wedge-shaped head, the small spikes atop his skull flopping to the side.

"Braaach!" he said.

"Well, don't you think you should return it? I'm sure it misses its mother. Think how *you* would feel."

"But, Mom, no one else was around. He's mine now and his name is Toutles. Please let me keep him! *Please!*"

No one can plead as prettily as a ten-year-old girl on a mission, and Mattie was more single-minded than Jane Goodall in the bush.

"Ughhhhh..." Mom groaned. "All right, but only for now. And put him in a cage—in *your* room. I don't know what dragon poop looks like, but I don't want it on my carpet."

"Thanks, Mom! Thanks!" Mattie ran up to her, planting a kiss on her forehead. "You're the best mom ever!"

Mom nodded wearily. She was old enough to know that there were two kinds of love: one based on favors and one rooted in genuine feeling.

"Use the cage from the crazy cat," Mom said.

"Okay," Mattie yelled as she bounded off to her room.

One cat Mattie brought home had bitten and clawed everyone. She'd finally been adopted by the cat lady upstairs.

Mattie skipped into her room, Toutles bundled in her arms. She set him on her twin bed, where he surveyed his surroundings. Her wildlife poster and miniature Breyer horses really seemed to intrigue him.

"One sec, Toutles."

She ran out to get the cage from a closet, plus newspaper to line the bottom. She rinsed and filled his water bowl, then stood before the fridge and wondered, *What do dragons eat?* She tried putting milk in her old doll's bottle. This was met with an upturned snout. Next, she filled his food bowl with her dog's Kibbles N' Bits.

"C'mon, Toutles. Good boy!" Mattie tried to coax him into the cage, holding up a Kibble. Or was it a Bit?

He looked beyond disgusted. He opened his mouth with its pointed teeth and said, "Brrrrrp!"

"Please. You have to eat."

Mattie felt maternal concern. She tried an age-old ploy. Snapping up a bath towel, she threw it over Toutles, then released him inside the cage, slamming and locking the door.

Toutles looked around amazed, whipping his head back and forth. Mattie noticed a strange change. His pupils, which had been blue and round, became vertical slits, as if he were a cobra. He stuck out his forked tongue, hissing like a radiator.

"I'm sorry, Toutles. I know, being in a cage sucks."

He looked down and gave a sniffle. Then, he actually started to sob! The scales of his small chest heaved as he whimpered and shook.

20

"Okay, I'll take you out. Just don't tell Mom."

She unlatched the cage door and freed him. His pupils turned back to normal. He headed right for her, settling into her lap. There, he seemed content, for he curled into a scaly ball. It was then that Mattie learned baby dragons can snore!

Over the next few days, she found out what dragons eat. Toutles devoured some Chinese take-out, then showed a real taste for tacos. Not the fake kind—but street tacos from the truck, *asada* and *pollo* and *carnitas*. He disdained soda, preferring bottled water, and revealed a real fondness for prime rib au jus.

"You're a strange one," Mattie told him as he nestled into her lap while she read from *Harry Potter*. He seemed to get very excited during the Triwizard tourney, though he frequently snorted. One time, he even blew white smoke through his nostrils!

"No, Toutles, no! No fire. You want Mom to have kittens?"

Toutles shot her a queer look. He pointed a small black nail at the pages of their open book.

"Oh, I get it." She leafed forward a chapter, making sure to skip any parts that mentioned his own kind. Who could have ever guessed that dragons could be so sensitive?

O n weekdays, when Mattie was at school, she could barely sit still. After the last bell rang, she ran to catch her carpool, bouncing up and down until she could finally get home.

"Ants in your pants?" Mrs. Spees asked.

"Mattie, settle down," Mom ordered.

It was hard to focus on fractions when you had a dragon in your room! Still, Mattie tried, though her thoughts were mainly with Toutles.

After their first week together, he'd convinced her that he was as smart as she was. He loved for her to read to him and really seemed to listen. When Dobby died, he cried. He could also make his wishes clear, with crossed arms or a toothy smile and front claws thrown in the air.

When she introduced him to Felicia, her rescue dog from the pound, he was so glad to have a friend that he did a happy dance! One day when Mattie came home, she was cradled in his arms and he was gently humming to her. Felicia, half-Chihuahua and fully hyper, seemed content to lie still for once.

"How I wish you could talk," Mattie told him at least ten times a day. Toutles would frown and sadly point to his throat. Mattie understood. For now, their exchange was only one-way.

On his third Sunday with her, she took Toutles out for a walk by the edge of her complex's pool. It was of course sunny, and what Mom called "wannabes" were laying by the water in tiny swimsuits.

"Hey Mattie," Mr. Gold called. He was an elderly man who lived with his grandkids downstairs.

"Hi, Mr. Gold."

"Whatcha got there—some kind of iguana?" He dipped his chili-cheese fries into a cup of ketchup.

"He's a dragon, Mr. Gold."

"Sure. The kids love *Animal Planet*. From the Komodo Islands, right?"

"Yes, *sir*." As Mattie lied, she found herself getting louder to make her words more believable.

"Aren't they vicious?"

"Oh no, Mr. Gold! Toutles is sweeter than Felicia."

"Well, he's a cute little thing. Now. Hope he doesn't get too big. There's a twenty-pound pet limit here."

"Oh." Mattie moved away quickly, hoping Toutles hadn't heard. But he was far more interested by her neighbor's red-tipped fries.

Mattie pulled him away, using Felicia's leash. In the space of just two weeks, he'd put on a lot of weight, about fifty pounds. This could be a problem, or "issue," as Mom said her bosses called it.

Only Mom, Mr. Gold, and Mattie knew that Toutles lived in the building. She wanted to tell her friends, but managed to keep quiet. Once they got a look at Toutles, they would know he was no "Komodo" dragon. He had *wings,* for Pete's sake! Old people could be so dense.

Toutles continued to grow. And grow. At one month, he was a quarter the size of Spitfire; at two, he was equal to half the pony. Cleaning his poop and keeping him fed was almost a full-time job. Yet as the dragon grew, Mattie felt the two of them grow closer.

They read *Eragon* together and watched *Reign of Fire* and *Dragonheart.* Toutles seemed shocked at the savage portrayal of his species. He watched the films with folded arms, shaking his now-blue head. In fact, all his scales had turned deep blue, which was more than fine with Mattie since that was her favorite color!

As spring gave way to summer, she found he was her best companion. When she came home from school upset because some boy had called her "Zoo Girl," Toutles put an arm around her, making a soothing sound. When *he* grew restless at being confined, she would take him out at night to walk the edge of the pool. It was really a perfect friendship, and all thoughts of Dad in New York faded from Mattie's mind.

Her whole world consisted of Toutles. She daydreamed that together they would live in a magic kingdom and fly away to the sun. It was so rare to find a friend who truly understood her, who didn't point out her faults, or leave when she was bratty. Toutles was that kind of friend, but Mattie didn't know then that nothing in life lasts forever.

As usual, it was an adult who ruined everything. And, as usual, that adult took the form of a parent.

So far, Mattie had kept Mom away by cleaning her room every day and shushing Toutles' sounds. Still, Mom was a mom, and she staged a surprise visit one weekend.

"*No!*" she shouted, looking like she'd just spotted her boss. On the sagging bed sat Toutles, now over three feet tall.

"Mrrrrm!" he roared upon seeing her.

"*Mattie!* Why didn't you tell me your pet was the size of Godzilla?"

"Um—"

Mom mumbled to herself. "My fault. Too much stress at work."

"It's okay, Mom. Toutles is good. He likes to read about Pern and dip his tail in the pool."

"Aiiieee!" Mom cried, like a movie villager running from dragons. "Do you want to get us thrown out? I could barely get into this place as is! This, this...*lizard* has got to go!"

"But, Mom—"

"No buts. Take him across to the zoo. They have people."

"But, Mom, he's not a pet—he's my friend." Mattie's eyes filled with tears.

"I'm sure. He's also huge, like he could destroy Tokyo. Get that thing out of my house or I'm calling 9-1-1."

Mattie knew her mom well enough to realize when begging was useless. Mom stood and watched as she slipped Felicia's leash, which was now ridiculously tiny, into Toutles' collar, one of Dad's old leather belts.

Mom backed off as Toutles rose from the bed, sliding sideways through the door. He waved a claw at her sadly as he and Mattie left.

Toutles was too heavy for the elevator, so Mattie took the stairs. Under the summer sun, they both walked down the block, heads drooping. A rider on horseback stared and fled, though his mount stayed strangely calm.

"I'm not taking you to the zoo," Mattie hissed, as fierce as any reptile. They passed the Circle K barn on the corner, went over a rickety bridge, and then went through a cool, dark tunnel until they emerged in the park. There, they treaded the dusty trail, trudging uphill by Forest Lawn.

"Here." Mattie took off Toutles' collar, freeing him from restraint. He looked sad as they stood on the spot where the egg had hatched only three months before.

"Run, Toutles. Don't let them find you. They'll just put you in a cage." Mattie went up to her friend, wrapping her arms around his blue belly. It was cool to the touch.

"Neeckkk," Toutles cried mournfully.

"I know." Mattie was sobbing now, her tears coating smooth scales. Toutles sighed with a force that shook his delicate wings.

"Goodbye," she whispered. "I'll miss you, I'll never forget you."

"Ahhhhhh," Toutles moaned. He bent and licked her face for what they both thought was the last time. Then he raised his head as if hearing a silent call. Gently placing Mattie to the side, he tensed, putting both claws on the ground. Loping forward with the aid of his tail, he crashed over the dirt until he hit an invisible barrier. On contact, the wall shimmered with waves, each of which swallowed a part of Toutles. Before he disappeared, he looked back at Mattie once, then was gone.

Chapter One

Trouble in L.A.

Present day...

Mattie couldn't remember buzzing herself in, unlocking the front door, or finding her way to her room, but she snapped to attention when Mom came in, her thin figure framed in the doorway, her head tilted quizzically. The first words out of Mom's mouth didn't seem to make much sense.

"Mattie, you're upside down," she said.

Through a haze, she realized that her head was at the foot of the bed while her feet were on the pillow.

"That's true, actually," Mattie replied.

"How was the party?" Mom asked.

Mom had finally let her go—reluctantly. Now as she got closer, she could clearly sniff the evidence.

"Don't answer. I can tell." She must have looked disapproving, since she put her hands on her hips. "Mattie, I haven't said much lately, but I don't like the way you're going."

"And wha' is tha'?" Mattie drawled.

Mattie's words, though slurred, were still tipped with sarcasm. She was seventeen now and the knack came naturally.

"*Down.*" Mom's voice was worn and scratchy. It was a weeknight, and she was tired. Tired from the contract jobs she worked to make rent on this tiny apartment and keep her daughter in boots, jeans, and smartphone equipped.

"I don't like your new group of friends. Mrs. Rodriquez says that one of the girls is pregnant and the boys are nothing but trouble."

"I think ther' a connec'ion—"

"I don't care. Let them worry about themselves. I am worried about *you*," Mom said.

Mattie couldn't see too well, but she could imagine Mom's expression: a downward turn of frustration. "It's okay."

"No." Mom stood over her like her own conscience made flesh. "It's not."

Mattie sighed, her breath nearly visible. But Mom wasn't done.

"You used to be so sweet. So caring—to people *and* to animals. Remember that lizard you found? And the bird with the broken wing?"

"Petey."

"You were going to work at a zoo and you used to study so hard."

"I've got new prio—prior—t—tt—"

"Like ditching every day? I am *so* tired of hearing from the vice principal."

"Miss B.? She jus' an old ax. Battle. Ax—"

"Well, her blade is sharp enough to notice you skipping class. And your grades are suffering. You used to be 4.0."

"Peopl' change." Mattie nodded at the seeming wisdom of her words.

"You think I'm going to stand here while your life goes down the drain? And tonight—actually getting *drunk*!"

"Whe' I eighteen—" Mattie whispered.

"I know, freedom awaits. In the meantime, you are so grounded. One week. I catch you sneaking out that front door, and you're going to live with your Dad. In. The. *Snow*."

Mattie tried to roll her eyes. It hurt. She thought she saw Mom purse her lips.

"I have tried to let him know what is going on with you. But he's too obsessed to listen."

Mattie wanted to argue—to say, *No, that isn't true!* But it was. Her dad was so engrossed in whatever he was doing in Manhattan that he didn't remember her birthday. She would hear mom on the phone reminding him.

"Fine," Mattie spat. If only mom had shown more patience—hadn't always fought!—she and dad would've never split. Mattie knew—as much as she knew anything—that it was all her mom's fault.

"*I hate you!*" she yelled.

"*Two* weeks."

Mom walked to the doorway and stood there, but to Mattie's eyes, she was six Moms, and floated above the carpet.

"I just can't understand how you've turned into Regan from *The Exorcist*."

Mattie plumbed her vodka-soaked brain for a snappy reply. "At least I not spitting pea soup!"

Mom just shook her head as she turned and shut the door.

Chapter Two

Transported

The next morning, Mattie woke to the sound of hammers, like Keebler elves inside her head.

"Quit it!" she yelled, sitting up. She was still upside down on her bed, but that didn't last. She sprinted into the bathroom, barely making it before paying homage to the Porcelain God. Again. And again.

She staggered back to her bed and switched on the TV. Some crazy old movie was playing about the Pied Piper. Every time he trilled a note, it burst right through her brain.

"Uggghhh," she groaned, feeling sicker than she ever had. This was worse than getting the flu. Worse than when she was two and had sat down on an escalator—her tush still bore the scars. Why had she let Lana convince her to try something called a "Screwdriver"?

Sometime around mid-morning, Mom came in to check on her. She must have stayed home from work.

"Do you want some chicken soup?" That was Mom's cure for everything, including broken bones.

"Ugggghhhhh." The only taste in Mattie's mouth was the lingering one of orange juice.

"I'll take that as a no."

Mom suppressed a smile before gingerly shutting the door. Mattie couldn't believe it. It was almost like parents *wanted* their kids to suffer! They actually enjoyed it!

Mattie touched her throbbing head and tried to think of the future, one beyond high school parties. From where she sat, it looked pretty bleak. Why bother going to college only to emerge thousands of dollars in debt when there were no jobs anyway? Why bother saving the world—or its wildlife anyway—when corporate greed was doing its best to destroy it? These were the thoughts that oppressed her as she dressed and tried to get ready for school. Being Generation Z really meant that you were last.

Pico Pico High sucked, as usual. Peter—the guy she liked—was with some other girl, and her new friends Lana and Lupe were fighting over some guy. In history class, Mr. Lewis droned on about the Revolution, giving her the urge to start one.

Her next class, Algebra II, went on—and on—with its quadratic equations and endless "find x's". Couldn't they mix it up a little, with a "q" or even a "w"? Why must it *always* be "x" and "y"?

Thankfully, the bell rang with an elderly clang and Mattie shuffled out. She thought she'd done all right on a pop quiz. She found the best student in the class, David Wang, by his locker.

"Yo, David, you get a hundred like always?"

"Yes. Thank you." He grinned, an armful of books practically pulling him to the ground.

"Can you say, 'STEM Nerd'?" Mattie asked, in her best snarky Lana impression.

"Um—"

"Guess what, David? You're condemned to a life of coding, just like my parents!"

"Actually, I hope to become a particle physicist." He gave her a little smile.

"Oh, great, that's even better—Nerd Squared!"

Behind David, Mattie spotted Lupe, who gave her a big thumbs up.

"Okay, nerd, don't trip on your *quadrilateral* on the way out!"

Lupe was practically busting a gut. This was funny, right? This is what passed for "high" high school humor. David looked hurt as he opened his locker and Lupe shoved him aside.

"Good one, sis! Put Bruce Lee in his place!"

"He's dead," Mattie said, already feeling bad for her treatment of David.

"Whatever."

Mattie looked around for him, but he was gone. She sighed. "I can't stand the thought of P.E. and batty old Miss Evans. Wanna cut and catch a movie?"

"Like to, sis, but I got a hot date under the bleachers. Later."

Mattie nodded, walking across the quad and slumping out the Pico gate. Students came and went all day, according to their schedules, so the coach who was stationed as a guard didn't ask for a pass. She crossed the street at the light, catching the Orange Line east. There was no such thing as a school bus, not at "community charter" Pico. Formerly the biggest school in the L.A. School District, it was also one of its worst.

Mattie rode into NoHo, walking to the subway station. She took the Red Line two stops into Hollywood proper. Lovely, as always. Crazies, addicts, runaways—all crowding the sidewalk along with bemused tourists. Welcome to the Land of Tinsel!

She walked west from Vine and Sunset onto Hollywood Boulevard. For once, she hoped she wouldn't be hassled. To her right was the Dolby Theatre, now the permanent home to the Oscars, and Highland Mall, with its life-size elephants modeled on an old silent film. Under her feet were stars—the "Walk of Fame" with its names, some famous and some forgotten.

Mattie ignored the come-ons of some guy in a Spider-Man suit, and a person dressed as Marilyn. She checked out the marquees at the Boulevard's famous theaters. The El Capitan had some Disney flick and a lame romance was at the Egyptian. She crossed the street with a mass of tourists and stood before the Chinese. An action flick was playing on the main screen, the one with the cool lobby. Mattie stepped up to the cashier—about the same age as she was—and forked over some cash.

The Chinese was really nutso. It was shaped like a giant pagoda with a huge cement square out front. This was not just any square: it held the foot and handprints of the greatest movie stars ever: Judy, Fred, Bogie. Mom was movie-mad, so Mattie knew all the names.

She stepped gingerly over Gable, letting herself be swept onto the central facade. *Could this place be more kitsch?* she mused, with its hanging gong, lion statues, and mounted carved centerpiece?

Mattie dodged the picture-snapping tourists to get a closer look. After a good five minutes, she finally figured it out: the white carving was of a dragon—a Chinese one, duh—replete with coils, whiskers, and antlers.

Mattie felt a pang as she thought of her old friend Toutles. What was he doing now? Had he survived his ragged departure? She had looked for him so often in the park by Forest Lawn. She'd searched the L.A. Zoo and the other fixtures of Griffith: Tiny Town, the Greek Theater, even the Observatory. Nothing.

As always, Mattie felt depressed. Was going on even worth it? She didn't want to be a statistic, but really, what was there to look forward to? Mom was obsessed with work. Dad was obsessed with whatever. She hated Pico; hated Peter; hated herself for bullying David. When she consulted her Magic-8 Ball app, all it said was, "Reply hazy try again." She was only seventeen and already sick of this world.

Mattie stared at the bas relief sculpture beneath the gong until it fell out of focus. Her vision faded to white as the faux-dragon moved its head, going from 2D to 3D just like the movie inside!

An eagle's claw followed, along with the tip of its tail. Thin sculpted whiskers wafted softly in the breeze.

"Hey," Mattie said, but that was all she could manage. She was overcome with desire to run *toward* the writhing stone. Then, with a cry, she jumped like Lebron James and actually went *through* it!

She tried to get a grip. She was inside a translucent cube that spun wildly on its vertices. *I don't like spinning!* she thought. When she looked out, she saw blackness flecked with dots—*stars?*—and as she turned upside down, she caught a glimpse of vibrant colors—blue, green, red— trailing her ascent like a demented plume.

9

Mattie yelled. If this went on much longer, she thought her lungs would explode. "Make it stop," she gasped.

Seemingly compliant, the cube halted its spin, ejecting her through one side.

She landed on all fours. Where had the cube taken her? *This* was not L.A.—of that she was certain. The dirt was soft and moist, as if it sometimes rained, and there wasn't a sprinkler in sight!

Bruised but basically fine, Mattie stood, brushing dirt from her jeans and palms. The cube had popped out of view, but she was in a pretty countryside lush with leafy trees. In the near distance, she saw a wooden fence sheltering some sheep and a herd of grazing cows, lowing softly and tinkling their bells. Guarding them fiercely were two collies.

This is nice, she thought. I could live with this. It sure beats hell out of Hollywood...

Her dreams of rural bliss ended with a whoosh of air. It took her a moment to process what was in front of her.

"*Toutles!*" she yelled as her old friend folded his wings after making a seamless landing.

He looked so...grown up. His color was now deep blue, like the sea in Malibu, and his scales were tightly packed. His front claws were three times the size of her hands, and he was over nine feet tall, not to mention three feet long! Floppy blue spikes now covered his spine and tail while his pupils—big as baseballs—retained their soft yellow hue. When he grinned, he revealed teeth the size of her thumb!

Without fear, Mattie ran forward and embraced his blue belly. It was just as she remembered, cool to the touch.

"Where are we, Toutles?" she asked, half expecting an answer. He lifted his eyelids, revealing those round yellow pupils, then did something strange. With one black nail, he drew blood from his opposite palm. He offered her this liquid treat, bending low so it approached her lips.

"Ech! Toutles, wha—?"

He thrust the tip of his nail gently over her tongue while she was in mid-speech. Then he gulped dramatically, indicating she was to do the same.

Mattie spit out blue blood, but she must have ingested a little. She knew because Toutles cleared his throat and said, "By the way, my name isn't Toutles. It's Artorius. Artorius Wyvernis." He bowed with courtly grace, or as much as a dragon could muster.

Mattie was so amazed that her backside hit the ground. "I...I can understand you!"

"Yes. A dragon's blood is magic. It allows you to understand the language of higher beasts."

Mattie was about to protest, until she heard one collie say to his mate, "Lovely day."

She drew a hand over her forehead. "And...could you always understand *me*?"

"Of course. Unfortunately, a dragon's voice doesn't mature for years. By the by, I really enjoyed our reading of *The Dragon and the George. Dragonslayer*, not so much."

Mattie lay full-length on the ground. "This is really too much. One minute I'm getting hit on by Spider-Man, and the next I'm talking to a dragon. You have to admit this is weird—even by Hollywood standards."

"I know it must seem odd, but Praeses will explain. In the meantime, we should go. We are far too close to Georgia."

Artorius stuck out a claw, helping Mattie to her feet. She was *so glad* to see him again! Still...

"Is *this* Georgia? Are we anywhere near Atlanta?"

Artorius laughed, puffs of smoke coming from his nostrils. He even belched a small flame.

"Okay, so is this like the Georgia in Russia? Are we going to be taken prisoner?" She glanced around for fur-hatted Cossacks.

Artorius patted her gently on the back and gestured with a talon that she was to follow. As they treaded a soft dirt trail, a horse trotted past and said, "Good morning."

Mattie tried not to stare. "Um...hi."

The horse nodded pleasantly.

Mattie decided to try this for herself. She saw a calico cat atop a pasture fence. "Hello there," she greeted it.

The cat tilted its head, giving her a look of utter contempt.

"So...cats aren't considered 'higher beasts'?"

"In *their* opinion, they're the highest. They can talk, but they're snooty."

"I see." She turned back to the calico. "Same to you then!" The cat stuck out its tongue.

Artorius smiled, then started to reminisce. "Remember when we read *The Wizard of Oz* together? And then we saw the movie? Boy, that Judy was something!"

"Yeah?" Mattie wondered where this was leading.

"Well, I can tell you that you're not in Kansas anymore. In fact, you're not on Mundanis."

"Huh?"

"Uh...what you humans call Earth."

"Come on, Tout—I mean, Artorius."

"This is not Mundanis. It's *Mundus Multi Cavernis*, 'The Land of Many Caves.' But we dragons just say Cavernis."

Mattie started. "There's *more* of you?"

Artorius grinned, showing off his gleaming teeth. "Many more. You'll see."

Mattie was getting tired as they kept trekking west. She wasn't that used to walking. Hello, she was from L.A.!

"Artorius—" the new name dropped off her tongue with difficulty, "—can't we just *fly* to wherever we're going?"

The dragon snorted. "*I* can, but what about you? I don't see any wings."

"But can't I ride on your back, like they do in all those movies?"

Artorius let out a gasp. He couldn't speak for a full minute. "How utterly...barbaric," he finally breathed.

"Sorry." Mattie shrugged. More than anything, she wanted to catch up with him. "Artorius, what have you been doing these past seven years?"

"Actually, twenty-one."

"No! It's been seven."

"Not for me. One human year equals three for a dragon."

Mattie tried to assimilate this. "Like dogs?"

"Gee, thanks. Well, to answer your question, I've been growing up, flying, breathing fire. Now I can finally go to school."

"You mean you haven't been? Not even to kindergarten?"

"Nope. We dragons wait till we're mature."

"Oh."

"No worries—we have plenty of time. Most of us live till at least three hundred."

"Wow!"

"Except for the Elders."

Mattie's head started to spin. She almost wished she was taking notes. There was so much to learn!

Still, she forgot about research to ask what was uppermost in her mind.

"Artorius, why am I here? Why did you wait so long to bring me?"

"*Me* bring you? Ha, that's a good one." As he laughed, his blue neck shook. "If only I had that kind of power! Please don't make me explain—I haven't even been to school. Praeses is so much wiser."

Mattie wanted to ask him more but she was fading in the heat. They had to trudge along slowly, since poor Artorius was forced to both crawl and slither. This brought something else to the top of Mattie's mind.

"Artorius?"

"Yes?"

"Will you ever grow back legs? Does it...take like twenty more years?" Still smarting from her riding faux pas, she tried to be tactful.

Artorius laughed in a series of bellows. "Oh no! You see, I'm a wyvern."

Mattie looked blank.

"We are a kind of dragon with only two front feet. We simply don't *have* back legs."

"Oh."

"Unless..." Artorius paused.

"Yes?"

"We earn them in battle. With a knight. If we slay one—instant legs!"

Mattie shuddered. "What a horrible way to get them."

He shrugged. "It's been like that for ages. Don't worry—we're leaving the knights behind."

They kept walking—and walking—and Mattie's legs kept aching. She tried to divert herself by asking more questions.

"So...Artorius."

"Yes?" He smiled over at her.

"From what I know about reptiles—"

"Not so much," he said playfully.

"Yeah. Anyway, don't they lay a clutch of eggs? Which means you must have a bazillion brothers and sisters!"

Artorius laughed. "Not exactly a bazillion. But the average clutch does have nine to ten eggs. What the moms and dads do here—to stop themselves from going nuts—is to farm out most of the hatchlings to Dunvernis."

"Dun-what?"

"It's a place where dragons live, including most of my family. The hatchlings are raised in foster caves in sets of about three."

Mattie wrinkled her nose. "I'm not sure I like that scheme. Don't you ever get to meet your siblings?"

Artorius sighed. "Some do, if they want to make the journey. But considering my family, it's probably best they stay where they are."

They passed a fenced pasture confining a small herd of horses, who seemed to be quite chatty.

"How do?"

"Top o' the mornin'."

"That's no Georgian, I hope." A chestnut eyed Mattie warily.

Artorius calmed the herd.

"No, she's no Georgian! *This* is the human who raised me. From Mundanis."

The horses all widened their eyes, but trotted off regardless.

"I take it my species isn't too popular?"

"Well..." Artorius scratched his chin. "We'll get to that in a bit."

Finally, as the sun set, they stopped before an arched entrance.

"Home," Artorius said, leading her through what seemed to be a cave's stone corridor. They went deeper, deeper still, and Mattie was glad that the cave wasn't freezing like a crystal one she'd once visited on a school trip. But this cavern was warm and comfy, with not a stalactite in sight.

After entering a copious hall, Artorius quickly halted, causing Mattie to step on his tail. It was just as scaly as she remembered—only a lot bigger.

He dropped contentedly onto a large moss bed, beckoning Mattie to join him.

"Hob! Oh, Hob!" he yelled.

An odd creature appeared, as small as the dragon was huge, for he was barely a foot tall. He had leathery brown skin, shoes made of dragon scales, ill-fitting trousers that came to the knee, and long, stringy, brown hair. A vest made out of fur and a Robin Hood cap completed this curious outfit.

"Mattie, this is Hob, my head house brownie. Hob, this is my old friend from Mundanis!"

"Hi." Mattie stuck out her hand, but Hob only stared at it in disgust.

"What's for dinner?" Artorius roared.

This seemed to cheer Hob up. "Ah, we've prepared a braw leg ay lamb, followed by Coq au vin, followed by pork loin. 'En a braw niçoise salad an' a side ay braised fingerlin' tattie coins."

"Gelato for dessert?" Artorius asked.

"What else?" Hob clapped his hands like a fancy maître d'. An army of brownies marched out bearing food on shining gold trays.

"Eat up, Mattie," Artorius told her. "At least *I* won't be serving you dog food."

Mattie blushed. Since the portions were dragon-sized, Artorius cut her tiny pieces, placing them on a plate so big that she actually had to stand on it. This was all getting too *Alice in Wonderland* for her, especially the lack of silverware.

"Sorry, Mattie, I'll have the troops dig up a knife and fork. I literally have *thousands*. And a spoon for the gelato, of course."

"Thanks."

After their long trek, Mattie was nearly famished and devoured the meal with gusto. She thought the pork loin especially good, though she secretly longed for an In-N-Out burger.

Artorius seemed to know this. "Still eating that crappy junk food?"

"Well, I wouldn't call it—yes." Why bother lying to the one who knew you best?

"None of that stuff here! Only fine fare supplied by Latro."

Mattie was too tired to ask who Latro was. But after dinner was over, she had an urgent request.

Artorius led her along the cave's periphery to its farthest recess. When they arrived at a vast pit, he immediately got the hint, perhaps aided by Mattie's terrified expression.

"Right. We don't want you to fall in."

Using his spade tail, he quickly dug a hole more suited to human proportions.

"So uh...no indoor plumbing?"

"Nope. We're not that fancy."

She nodded.

"Well, guess we're even."

She stared uncomprehendingly.

"In waste disposal, I mean."

Artorius left her in privacy. After she washed her hands in an ornate marble bowl, she used a torch as a landmark to guide her back to him. Taking the central path, she realized as she walked that the cave floor was crunchy and wildly uneven since she kept tripping on odd-shaped objects, some of which emitted a glow.

"Oh!"

She looked down. She was walking on mounds of riches. There were heaps of golden coins, silver goblets, kingly crowns, diamonds and rubies and sapphires that gleamed in the uneven light. Mattie felt almost giddy as she bent to touch a tiara.

"Artorius!" she yelled, once she reached him on his bed. "You're rich. You're like richer than a rock star!"

"That's nothing. You should see the treasure at ASH. Speaking of which, we have a meeting first thing tomorrow. Time to get some rest."

He beckoned her to come close, stretching a webbed wing around her. For the first time in seven years, she actually felt happy. It reminded her of the days when *she* would cradle him. Snuggling under a sea of blue, Mattie dreamed of vast oceans blanketed with gold.

Chapter Three

A Meeting with the President

She felt completely refreshed when she woke up the next morning. She was nestled in her friend's arms, held as closely as he'd held Felicia. Mattie didn't want to move, she wanted to stay this way forever.

"Rise an' shine!" Hob yelled, jumping up as close to her ear as possible.

"Ugh."

Artorius had always been a morning dragon, and now he rose with one stretch and started his toilette. A host of brownies handed him a silver basin and mirror. This got Mattie thinking. She took up a napkin and knife, trying to recall her skills from her Oriole days. All she could remember was that she'd gotten sick on a camping trip.

"Hob," she said, after downing a breakfast of poached eggs, ham, bacon, a side of caramel toast, and a strawberry muffin.

"Hmmm?" the brownie asked curtly.

"I...I want to give you something."

19

She held out a tiny apron, the result of her improvised craft project.

Hob's eyes widened. "Weel, Ah ne'er!"

"I know." Mattie smiled with pride. "Now that you've accepted clothes, you're free."

"Ye hae got tae be jokin'!" Hob spat, tearing the apron in two. "Ah hae ne'er bin sae insulted in mah life! That's it, I'm gain. Brownies, we're ootta haur."

And with that, the whole brown-clad army vanished.

"What have you done?" Artorius cried, crawling up behind her. "Don't you know it's considered an insult to offer a brownie clothes?"

"But—Hermione—Dobby—"

"Those were *house elves!* These are *brownies*—from Scotland. Taking pity on them or offering pay is terribly impolite. And whatever you do, do *not* criticize their work!"

Mattie looked down, embarrassed. She had only meant to free them.

"Hob!" Artorius called. "Mattie has something she wants to say to you." He turned to her and nodded.

"Yeah, uh...Hob, I'm really sorry for making a noob mistake. It's just...I don't know the rules. I'm sure you take great pride in your work and seriously...I've never seen such pep. Brownies rule! You guys are *sick!*"

With a snap, all of the brownies returned, resuming their various tasks as if nothing had happened.

"Hrump," Hob said. "Apology accepted. An' aam in perfect health, thenk ye!"

"Thanks." Mattie smiled down at him.

"If yoo're gonnae meit th' President, yoo'll need some brain new clase."

Hob looked in disgust at her blue boots and skinny jeans—the only articles in his sightline. "Main 'en."

That must have meant "come on" since he gestured for her to follow. She traipsed after him to the back of the cave, trying not to break a leg on the booty underfoot. It was kind of strange, Mattie thought, following a brownie. He was no bigger than G.I. Joe, but, unlike the toy, he was real and very grumpy.

"Thes is guid!" Hob yelled, stomping on some delicate fabric. He almost did a little dance. As Mattie stared down, she saw it was a Ren Faire-type dress with sleeves as big as your leg. Plus, the whole thing was brocaded with what looked like *real gold thread.*

"You've got to be kidding," she said, but Hob was as stubborn as she was.

"If ye see th' President, yoo've gotta swatch presentable! Reit noo, I'd mistake ye fur th' milkmaid."

"Nice." Mattie shooed him away and started changing. She didn't want to look in a mirror since she was sure she'd start laughing.

"That's mair loch it!" Hob nodded when she reappeared next to Artorius. He turned to his master. "Don't ye hink she needs some sparklies?"

"Of course."

Artorius crawled to the back and emerged with a clawful of jewelry. "Take your pick," he told Mattie.

She felt like one of those starlets who rents jewels for the Oscars. She made what she felt was a modest selection: a gold necklace dripping with sapphires, two solid silver bracelets, and a ring with a knuckle-sized diamond.

"You look great," Artorius told her, clapping her gently on the back. "Like a princess!"

"Ech," Mattie said. "I'm not ten now, you know? My princess days are over."

"Okay then—a queen."

"How about Maleficent?"

"I like your new haircut."

"Oh." Mattie fingered her neck-length brown hair. It had actually been short for the last three years. "Thanks."

"Now we can see those dark eyes!"

She laughed.

They walked out of his cave together, Hob and the brownies waving goodbye. It was nice to be back in the light, and there certainly was no lack of it. Mattie saw a series of archways, each spaced a tasteful distance apart. She supposed this was due to dragons' solitary natures, or so the storybooks claimed. It still must have been early, dragon-wise, for no neighbor poked out a head or emitted a stream of flame.

Mattie and Artorius turned onto a street that was densely clustered with caves. Each was painted a cheery color and bore a wooden shingle.

"What is this?" she asked.

"The *Platea Fures*. Literally, 'Street of Thieves.' We call it the Plat."

"What are these places?"

"This is where the professionals—doctors, lawyers, CPAs—hang out. See that big street off to the right? That's Restaurant Row. My favorite!" He rubbed his flat blue stomach.

"So uh...dragons have a real city? Like L.A.?"

"Feh!" Artorius spat. "Not like there. We don't have SUV's, self-important Hollywood types, and pools shaped like guitars. In Cavernis, the state offers free housing, we bathe in natural lakes, and when we want to travel, we fly."

"But the lawyers and CPAs?"

"Ever so often, there's a trial. And the CPAs take inventory. Of treasure, naturally."

Mattie tried to picture this. "How...odd."

Artorius shrugged. "We dragons are a practical lot."

Mattie nodded, trying to picture a dragon with a calculator or one before the bench. She wondered if they wore suits. And if so, *who* were they wearing?

She ran to catch Artorius as he crawled toward a series of caves just south of the Plat. It was the biggest compound yet, with several tightly-spaced entrances.

"What's this?"

"This is the Academia Sollertibus Hydris."

Mattie looked utterly blank.

"It really means 'An Academy for Clever Hydras.' Guess something got lost in translation. We just call it ASH."

"What is it?"

"It's a *school*. ASH is a school for dragons."

"No way."

"Way." Artorius' stay in L.A. had obviously affected him.

"Is this *your* school?"

"It will be." His scales swelled with pride. "First quarter starts tomorrow. C'mon."

He took her by the hand and they entered the largest archway. What Mattie saw within rooted her to the floor.

The cave's exterior was nothing, just made of boring rock. But the inside was like a palace, or at the least the Pantheon! The walls were dark-veined marble, paneled with heavy gold. The *floor* was made of gold so bright it hurt her eyes. In niches lining the walls stood priceless artifacts: what looked like the Holy Grail, though this one was made of rubies, a lyre inlaid with silver, etched by an artist's hand. There was an immense cut diamond that made hers look like a dust mote and a jeweled scepter and crown that might have belonged to the Tudors. Beneath the platinum roof hung a full-size pharaoh boat overflowing with gold sarcophagi.

Mattie almost felt dizzy as she took in this display. If this was the school museum, it put *her* world's best to shame!

She felt Artorius shake her and she gradually came back to Cavernis. They were facing a seated red dragon who guarded a walled-off entrance. She was busy transcribing something *with a stone slate and chisel.*

"Miss Fang." In her presence, Artorius became a schoolboy. He practically shuffled his tail. "I've brought the girl from Mundanis."

"Yes. The president is expecting you." Miss Fang was crisply efficient. Mattie noticed that she wore a gold medallion around her bristling neck.

Miss Fang rose. She was at least twenty feet tall. Walking on two legs—even though she had four—she rolled a flat rock aside.

"You may enter."

Mattie followed Artorius into the drafty space. They walked and walked down a hallway hung with paintings. The first was titled *St. George and the Dragon*—but here *the dragon* was winning! Another showed a flame-spewing beast lifting the broken body of a warrior. "Beowulf" read the plaque. There was a vicious feathered dragon digesting a man whole. And a Chinese one, levitating. Mattie felt uneasy when she came to the end of the hall and a sign pointing back at the portraits read "ASH Senior Faculty".

She had a sinking feeling as Artorius led her into the inner sanctum. She trusted him more than anyone, but what *was* this place? On every wall, and rising to an unseen height, she saw the remnants of history. There were scores of papyrus scrolls, most yellowed and frayed around the edges and actual *tablets* bearing cuneiform. There were pamphlets and hanging maps, some bearing the legend at the end of the then-known world, "Here there be dragons". Mattie noted that the landmass of Cavernis looked like a squashed cloud. Also, the name applied to the whole planet.

But mainly, she saw books. She had never encountered so many, not even at the downtown L.A. library. And that was the largest public one west of the Mississippi!

Seated amidst these riches was a dragon—the largest Mattie had seen. He looked to be forty feet tall, his head just inches from the rounded roof of his office.

"Welcome, Mr. Wyvernis. And of course, Miss Sharpe."

Artorius bowed, looking like a hatchling beside the president. What made the latter more imposing were the many medals around his neck coupled with his long dark robe, which to Mattie looked like a scholar's. In front of this gold-colored beast rose a mountain of open books. Some were huge but still readable by a human.

"Miss Sharpe, won't you sit down?" He gestured toward a small chair placed before his desk, which in fact was a massive tree trunk.

"Please—call me Mattie," she said as Artorius winced with embarrassment.

The president seemed unaffected.

"Excellent." He bent his giant head, and she saw that he bore a natural crest shot through with three vibrant colors.

Mattie found herself staring into hazel pupils. This, along with the dragon's snout, was all that she could fit into her field of vision.

"Mattie, I am Praeses, president of ASH. I'm sure you have some questions about why you've been brought to Cavernis."

"Artorius says you can explain."

"Yes. But before I turn to the present, I should confess that *I* was the one who planted the egg in a place where you'd see it."

"*You?* What about the eight-point buck?"

"An accessory, I fear."

Mattie gave a loud huff. What kind of a world was it when you couldn't even trust a deer?

This brought up another question, and she turned to the standing Artorius. "Did *you* know about this?"

Her friend nodded sheepishly.

"Thanks for telling me." She pretended to be mad, but she really wasn't. *He* couldn't help it if Praeses had left his egg in the park.

Praeses raised a gold claw. "Please, I was the one who counseled silence."

Mattie said to Artorius, "Okay, you're off the hook." To Praeses's looming face she asked, "Well, what happens *now?*"

The President crossed his claws. "You may find this odd, but we actually brought you here *to fight.*"

Mattie tried to absorb this. "With all due respect, you've got the wrong girl. I'm in *corrective P.E.!*"

Praeses smiled gently. "I can well imagine your shock. Nothing in your life would have prepared you for this. But know that you have a very special relation."

Mattie thought. "Uncle George?" She pictured the ex-talent agent with his waxed moustache.

"A little farther back. Let me tell you the tale of Matilda."

Mattie stifled a groan. Why were old people—and dragons—always so long-winded?

"In the mid-1300's, a small dragon—or wyrm as they were then called—set up shop in a well in Chiborough. It followed that the villagers wanted to slay him and sent off for a noble knight. Fortunately for the poor beast, Matilda took pity on him, and one moonless night, spirited him out of town. Since then, she has been our greatest heroine."

He bowed his head in homage.

Mattie rolled her eyes. "So something that happened uh..." She tried to do the math in her head, then promptly gave up. "Hundreds of years ago has something to do with *me?*"

Praeses nodded. "It was prophesied in 1612 that an heir of Matilda would be our greatest ally in a war between dragons and men."

Prophecy? This at least sounded familiar. "Well, can I see the little globe with the paper in it?"

Praeses looked puzzled. "We just pass our prophecies down. Orally."

"Oh."

"In any case, the other Elders and myself have felt intimations of war with Georgia." He looked sad. "There hasn't been even one skirmish since the Great Peace broke out."

"And that was—?"

"303 A.D."

Mattie felt like she was back in history class. She tried to stay alert.

"So what's up with these 'Georgians'? What are they— people?"

"People who hate dragons."

Mattie rose to her feet. "No offense, Sir, but this has *nothing* to do with me. And I think it's pretty rank to steal someone from their world and make them rotate in a cube!"

"I fully appreciate your anger. But from *our* point of view, there really was no choice."

"And from *mine?*"

"We're giving you a chance to prove yourself. Doesn't that mean anything?"

Mattie thought of her dead life at home. "Maybe," she mumbled. "Why was I brought here again?" Like most teenagers, her attention span was short.

"To fight."

"Against Georgians?"

"Right."

"Who are people."

Praeses nodded.

"So I'm supposed to fight for dragons against my own kind?"

"Exactly."

Mattie turned to Artorius. "Am I missing something here?"

Praeses answered for him. "Miss S—Mattie—you love your friend here, do you not?"

"Of course!"

"And you are willing to fight for him?"

Mattie stared at Artorius' face. Her reply was instant. "Of course."

"This—and the prophecy—should tell you what you need to know."

Mattie exhaled, deciding to play along. "What exactly do I have to do?"

This caused Praeses to brighten. "First you begin training."

"Like Rocky?"

Praeses thought. "Not exactly. You'll start training as a page."

"Don't waste your time. I auditioned at NBC and somebody's niece got it."

"This is the type of page who eventually becomes a squire who finally becomes—"

Mattie and Artorius leaned forward.

"—a knight."

Mattie let the president's words sink in. Then, she laughed. "You can't be serious. I got sick at Dark Ages Park—and that was just from the food! Sir, with all due respect, you have got the *wrong* Mattie Sharpe."

"I'm afraid there is only one of you related to blessèd Matilda."

Couldn't that medieval lizard lover have left Wyrmie in the well?

For the first time since they'd entered, Artorius spoke. "Think of it, Mattie, you get to learn a whole new trade. When you go back to Mundanis, you can kick some serious—"

"Thank you, Mr. Wyvernis," the president broke in smoothly. "There are so few knights these days who aren't make-believe. *You* will be the 'real deal,' Mattie. With armor of your own and a broadsword by your side."

Mattie thought a little. She had always liked the Renaissance Faire. "Let's pretend I agree—"

Praeses clapped his claws together, which nearly caused a sonic boom. "I *knew* it. The blood of Matilda runs strong. I have just the Master for you—one brought up in the world of chivalry. You'll start your training along with your other classes."

Mattie stared.

"I want you to fit in at ASH, be friends with the other dragons. No better way than taking courses beside them."

Beside *her*, Artorius clenched a claw in victory. Of course, he would be elated that they would soon be classmates.

"Fall quarter starts tomorrow, and Miss Fang has arranged your schedule." Praeses gestured toward a piece of paper, which Artorius grabbed. "I'm confident you will learn some new and instructive things. For example, how we dragons think."

Mattie thought to herself, *I already know that, duh.*

"Usually, we have females room in the girls' dorm, but I'll make an exception here. You may continue to stay with your friend."

Mattie exhaled with relief. That's all she needed, to be bullied by mean-girl dragons.

"I'll say goodbye for now. Good luck, and may you succeed not only in battle but in fighting your own dragons."

Mattie turned to Artorius the minute they left the chamber. "That dude is cra-cra. Shouldn't he be in a home?"

"I've known Praeses since I came back, and he is our wisest Elder."

"But...picking *me* as some kind of hero? I'm flunking junior year!"

"Now's your chance to turn things around."

Mattie sighed. "What about my mom?"

"She'll think you ran away?"

"That'd be a relief for her."

"Don't worry." He put up an arm to pat her. "I have faith that you can do this."

"Based on—?"

"Because you said you would. And you *are* one mean little cuss."

She playfully reached up to sock him.

"Remember, you have me. And I won't let you be harmed, or do anything you don't want to."

Mattie felt herself calming. She tried to ignore the portraits of her new "professors". "Who is this 'Master of Knights'? Some ghost from the Round Table?"

"I have no idea. Guess you'll find out pretty quick."

At last, they emerged from the hallway to face Miss Fang again.

"What did you think of the President? Isn't he simply *wonderful?*" She wore a near-dazed expression.

Mattie wondered if the side eye was part of dragon body language. If so, she gave one to Miss Fang that she hoped combined contempt, pity, and the unspoken belief that the recipient should be medicated.

Chapter Four

ASH U

Mattie barely slept at all that night, and neither did Artorius. They were both too filled with excitement—or dread—to do anything but toss and turn on the big moss bed.

"I'm scared of ASH, Artorius," Mattie said, sometime before dawn.

"So am I," the dragon whispered, putting a protective wing around her. For some reason, she clung to his tail until it was time to rise.

Mattie then did something she'd been dreaming of all night—she completely cut off the sleeves of that damned medieval dress. She stretched out her arms. So much better! Now, if she could just find something like a shower...

Hob and his troops moved crisply as they supplied a supersized breakfast. Still, the two future students could barely touch their pancakes.

"Yoo'll baith be stoatin—Ah ken!" Hob shouted, which Mattie took as encouragement.

Hand-in-claw, she and Artorius retraced their steps toward the ASH campus. Mattie had no idea what awaited. From Artorius' glazed expression, she saw that he didn't either.

They passed through the school's main entrance, still guarded by stern Miss Fang. Again, Mattie was struck by the main hall's opulence. Only this time, the solid-gold floor was literally *crawling* with dragons!

She'd never known there were so many kinds. She saw so much variety that she actually took out her smartphone and tried to snap a picture. Unfortunately, the battery was dead.

The first thing she saw was a creature so small it could fit in the palm of her hand. As it buzzed close to her face, she saw it was a tiny dragon with just two front feet like Artorius.

"You must be a wyvern," she said, trying to be friendly.

"And you must be an ass!" The put-out reptile exhaled a puff of smoke. "Could it be more obvious that *I* am a dragonet?"

"Sorry," Mattie mumbled, feeling her cheeks burn. "My name's Mattie. What's yours?"

"Twinkletoes," the dragonet spat, flying angry circles around her head. "I freaking *hate* that name!"

Mattie tried to think of the toughest woman she knew. "Hey, there was this movie *Alien,* and the heroine, Ripley, kicked some serious butt."

"Cool." The dragonet nodded. "Starting now, my name is Ripley." With that, she flitted off.

Artorius, standing by, seemed glad that his friend had survived.

"Mattie," he said, "I'd like you to meet a good friend—this is Jimmy Chow."

Mattie saw him gesture toward the model of a Chinese dragon. His snakelike coils, tiger paws, and fish scales mirrored the one at the Chinese theater. The main difference was that Jimmy's scales were orange and black, and he didn't look at all menacing. Thankfully, he was *not* a giant, just slightly taller than Artorius.

"Nice to meet you," Jimmy said, sounding like a California kid. He extended an eagle claw. "Let me be the first to welcome you. I hope we have classes together."

"Me too," Mattie said.

"Oh Mattie, this is Sudha."

Jimmy pointed to a nearby girl, surrounded by a crush of admirers. She wore a dark red hood and saree and was so stunning she could have passed for a Bollywood star. Her flashing green eyes, long, luxuriant hair, and flawless skin almost made Mattie scream.

And then, she did scream as a gap opened up around Sudha. From the waist up, she was sheer perfection, but from the waist down, she was *a snake*, her lower half composed of coils! Mattie recognized the football-like pattern: this girl was *half-cobra*.

"Seems that *creature* has never seen a *nāgī*," Sudha snapped. Sarcasm dripped from her like poison.

"This is *my friend*," Artorius said, stepping forward. "Her name's Mattie and she's from Mundanis."

"What is she doing *here?*" Sudha's forked tongue emerged from red lips. "ASH is a school for *dragons*."

"The president enrolled her," Artorius answered, keeping his cool as always. "She has special permission."

"She's *hideous*." Sudha sniffed the air with distaste. "Praeses must have a scale loose."

"C'mon, Sudha, chill," a voice said, and with relief, Mattie saw it belonged to an actual *human*. His bare, deeply muscled chest and flowing black hair made her think of an

35

Indian Fabio. *He's hot,* she thought, giving him her brightest smile. As he passed, he did the same, flashing a closed-lip grin.

"May the Frost Dragons chill *you,*" Sudha hissed at this vision's back. "*Geetha.*"

She glided off haughtily, revealing more appendages. Mattie saw that she had *six arms.* Man, what an A1, first-class beyot—

Ding! Ding! Ding! Ding! Ding! Miss Fang rang a golden triangle and the dragons crawled off to their various classes. Mattie just stood there and looked at Artorius.

"C'mon," he said, sounding cheerful. "We both have the same first class: TNS."

Mattie had no idea what that was, but she was glad to get moving. Artorius led the way to a modest cavern. Once inside, she saw twenty dragons seated on benches large enough to hold their bulk. In front, there was a raised podium occupied by a teacher. She and Artorius slipped to the back.

"Quiet!" the teacher admonished, and not a dragon's breath could be heard. She was clearly a woman, with several strands of pearls encircling her green neck. She was huge—about the size of Miss Fang—and brandished some decidedly gnarly antlers. Mattie also noticed that her tail bristled with clubs. She was clearly *not* a dragon to be messed with.

"I am Professor Fraxinus," she said, her voice slightly shrill. "Welcome to TNS: Care of Tails, Nails, and Scales."

Mattie thought for a second, then gingerly raised her hand.

"Yes?"

"Um, Professor, I don't have those. I mean, I don't have a tail or scales."

The other pupils—with the sole exception of Artorius—began to snort with laughter.

"Enough!" Professor Fraxinus rattled her pearls, turning back to Mattie. "Regardless, you will participate just like any other student."

"But—"

"The goal of this class is to learn how best to preserve our hygiene. You can certainly apply the lessons to your own hair and nails."

Mattie nodded, somewhat feebly. She noticed a dragon in front of her turn from white to a willowy silver.

"Chameleon," Artorius whispered.

"We will begin with proper care of the nail sheath. You all are now at an age where you can start doing this *right*."

All of the students whipped out slates about the size of a hardback. They started taking notes, raking the stones with their nails

Mattie glanced at Artorius.

"Don't worry," he assured her. "I'll take notes for both of us.

Mattie felt another presence sliding into the space next to her. It was Geetha. He slipped into the place on her other side. "Hi," he whispered. Mattie caught his scent. It was more fragrant than a bouquet.

"Hey. I'm Mattie."

"I'm Geethavarden, but everyone calls me Geetha."

"Right."

She stared into his green eyes—so much lighter than her own. With effort, she came back to herself.

"I'm glad you're here," she whispered in his ear, accidentally touching his pumped-up bicep.

"Oh yeah?"

He flashed a closed-mouth grin and actually took her hand in his. "Why is that?" he asked in his deep voice.

"It would be beyond awful if I was the only human. But we have each other, right?"

"Oh...right," he muttered, lightly stroking her arm.

Artorius turned from his slate, shooting her a stern look. She did her best to focus as Fraxinus demoed a Brazilian tail wax, but her thoughts were wholly centered on the hottie beside her. She wondered how often he worked out...

"Oh Mattie," Artorius shook her. "Class is over."

"What? Oh, right."

Geetha gave her the once-over before trailing them out of the cave.

"You look better standing up," he told her.

"So—so do you," she sputtered, unable to pry her gaze from his ten-pack.

"Where do you live?" he asked, walking her out to the hall.

"Burbank," she said instinctively. "I mean, with Artorius."

Geetha drew himself up to his full six-foot-four inches. "Maybe I can drop by some time."

Mattie started to answer, but Artorius stepped in.

"I don't think so," he said sternly. "Mattie just got to Cavernis and she has a very full plate."

"You her dad?" Geetha asked.

"I'm her friend. And protector. I suggest that you get moving."

Artorius extended his talons, arching his tail so its spade grazed Geetha's face.

"Okay, man, no sweat."

Geetha backed off and shrugged at Mattie, then strode down the hall. She immediately whirled on her friend.

"What do you think you're doing? I can speak for myself! Is this a school or a prison?"

"Take it easy," said Artorius, escorting her to their next class. "Remember—I've lived here a while. Not everything is as it seems."

Mattie was not at all satisfied with this lame explanation. Was it possible, she thought, that her old friend was actually jealous?

They chose another bench for Dragonlore, taught by Professor Beowulf. Ripley, Sudha, and Jimmy squeezed in beside them.

"How's that scale care going?" Sudha asked Mattie sweetly.

"Shut it, Sudha," said Jimmy, "or you'll be wearing your coils on your head."

She stuck out her forked tongue, then feigned demureness. "Wise dragon speaks and I am silent."

"All right, class. Come to order."

Beowulf stood before them. He was at least the height of a house. He was the typical Hollywood dragon: gray head shaped like a steam shovel, spade tail, and flickering yellow eyes like Halloween candles.

"Most of you know who I am."

The students murmured in assent.

"Along with Praeses and Dr. Lung, I am a founder of ASH."

There was a light scatter of applause.

"Previously, I earned my name by killing a certain Geat."

Mattie rifled through her school knowledge, most of it not very current. But she did remember something Mrs. Stern had said in English.

"Excuse me, sir."

Twenty heads snapped toward her on scaly dragon necks.

The professor waited patiently, smoothing his long brown cloak.

"I was led to believe...by a teacher...that *Beowulf* killed the dragon."

This Beowulf started to laugh, his guffaws booming off the stone walls.

"That is the myth on Mundanis, but it couldn't be more wrong. In fact, *I* was the victor, and the Geat promptly expired."

Most of the class—especially Sudha—broke into hilarity, of course directed at Mattie. She decided at that moment that Sudha was a mean half-girl.

"Very well, let's get started. I want to begin with the difference between the Western and Asian dragon. You may think you know this, but let's review."

Again, twenty sharp nails scratched onto twenty slates.

"The Occidental, or Western, dragon has a fierce reputation. He is known for jealously guarding treasure, demanding children or virgins as sacrifices, and in general, being a mean-tempered old sow."

Some of the students giggled.

"The Oriental, or Asian, dragon, is thought to be kind and wise. He or she is a symbol of good luck, and one of the Children of Heaven. They control water and the four winds. There are nine different types, beginning with the Qiulong—"

Mattie was surprised to find herself listening. At least this was something new. While Artorius scratched their notes, she found herself surprised when the golden triangle dinged after a brisk two hours.

That was it for the first day. No sign of knights or armor. Mattie was so tired that by the time they reached home, she flopped full-length on the moss.

"Artorius, do you have any burgers?"

Hob shook his head in disgust. "Latro don't trade in 'at guff," he said. "Only th' finest in th' twal worlds."

Mattie sighed, asking her friend, "Do we have any homework?"

"Nope. They don't give it on the first day."

"Yay." Mattie closed her eyes as Artorius sat beside her, but she opened them quickly when she felt a small whoosh of air.

"Hey, blue guy!" Ripley shouted, landing on her friend's nose. Mattie saw that she bore a tiny red knapsack on a stick. "I'm s'posed to be your new roomie."

Artorius crossed his eyes as he tried to focus on her.

"Yo, dude," the dragonet addressed Mattie. "You better not hog the bathpit or brush that hair like a million times." She added in a low tone, "By my tail, I hate girlie girls!"

With that, she flew onto the bed and started to unpack her things. Mattie saw a doll-size sword and dagger.

Ripley turned to Hob. "Yo, little man, chop chop with the grub. I'm starving!"

Hob's face flamed. "Who ye callin' wee, sister?"

"You, brownie boy. Wassup with din din?"

Hob's not-quite-foot-tall body began to shake with rage. "Either ye learn some manners, missy, ur yoo'll be it oan yer wee butt!"

Ripley snorted two tendrils of smoke. "And who's gonna put me there? You?"

"That's enough," Artorius ordered, tired of all the bickering. "Twinkletoes—"

"It's Ripley now!"

"Okay, Ripley, who told you to come here?"

"That lovesick loon, Miss Fang."

"All right then, you can stay. But only if you behave nicely. To *everyone*." He looked pointedly at the hopping-mad Hob.

"Okay, okay," Ripley said. "Don't get your scales in a bundle!"

41

After another sumptuous meal, involving the Benihana-like chopping of meat by brownies, Mattie lay back to rest.

"C'mon dude, no time to crash. It's karaoke night at The Three Dragons!"

"I can't, Ripley," Mattie groaned. "I am totally fried from today."

"Miss Boring." Ripley flew out on her own to seek some form of amusement.

Mattie turned to Artorius. "Does she *have* to stay with us?"

"According to ASH, yes."

"But why?"

"She probably got kicked out of the girls' dorm."

Mattie stared at Artorius, and they both started laughing. Despite Sudha—and Ripley—Mattie felt that she could make it through ASH with her best friend at her side. *Maybe joined by a certain hunk,* she thought...

Still, there was something bothering her, something that set her apart from the others, besides not having scales. She made up her mind right then that she would address it tomorrow.

Chapter Five

How to Preserve Your Treasure

The next day, when she entered the main hall, which she learned was called the quad, Mattie turned and waved goodbye to Artorius. She decided to make good on her resolution.

"Miss Fang?"

She tried to get the red admin's attention, but she was busy filing scrolls.

"Excuse me?

Miss Fang reluctantly turned to her.

"All of the other students take their notes on tablets, but obviously I can't do that."

The admin stared down at her.

"You see, I don't have any claws." Mattie presented her short nails.

"You don't say. Well, as always, the president has thought of *everything.*"

She sorted through some tablets, half-muttering to herself. Finally, she pulled one out, but this wasn't of stone.

It was an actual *tablet,* with a screen and apps and everything!

"This is for you," the admin drawled, bending double to pass it to Mattie. "Oh, and the president says this model has its own power. Also, there are no 'Nets' or 'Googlies.' I swear, that dragon's a genius!" She gave a worshipful sigh.

Mattie backed off across the gold floor, her new treasure in hand. Pity that it didn't have wireless, but at least she could play some games. As she hurried off for class, a hunky form approached her.

"Hey," Geetha said in his husky tone, pushing back his long black hair. His features were so chiseled that he looked like a Greek statue.

"Fellow human," she greeted him, not wanting to be late but then again...

"Mmmm. You a fan of Bollywood?" he asked.

Mattie crinkled her nose. "Not really." Her mom ate up that stuff, but she couldn't get past all the corny—and long—musical numbers.

"You know how Indian guys and girls do all this hot dancing, but aren't allowed to kiss?"

Mattie was getting nervous. "Yeah, my mom—she's an old—thinks that it's really sweet but I think it's totally lame and can't stand all the bad disco moves and most of all the lip-syncing—"

Speaking of lips, his were moving closer to hers. She focused on his green eyes, which drew her in hypnotically. Geetha moved his half-naked body toward her, putting his hands behind her head and kissing her on the mouth. It felt good, but when he stuck his rolled tongue in, she recoiled.

She pushed him away—hard. "Hey, not so fast, lover boy!"

Geetha looked disappointed as he struck a model's pose.

"Greetings from Cavernis," he whispered, stroking her arm as he passed. Mattie stood rooted to the floor in a flower-scented daze. She really had to resist running after him.

"Ecch," she heard, then turned to see Sudha, who stared at her in horror.

"How positively...bestial," she spat, looking physically ill, then slithered in a hurry after Geetha.

Guess she's not too fond of PDAs. Mattie hurried into a cave marked with a slate reading "Treasure." She slid next to Artorius, who had kindly saved her a seat.

"All right, all right, let's begin, no time to waste."

A nervous little dragon, his color a pale yellow, practically ran to the podium.

"I am Professor Avarus, and this is How to Preserve Your Treasure."

Mattie noticed that around his neck hung a tangle of gold chains.

"Very good, okay, let's get started. We have so much to cover!"

Mattie withdrew her tablet, prepared at last to take notes. Artorius widened his eyes and gave her a "talons up."

"First of all—and I cannot stress this enough—treasure must be treated as nicely as you'd treat your wife. In other words, with loving care and respect!"

Professor Avarus stroked one of his chains.

"Let's begin with gold. It must be polished, it must be burnished, it must be rubbed to a brilliant sheen until it is almost blinding! Anything less is a crime." He lowered his head sadly.

"Is this guy for real?" Mattie whispered to Artorius. Her friend nodded slowly, as if he could hardly believe it himself.

"Silver. Ah, silver! Is there anything so beguiling? It must not be allowed to tarnish, to lose its sparkling patina. That is why I recommend Royal Polish every day."

"Who has the time?" Artorius mumbled.

"In this class we will learn how to tell cubic zirconia from diamond, and how to use the bite test on pearls." Avarus clasped his claws. "Any questions? Be quick now! Our syllabus is huge!"

Mattie was still shaky from her makeout session with Geetha. She really wasn't that into treasure, so this class would go by slowly. To her, hoarding a bunch of metals—precious or not—was a big ol' waste of time.

"Thank God," she told Artorius as the triangle dinged.

"I've never seen anyone get so upset by topaz."

"I swear he was gonna have a stroke when Ripley asked about rhinestones. What's next?"

"Varsity Crew."

"Is that some kinda sport? You know I suck at P.E.! And I'm not changing in front of dragons!"

Artorius looked puzzled. But before they could head off, Sudha slithered up with a cadre of dragons in tow.

"You," she spat at Mattie. "Mundani. I knew your kind was primitive, but really, *interspecies* relations? How low can you humans go?

"What?" Mattie asked, genuinely confused.

"She didn't know—" Artorius started to say.

"Cow dung!" Sudha cried. "He kissed her and we all know what's in his mouth."

Artorius sighed. "He looks like a *human* right now. Same as the ones on Mundanis."

"On her side, wyvern? For all we know, she's dating you too!"

"That's disgusting!" Mattie shouted.

"Go home, unnatural girl! Go to your own school. And leave *our kind* alone!"

"Perv!" a pink dragon sniffed.

Sudha and her fans lumbered or slithered away.

Mattie was so shaken that her hands literally shook. She turned to Artorius.

"What the heck was that about?"

He sighed. "I should have told you. Geetha isn't human. In fact, he's a *nāga* just like Sudha, but he can take an all-human form."

Mattie stemmed a tide of nausea. "*You mean I kissed a snake?*"

"I'm afraid so. Didn't you feel his fangs? Or his forked tongue?"

"Ech, no! He must have curled it up. Why didn't you say something?"

"You seemed so glad to see another 'human.' And I didn't realize things had gone so far."

"Ugh." Mattie flicked her own tongue, trying to expel snake cooties. "This is so wrong."

Artorius looked concerned. "Do you want to talk to a counselor?"

"No! I want to turn back time to like two hours ago."

"Well, try to forget it. Though I'm afraid that Sudha won't."

Since they were already late, Artorius hurried her outside the quad. They walked across the ASH compound, stopping before a broad river that twisted behind the Plat.

Mattie recoiled. "Not water." Memories of old Miss Evans making them swim in the rain quickly flooded her brain. But Artorius led her down to a small group at river's edge: among them Jimmy, Ripley, and—oh joy—Sudha.

The *nāgī* didn't wait before lobbing the first of her missiles. "So snake lover's gonna row? With what? Those puny arms?" She outspread her six in derision.

"Shut it, Sudha," said Ripley, landing on her head. "That's *my* homegirl now!"

"You're probably part of her threesome. What a bunch of freaks!" Sudha swatted Ripley off with three hands.

The dragonet was nonplussed.

"Anybody got a flute? That snake needs some serious charming."

"Helo helo pawb!"

A bright-red dragon with an arrow at the tip of his tail and four claws with four talons each sprinted up at a run. Mattie thought he looked familiar.

"I am Coach Dragon sy'n ymddangos ar faner cymru, but heck, just call me Cymru. Fi yw'r draig cenedlaethol Cymru."

Everyone looked blank.

"Sorry! I'm the national dragon of Wales."

Now Mattie remembered where she'd seen him—the Welsh flag. Here he looked less like a symbol in his backward sports cap and tee which bore the logo "S&B."

"You've all been specially chosen, and I'm happy to welcome you to S&B." His voice was a rich baritone, like that guy who'd played Arthur in *Camelot*.

"That's Scull & Bones," Cymru said. "You'll be rowing Varsity 8's, with the strongest dragons in the middle."

Mattie looked at her fellow rowers, most of whom were ten times her height.

"Uh—" she began.

"Right." The Coach noticed her presence. "No need to fret, young lady. You're not expected to row, but you're our most important crewmate: the coxswain!"

He smiled brightly, revealing two rows of perfect teeth. Mattie nodded. The coach was so exuberant, she didn't have the heart to tell him she didn't know what a "coxswain" was.

"Training starts on Drakeday at 6 a.m. *sharp*. And I do mean *training*, boys and girls. Weights, rowing machines, stationary bikes, and push-ups. We'll work *three months* before the big boat race."

Mattie put her hand to her forehead. God, she hated sports. She had even lied to get into Miss Evans's class. And now, she was the key member of a *sports team?*

"Don't you worry, Missy, all you do is sit. You're excused from training."

This made Mattie feel better, but not really by much. "Artorius, I am so not into this," she said, as the first session ended and they walked away from the bank.

"Don't worry," Jimmy soothed her. "The coxswain barely moves. You just call out the strokes and shout 'good job!' Oh yeah—you also steer the boat."

"I don't even have a driver's license! I failed the written *twice*." Mattie felt tears start to sting her lashes.

"Now, now," Artorius said, enveloping her in a blue wing. "I'll be there, and I'll get you through this. Isn't that what best friends are for?" He gave her a tight squeeze.

"Thanks, Artorius," said Mattie, running a hand over her eyes.

"I'll help too," Jimmy said eagerly. "I can demonstrate steering. I'm getting an A+ in Navigation for Dragons."

Mattie smiled toward him. He was really a nice kid. Then, with a pang, she remembered David Wang.

"Jimmy..." This was a sensitive subject, so she wanted to be sensitive. "Why do Asians study so hard? Is it that they want to be better than everyone else?"

Jimmy laughed. "Not exactly. You can't believe the pressure we get from our family. My dad says if I don't become a cosmologist, he'll never speak my name again."

"Oh." Something like light flooded over Mattie.

"We're supposed to be perfect. You should hear my dad go on about the cataract I had to have removed."

"Why?"

Jimmy struck a solemn stance, deepening his voice. "'A dragon's vision is perfect: in the physical, spiritual, and mental realms. You are a disappointment to me. At least I have your eight brothers.'"

Jimmy removed his talons from his upper coils, which passed for hips.

Artorius laughed merrily, but Mattie stood there thinking.

"So there are these...*expectations* put on you?"

"Like you wouldn't believe. If I ever get a B, my mom won't leave the cave."

"Wow," Mattie said.

"She means the best. She just wants me to succeed. Doesn't your mom?

"Yeah."

When Mattie thought about her, she started to tear up. She had to say, Mom had never nagged her that much about grades. Until she started failing.

"Artorius, do you think my tablet can send a text? To Mundanis?"

He frowned. "I doubt it. There's just two portals between the two worlds, and I'm sure Praeses has closed them."

Mattie felt a rush of sadness. For the first time in years, she actually missed her mom. Artorius—her best friend— knew immediately what was wrong.

"Hey, let's see if Latro can smuggle a burger and fries!" He winked broadly at Mattie.

"Can you throw in a chocolate shake?"

"Sure! Latro can get anything."

Mattie felt her spirits rise as they said goodbye to Jimmy and headed back to their cave.

Once there, Artorius whispered to Hob, and in what seemed like a flash, she was dining on her favorite foods: an In-N-Out Double Double and Animal Style Fries!

Ripley wrinkled her nose. "You actually prefer *that* to coq au vin?"

"You better believe it, sister."

Mattie bit into a spray of ketchup, mayo, and sauce and washed it down with a thick shake. The meat of that burger and the pickles on those fries made her happier than Ronald McDonald. With the minor exceptions of dragons— and oh yeah, brownies, and a cave—this was getting to be like home. Which, now that she thought about it, wasn't all gloom and doom.

Chapter Six

Master of Chivalry

Mattie guessed that Praeses had given her time to adjust to ASH. "Mr. Chivalry," as she'd come to call him in her head, didn't appear for four days. But when he did, he entered with a bang—albeit a silent one.

On Thorsday, the Cavernis word for Thursday, a small, nondescript brown dragon grabbed her in the quad. In fact, his sharp talons raked her bare arm.

"Ow!"

He didn't look the least bit sorry, giving her a quick once-over, which ended in an eye roll. Before Mattie could speak again, Jimmy came slithering over to join them.

"Matilda," he said formally, "allow me to introduce Master Eliwlod. President Praeses has asked him to provide your training."

Mattie returned the small dragon's contempt.

"In what? Breathing fire? I need a *human* instructor. I thought maybe someone like Geetha—"

"No," Jimmy said quickly. "Eliwlod here is a master of knightly arts."

"Okay," Mattie felt herself soften slightly. "Nice to meet you," she told him. "Please, call me Mattie."

He made a series of signs with his claws, which Jimmy then interpreted. "He says to call him Eli."

"Ah. What are you guys doing?"

"DSL—Dragon Sign Language. You see, Eli is mute."

"But he can hear?"

"Oh yes."

Eli gave her a side eye. Mattie saw that he had webbed ears and disturbingly curved horns. Plus, there were unsightly bumps all over his face. *Poor little guy,* she thought.

Eli's claws were a blur as he made some more signs.

"He says you are to follow him. He's going to try to make you a page. That means..." Jimmy hesitated, trying to get it right, "...you must master the couch."

"I think I already have. You just sit on it, right?"

Eli put his claws to his ears. Another series of signs.

"He says you better take this seriously. He uh...hesitated before taking this job. But feels that Praeses is counting on him."

"Are you sure you're translating *exactly* what he means? Is this like those Japanese movies where somebody speaks for three pages but the subtitle just says, 'The giant lizard is coming'?"

Jimmy laughed nervously, which told her all she needed to know. Her very polite friend was softening Eli's sentiments.

She and Jimmy followed "the Master" to an empty dirt lot by the river. It wasn't much to look at. Eli whirled toward them and signed.

"He says pages usually start training at seven years of age, so you have ten years to catch up on. First, he's going to institute basic fitness. You're to run around this lot five times."

"Did you tell him I was in *corrective* P.E.?"

Eli clearly had no trouble hearing. He dug his claws in the dirt, flashing some angry signs.

"He says he doesn't give a rat's—"

"I get it. And I'm supposed to run dressed like Snow White?"

"He says next time, bring appropriate clothing. For now, just make due."

What an ass, Mattie thought.

Eli slapped her on that very part of her body, gesturing she was to start. Reluctantly, Mattie did. To her not-so-surprise, she managed to complete one lap before collapsing at Jimmy's coils.

Eli's expression ran the gamut from disgust to despair. He shook his bumpy brown head.

"He says, uh…"

"Don't sugarcoat it, Jimmy," Mattie gasped from her place on the ground. "Give it to me straight."

"He says that you run like a girl, one who is flabby as a swine. As to why you were chosen, it is like a Religious Mystery. They'd be better off with a brownie."

"Sweet," Mattie answered, rising to her feet. She thrust her face toward Eli. "Listen, dude, I'm not exactly a volunteer. Some damn cube rotated me here. I *know* why I was chosen, and even *I* don't understand it."

Eli just stared at her.

"Do you *always* have to look constipated?"

The brown dragon almost grinned. He shook his head slowly, then signed to Jimmy.

"He says be here tomorrow and every day at four. If he can't get you to the level of a child, he'll be the laughingstock of his friends."

Despite her desire not to, Mattie kept showing up. She tried to picture Artorius and her pledge to keep him safe. But it took all her willpower not to knock Eli flat on his tail.

She kept running around that damned lot—dressed in a sensible tunic, pants she'd cut down to shorts, and her blue boots from home. Each day, she managed to jog a little further until she could do five laps. The truth was, she'd forged a doctor's note to get out of normal P.E. There was nothing really wrong with her—except a lousy attitude.

After all that running, Eli decided to step it up. One day he showed up with props: two wooden swords and two wooden shields.

Mattie crossed her arms. "And who is it I'm supposed to fight? *You?*"

In response, Eli took up the "weapons" and it was clear from the way he handled them that he really was a master.

Mattie followed suit, attaching the shield to her left arm and raising the sword with her right. Eli issued such a barrage of strokes that she hit the ground like a meteor.

"C'mon," she told him, dropping her stick with fatigue. "I'm new at this, right?"

His answer was to mete out a series of blows against her shield. She grasped it with both hands, trying to cover her head.

"I give up!" she cried. "White flag, peace with honor!"

Eli resumed his usual look, as if he smelled something rancid. He dropped his weapons and signed to Jimmy.

"He says there is no surrender. The only way to get you trained up is practice, practice, practice. Soon these moves will become natural and you won't have to think."

"Wanna know what I'm thinking right now?"

"He says no."

"I think that if this goes on much longer, I'm gonna take that wooden sword and plunge it into my heart."

Jimmy paused to gather his friend's DSL. "He says go ahead. You're not a vampire, so you won't die."

Mattie leaned against a tree, every cell in her body aching. God, how she hated that do-gooder Matilda! But even more, she hated Eli. With no compunction, she turned to him and said so.

For the first time since she'd known him, she saw his mouth form a smile.

Chapter Seven

As Good as a Seven Year Old

Over the next few weeks, Eli had many reasons to smile. Mattie earned so many bruises that she looked more purple than Barney and her body was so sore it became her natural state.

One day at four, when Mattie hobbled into the lot, she saw a wooden contraption set up in the dead center.

"What is that?" she asked, taken aback by the thing's wheels.

Jimmy waited for Eli to finish signing. "*That* is what you're going to practice on now. We're going to roll you toward a target and you will try to hit it with this." He held up a wooden lance.

"Psycho," Mattie muttered, ignoring her Master's evil eye. He and Jimmy each took a side of the "horse" as she clambered on. They rolled her toward a paper target, making her feel like a toddler riding a Big Wheel.

"Gimme a break," she groused, holding the lance horizontal. As they approached the bullseye, she struck—*and hit!*—a nearby bush.

Eli put his head in his claws. He gave an audible sigh. Then, he signed to Jimmy.

"He says again."

"Naturally."

"He says you must master the couch. Put the lance *under your arm* for stability."

"I'd like to put it under his—"

"He says, 'If I were you, I'd stop there.'"

Mattie got back on the contraption. Her legs, strengthened from running, gripped the wooden frame. She rested the lance under her armpit, and—amazing—actually *hit* the target!

"Yah!" Jimmy yelled, extending a tiger's paw to be shaken. Even Eli nodded as he signed.

"He says, 'Congratulations. You are now seven years old.'"

Mattie felt plenty full of herself as she vaulted off the device. In just a few weeks, she had been promoted to Page!

"Whoa," Jimmy exclaimed. But he wasn't talking about her. He pointed a claw to the sky where a wisp of smoke wafted. "I saw flame!"

The three of them ran to the river, clambering up its steep west bank. From the elevated viewpoint, Eli and Jimmy both gasped.

"What do you see?" Mattie asked, wishing she had dragon vision.

"It's one of us," Jimmy whispered. "A female. She's on the ground and...she's dead. There're gallons of blue blood. And there are lances—real ones—embedded in her throat."

"Should we go over?" Mattie asked, her own blood boiling. "Maybe we can find out who did this."

"Too dangerous," Jimmy said. "It's better if we report this."

"Okay."

She and a grim-looking Eli followed Jimmy back to ASH. He entered a cave where a double of him—only bigger—sat alone at a podium.

"Dr. Lung!" Jimmy cried.

"Jimmy Chow, what's wrong?"

The Chinese dragon stood up. Oddly, he bounced a flaming pearl up and down with one talon and held a club in his tail. His voice was soft and calm, but Mattie had the feeling that, if challenged, he could kick some serious tail.

"Sir, a dragon has been killed. In a ravine near the Flavius. By—by Georgians."

"How do you know this?" the doctor asked, throwing aside his pearl.

"We—we saw it. There were...many lances sticking from the dragon's throat."

Dr. Lung closed his eyes. Still, he betrayed no emotion. "Did you recognize him or her?"

"No, sir."

"I will inform the other Elders. In the meantime—" he turned to Eli, "—I must ask you to fast-track your training." He shifted his gaze to Mattie. "Our need for a champion grows."

"Yes, sir," Mattie said. She now realized that training wasn't all about hating Eli. The war that Praeses predicted was clearly on its way.

"One thing more." Dr. Lung addressed the three of them. "Say nothing of what you've seen. We do not wish to create a panic, especially at ASH."

The two dragons and Mattie assented. This meant she couldn't tell Artorius, and somehow that didn't seem right. Still, she was determined to stand by her word. The thought of that poor dead dragon was more than enough to still her tongue.

Wolf

Chapter Eight

The Imposing Professor Fraxinus

The next morning, Mattie dragged her aching body to the Matilda of Chiborough Library. Artorius was off training, so she sat among the stacks alone.

The cave was vast. As with Praeses' office, there were countless papyrus scrolls, aging pamphlets, and human-size books. There were no windows per sé, but some holes drilled into the walls allowed light to strike all that learning.

Mattie bent over her tablet, intent on studying her notes. After yesterday's shock, this was easier said than done. But quarters went by so fast, and midterms were only one week away! Mattie clutched a text titled "Midas: Was He a God?" by Dr. Franklin Avarus.

"Hey."

A black dragon with a mournful face and posture that shouted, "Don't look at me!" shyly approached her seat.

"Hello," Mattie said brightly. None of the dragons outside her circle wanted much to do with her. Especially after Sudha had spread the word.

"We've got TNS together."

"Oh." Mattie hadn't noticed him.

"You're Mattie," he told her, sounding a bit stuffed up. "My name is Schmuck."

"Excuse me?" Mattie was from L.A., and she knew this was not a nice word.

He slumped even further. "I know. In Yiddish 'schmuck' means dragon. But you can call me Sid."

"Okay." Mattie tried not to grin.

Sid fidgeted for a minute. Something was on his mind.

"Hey, wanna see the secret rooms?"

"What are they?"

"Dunno, but they have secrets."

"Sure." Mattie was always up for an adventure. Besides, it was early, and her head hurt from studying.

"C'mon." Sid motioned her out of the library, and they walked through ASH's dirt quad to the nearby quad.

"You ever been to these rooms before?" she asked.

"Nope." Sid walked on all fours beside her, rushing her past the formidable Fang.

Mattie followed him to the very back of the hall under the pharaoh's boat. All those gold mummy cases kind of gave her the creeps. Especially the ones staring down at her, their eyeliner fierce as a model's.

"This way," Sid whispered, leading her to a silver pole stretching up past their view. He grasped it with four taloned claws, inching his way up.

"What do I look like, a fireman?" Mattie hissed.

Sid extended a hind leg, and Mattie took the hint. Cautiously, she clung on until they both landed on a smooth floor. Which, Mattie noted, was composed of rich white marble interspersed with squares of black.

After all that climbing, this second story was meh. Nothing was on display, and the space seemed cold and empty. Still, Sid bore a wide smile.

He crept forward, low to the ground, and Mattie slithered on her stomach, as if she were part *nāgī*. Sid halted abruptly, causing Mattie to smack his tail.

"Ow!"

"Shhh!"

Sid rose on his hind legs, and if a dragon could walk on tiptoe, that's exactly what he was doing. His black shape on the white marble looked like an old movie.

Sid approached a narrow door, which, if it were secret, certainly wasn't guarded. He stepped back, then propelled forward like a hurdler, intent on breaking in.

Before Mattie had time to think, Sid was on his back, covered with a layer of ice. He certainly wasn't moving.

"Wha—?" Over his prostrate body, Mattie had a quick second's view of the room through the half-closed door. Dangling from the ceiling by delicate silver wires was a fossil. It was of a small dinosaur with huge bumps on its face, bristling horns on its head, and a wide, gaping mouth. Its arms were tiny and clasped, like a mini T-Rex.

Before Mattie could see any more, a hulking shadow fell over her. Looking up, she saw Professor Fraxinus, her pearls angrily clanking.

"So," she said, treating Sid like a frozen fish stick, "this is our future champion?"

Sprawled on the marble floor, Mattie felt like she was *not* in the power position. She rose stiffly.

"Schmuck, um, Sid—"

"You both violated ASH rules."

Fraxinus' antlers shook like an angry deer's. "Just when we need you most, you *try* to get expelled?"

"No, professor, it's just..."

"Yes?" She constricted her green scales.

"I don't actually *know* the rules."

The teacher gave a deep sigh. "I will ensure they are delivered so that you may study them thoroughly."

"Thanks." Mattie straightened her hair, then noticed the inert black lump at her feet. "Um, Sid—"

"He will unfreeze in time for lunch. I strongly urge you, Miss Sharpe, not to venture up here again. And say nothing of the secret rooms." Fraxinus gave Mattie a scathing look that meant business. "Now, report to your morning class."

"Yes, ma'am."

The professor stepped toward the door, closing it with a wallop. Mattie felt lucky she hadn't been thrust inside.

She scurried back down the pole, running into a cave. Of course, her first class was TNS, with Professor Fraxinus. That dragon must have sprouted wings—what was she saying?

"We are going to cover tail care: clubbed and non-clubbed. Mr. Wyvernis, could you please step forward?"

Poor Artorius dragged to the podium, sticking out his small spade tail.

"I recommend a product known as Scale N' Tail. It coats with a nice sheen, and has a lovely smell…"

Mattie was too frazzled to pay the professor much mind. Instead, she heard her tablet "ding" and, on an off-chance, checked email. Sure enough, there was one from Miss Fang. "No Nets" indeed!

"SCHOOL RULES" read the subject line. Mattie scanned the body:

The following are considered the Ten Commandants of ASH. Any failure to obey may result in Immediate Expulsion or forced tail trimming:

1. NO **BREATHING FIRE** on campus unless it's in IEF.
2. **NO FLYING** unless instructed.
3. **NO FIGHTING** (including clawing, biting, raking, head-butting, and/or striking with tail).
4. No **NAME CALLING** or insults.
5. Dragons should **STUDY** 3 horas a night.
6. **RESPECT** at all times cultural & elemental differences.
7. ZERO TOLERANCE for SULPHUR.
8. No **DRAGONSMEAD** allowed on school grounds.
9. Senior Faculty may **NOT DO MAGIC** except in a classroom setting or Council Emergency.
10. NO ENTERING SECRET ROOMS!

Ugh, Mattie thought, *this is worse than Pico Pico!* And some of these were a crock. "No insults"? What about Sudha? "Study three hours a night"? She hadn't done that since middle school!

Yet Number 10 was strictly enforced. While Fraxinus lectured on cuticles, Mattie thought about what she'd seen upstairs. What had turned Sid to ice? She really had no clue. And the fossil, of that…thing. Mattie knew her dinosaurs, and she was sure that's what it was. Yet it *did* look like her classmates, with one main difference: the fossil had no wings.

Granted, neither did Jimmy or Sudha, but they were kind of snake-like. Those bones were from something that walked on legs.

Are dinosaurs dragons? Mattie wondered. *Or were dragons descended from dinosaurs?* She bet that scientists at home weren't debating this topic.

She wanted to ask Artorius, who was now getting a manicure in front of the whole class. But Fraxinus had warned her, and she was terrified of the imposing green dragon.

So when it came time to pick up her books and move on to Dragonlore, she didn't say a word.

Chapter Nine

Latro

To Mattie's great relief, she never made it to her next class. Miss Fang appeared by the classrooms, squarely blocking her progress.

"The president wishes to see you," she said, with as much feeling as a recording.

Oh boy, Mattie thought, *I'm really gonna catch it now.* Breaking the biggest ASH rule, and she was only a freshman. Matilda or not, she expected to be expelled faster than Praeses could say buh-bye.

She took the long walk down the hall, feeling more dread than the first time.

He was crouched over a papyrus, reading the relatively small scroll. When he saw Mattie approach, he gave her a wide smile, which quickly lightened her mood.

"Good thinking on the ravine tragedy, reporting it to Dr. Lung."

"That was Jimmy."

Praeses nodded. "He's one of the good ones. Make sure to keep him close."

"I will. Who was it, sir? The...the victim, I mean."

"I'm very sorry to report it was Professor Avarus's wife. Of course, he's on temporary leave."

Mattie felt a stab of shock. "Why her?"

"I wish I knew. But the lances were definitely Georgian."

"Does this mean the war's begun?"

"Perhaps. We've filed a Council protest."

"You mean...you aren't sure?"

Praeses bent his neck to come closer. "The lances may have been planted to make us think the Georgians were here. One can never be too careful."

"Yes, sir." Mattie must have looked uneasy.

"Eliwlod tells me you've made tremendous progress."

"Really?" She couldn't imagine *Eli* praising her.

"Oh yes. You'll be trained up in time—just in time, I should say. Everything else all right? Tablet working out well?"

"Yes, sir. I just wish—"

"Mmhmm?"

"That I could send a note home. I'd like my mom to know where I am."

"Understood. I had a mother too. But if yours knows where you are, it can only lead to confusion. The worst that can happen is if Mundanis discovers your portal. I imagine their 'love' for dragons exceeds even the Georgians."

"I see."

Mattie was disappointed, but she could more or less follow his logic. Man, when she got home, Mom would ground her for a year!

For now, she found her mind racing—settling on the sight she'd seen that morning. "Uh—"

"You're curious about that fossil. The one in the secret rooms."

Mattie wondered if Praeses was telepathic.

"Not really. I'm just an excellent guesser."

Mattie took a step back.

"That fossil is a dinosaur—as you correctly surmised. It was recently found on Mundanis, though *we've* known about it for ages. It's called the *Dracorex*—'Rex' for short."

"It looks so much like a dragon."

"Yes. Our experts believe that we evolved from this species. Over time, we developed wings and the ability to breathe fire."

"Cool!"

"It is. I must tell you that Rex has 'gifts,' which is why he's in that room!" Praeses bent his head until his crest nearly touched her face. "Mattie Sharpe of Mundanis, you've been asked to keep one secret. Do you think you can keep another?"

She stiffened. Did the President know what he was asking from a teenager?

"I...I think so," she stuttered.

"Excellent. I will rely on you to say nothing until Rex is known to Cavernis."

Mattie nodded. This was going to be really hard.

"Very good. Well, you may retu—"

Mattie felt a kind of energy electrifying the air. A clear object popped into sight at the side of Praeses' desk. Mattie knew what it was all right—some things you never forget. The Cube.

As one side slid open, a man emerged, dressed in futuristic garb that made him look like an extra from *Star Wars*. He was in his thirties, with a long brown cloak and hood. On his face was a dark bushy beard and a deep slash across his temple.

"Latro!" Praeses greeted him with delight.

"*You're* the guy who gets stuff," Mattie said to the visitor.

"That's right, little lady." The trader gave her a smile, marred by a few missing teeth.

"Bring it in, boys!" he yelled to the back of the Cube. The device spilled out four men heavily burdened with goods.

"What's in this shipment?" Praeses asked.

"Well..." Latro consulted some kind of space-age PDA. "Three hundred pounds of New York steak, seventy-five of white truffles, burgers for Missy here—" He threw a small package at Mattie, "—fifty DVDs of *How To Train Your Dragon 3*, *ludenhosen* from Jötunheimr—trust me, they're delicious—and a rowing machine for the coach. That's all we could carry this trip."

"So you can go...anywhere?" Mattie asked. "Not just Ea—Mundanis?"

"Pretty much," Latro crowed. "We can portal into any of the twelve worlds. Since we supply goods, *everyone's* happy to see us!"

Mattie nodded. Latro gave her a wink.

"Hey, you're not bad-looking for a Mundani! Next drop, maybe we can meet for a Dragonsmede?"

"Mattie is underage," Praeses pronounced.

"Damn!" the trader spat. "All the good ones are. Well, when you're are older—"

"Thank you, Latro," Praeses said, with an air of finality. "You're making many dragons happy."

The president placed a mound of coins into Latro's glove.

"Prez, you're making *me* happy." Latro happily counted, shoving his bounty into a bag. "Thanks for the tip!" he yelled, striding into the Cube. His men followed, and the portal shot through the roof, trailing primary colors.

Praeses looked down at Mattie. "Don't let Latro offend you. He's just an old space trader."

"Oh, he doesn't bother me."

In fact, it was nice to be noticed—by someone who wasn't a snake.

Wolf

Chapter Ten

Agravaine Gets Aggravated

The next day, Mattie finally got to Dragonlore. Artorius had dropped this class in favor of Wyse Wyrms, so for the first time, she was alone.

But who of course had transferred in to take his place? None other than "Master of Chivalry" Eli, his unmistakable form slouched on the bench in front of her.

She turned her attention to Professor Lung, who shared the class with Beowulf.

"Did you know that dragons symbolize the yin in Chinese philosophy? This is sustained energy, connected with the earth, dark, and cold. Tigers are the yang, and symbolize heaven, heat, and light."

Dude, I'd so rather be a tiger, Mattie thought. She doubted that the yinsters around her agreed.

"There are *nine* kinds of Chinese dragons. The first is the *Huanglong;* then comes the *Lóng Wáng—*"

Mattie typed away furiously on her virtual tablet keyboard. Eli looked back, alarmed, sliding down as if her device might attack. Mr. High Tech he was not.

Finally, the golden triangle dinged and all the students rose. Mattie turned to Eli, deciding to be nice for once.

"Wow, that was some lecture! It'll take me to midterms just to catch up."

He nodded as another classmate approached. This one was two-toned, red scales with gold stripes running down both his sides. *Like a running shoe,* Mattie thought. This vibrant fellow exchanged a flurry of signs with Eli.

Mattie stood there, feeling left out, until Dr. Lung floated up. "I should tell you that Eli's friend Superbas is deaf."

"Oh." Mattie nodded to him shyly. "What's the sign for dragon?" she asked, making sure he could see her lips.

He formed an outward pushing gesture, both claws extended to the sky.

"Cool!" Mattie made the same gesture. "What does Superbas mean?"

The striped dragon made some graceful gestures.

"He says his name is *Superbas Visum,* which means 'superb vision,'" Dr. Lung explained.

"I like that." Mattie put out a hand, which Superbas clasped with his claw.

She turned to leave, followed by her new friend and Eli. Once out in the quad, she saw a dragon swagger toward her—one she didn't recognize.

"Mundanis!" he addressed her, showing his fangs. "Hanging out with the freaks?"

"Shut it," said Mattie without thinking.

"What did you say?"

The large dragon lumbered closer. He was a chameleon and changed from silver to orange.

"I said shut it," Mattie repeated. "Nice move, making fun of people—um, dragons—with challenges they can't help."

"You're the biggest freak of all!" he yelled. "A Mundani going to ASH? Did you get lost, *hon?*"

"Don't patronize me," Mattie spat.

"Oh, she uses big words. Too bad her dumb friends don't know them."

"Deaf isn't the same as dumb, fool. And Eli simply can't talk. Neither can Stephen Hawking and he's the smarted man on earth!"

"Never heard of him."

"No duh. You probably never heard of Einstein."

The nasty dragon turned a bright shade of red, either from shame, anger, or both. He approached Mattie with menace, lowering his horned head and growling in the back of his throat.

"C'mon, Agravaine."

A voice emerged from one of the students who'd clustered around them.

Agravaine continued his march, pinning Mattie against a wall. She saw smoke waft from his nostrils and the cutting edge of his teeth.

"Get her, Aggie!" someone yelled. Mattie recognized that voice—silky, sensual. Of course, it was Sudha.

"Back off, dumbass," a deep male voice sounded.

Agravaine wheeled. Both he and Mattie saw Geetha, now in his *nāga* form, all six arms extended. His coils vibrated soundlessly.

"How perfect. It's her *snake lover!*" Sudha waved three of her own arms.

"I am no such thing." Geetha shot Mattie a look of shame. "I fooled her. She did not know my true essence."

"Double cow dung!" Sudha shouted.

"Do not heed her poisonous gossip! And speaking of poison..."

"What of it?" Agravaine snarled.

"You must be failing Dragonlore. Don't you know that the *nāga*'s bite is so poisonous, it's been described as 'setting fire'?"

He bared his toxic fangs.

Agravaine looked around. He seemed to be weighing the odds.

"Hey, I was just joking." He waved a large claw in dismissal as he lumbered off.

"Losers," Sudha muttered, flicking her tongue at Mattie before she glided away.

"Thanks, Geetha," Mattie said, peeling herself off the wall. "I forgive you for being...kind of a snake."

He shrugged his broad shoulders, giving her a look of regret. "Ethics was never my strong point."

Mattie turned to Eli and Superbas, who both cowered behind her. Her own legs were shaking as she thought of how close she'd come to being a dragon sacrifice. Frantically, she turned and searched the hall. Where was Artorius? If only he had been there, none of this would have happened.

At home in the cave that night, Mattie kept to herself. For the first time, she really *thought* about her ASH classmates. Her new Pico friends were trouble, that was true. But this crowd could rip your throat out, reduce you to a lump of charcoal, or with one bite cause a painful, toxic death.

Ripley was off at some party, and Artorius was enjoying Flambé Night at The Three-Headed Dragon. Yet Hob sensed her unease.

"Everythin' aw reit, miss?" he asked, his small face wrinkling with concern.

"I guess," Mattie said, but her flat tone betrayed her.

"Listen, lass. Ye jist keep studyin' at skale. Don't lit th' *bampots* gie ye doon." He pulled on his cap for emphasis, tapping a pointed dragon-scale shoe.

"Thanks, Hob. I won't."

He was right. Despite the prospective danger lurking behind most students, she was mainly enjoying ASH, and wanted to do well. Even, she admitted, as Eli's Page.

Over the next two weeks, she really listened in class. The memo app on her tablet filled with hundreds of notes. She and Artorius crammed for midterms—with the considerable aid of coffee—during two sleepless nights. Finally, Professor Fraxinus took her aside and told her she'd earned six out of six Dragon Teeth, ASH's equivalent to straight A's.

As the Professor strode down the quad, Mattie whispered, "See, Mom?"

She would have been so proud.

Wolf

Chapter Eleven

A Break

M attie could hardly believe it. The first quarter had flown by, and she had aced her finals. She and Artorius earned The Golden Dragon, reserved for the highest scorers. Jimmy was First in Class, followed by Sudha, while Ripley had to settle for two Dragon Teeth and a warning.

"I don't give a rip!" Ripley said, home with the roommates on break.

"Stop going out every night and you can shine too," said Artorius.

"I just wanna have some fun," the dragonet wailed, chomping down on a quail bone. "Is that so wrong?"

"I used to be that way," said Mattie, enjoying her French onion soup. "It's kind of a road to nowhere."

"That's th' spirit!" Hob interjected.

Assailed on three sides, Ripley exhaled smoke. "I need to bring up my teeth, or I'm gonna be expelled."

"I'll help ya," Hob said.

"What? A *midget?*"

"Maybe you should repeat Proper Treatment of Our Brownie Friends," said Artorius. "You're not exactly Praeses yourself."

"Humph." Ripley thought for a second. "If I flunk, my dad'll thrash my tail. Okay, little man, we're on!" She extended a tiny claw.

Hob grasped it in his own small hand.

"Thanks. Ah hink."

Mattie had found a solution to her shower issue. In the privacy of the back cave, she dumped water—from a solid gold bucket—over her head. It wasn't ideal, but at least it got her clean. Artorius lent her his Scale N' Tail, which she used as shampoo. She would have to ask Latro to bring her some human products.

In the middle of their two-week break, Artorius turned to Mattie and said, "Let's go."

"Where?" she asked, walking with him out of the cave.

"You'll see."

"Last time I went to a secret place I got in a lot of trouble."

"Really?" The dragon arched what would have been an eyebrow. "Wanna tell me about it?"

"I can't," Mattie mumbled, looking down.

"If you can't tell your BFF, who can you tell?"

"I know but...I made a promise."

Artorius put up a claw. "That's different." He cheerily changed the subject. "We're going somewhere I think you'll like. No rule-breaking, trust me."

Mattie nodded. She saw that they were tracing the Flavius behind the Plat. It was sunny, the Cavernin star generous with its warmth.

"What's your sun called?"

"Lumen."

"It works hard for the money."

"Yeah."

Close in by the river, it was slightly cooler as Mattie walked and Artorius crawled through sand and broken-off branches. It was nice being together, nice to know she didn't have to talk—didn't have to do anything.

At last, after a half-mile trudge, they came to where the river emptied into a green pool fed by cascading waterfalls. Mattie had never seen anything so pretty. Not in L.A., anyway.

"C'mon!" Artorius plunged ahead, leaping into the deep pool.

Mattie took a breath, then followed. She was relieved to find the water lukewarm, as comforting as a bath.

"Awesome!" she declared, swimming toward triple waterfalls. The crash of water over rock made a beautiful white noise.

"Here."

Artorius flipped over and offered a claw. It was like hitching a ride with an alligator as she clung to the slippery surface of his belly.

"This reminds me of something," he said.

"What?"

He stretched out his neck and recited:

"In ancient Hall of Kings, the fear of dragons was high.
A blast of streaming flame told villagers he was nigh.
But the beast of that old Kingdom was a kindly, peace-loving drake,

And wanted nothing more than to have a bathe in the lake."

"Ha!" said Mattie. "That's a good one."

"It is."

Artorius spread his wings so that they served as a kind of life raft.

"I wish we could stay here forever."

"But then we would never graduate. You wouldn't want that, would you?"

"No."

Although her tunic was weighing her down, Mattie felt at peace. She made sure to memorize every detail around her. The beauty of the falls and the fastness of their friendship made a memory to be taken out and cherished...even revived in darker times.

Chapter Twelve

Ugly Times

Mattie and Artorius tried to spend the week hiding out in their cave. Of course, Eli couldn't leave her alone. He sent word via Jimmy that she was to report to training.

"Why me?" Mattie groaned to Artorius, who lounged on the moss bed lazily reading a book.

"You know why."

"That damned Matilda! Couldn't she have helped Wyrmie in secret?"

Artorius laughed. "I know you don't really believe that. That's why I'm not engulfing you in flame."

"You're a pal."

Mattie set out for the dirt lot, passing the now-quiet ASH. At least it was a nice day. The sky was nearly cloudless, trees sheltered her from Lumen's rays, and she even found herself humming as she traced the path of the Flavius.

But, as she had before, Sudha ruined her day.

She and her mean dragons came marching over the bank and spread out to surround her. Mattie asked herself, "What would Eli do?" She decided that he would display no outward sign of fear.

"Find another snake to play kissy-face with?" Sudha hissed through her fangs.

"Is this how you spend your time off? Looking for someone to bully?"

"Not just anyone. *You.*"

"Time to stop, Sudha," Mattie said. "How many times do I have to say I thought that Geetha was human?"

"Sure. And you thought I was Ash Rai!"

Mattie rolled her eyes. There *was* more than a passing resemblance between her and the Bollywood star.

Sudha's female followers let out a collective snicker. They seemed to be evenly divided: three Westerners and as many Asians.

"What do you want, Sudha? I'm gonna be late for training."

"Ah yes, 'Our Lady of Cavernis.' Little girl never fought a day in her life but she's planning to save us all."

"I never said that! You might recall I was brought her *against my will.*"

"To become Praeses' favorite." Sudha shot out her forked tongue. "Guess he wants a Mundani for a pet."

Now Mattie was getting angry. "Let me pass. I'm warning you."

"You dare to threaten me? A *nāgī* of the blood!" Her cobra bottom half began to vibrate.

"Look, I don't want any trouble. Just let me go on my way."

"*Your* way is not that of the dragon."

"I am trying to learn. That's why I'm at ASH."

Sudha's features contorted, giving her an ugly look. "You violated our laws by consorting with one of ours. Now, I'm going to deliver the penalty."

She spread out her six arms and tossed off her red hood. Mattie looked around desperately, trying to spot a weapon. She finally settled on a downed branch, stripping it of its leaves.

"It's not too late to stop this," she said, her voice starting to tremble.

"Little girl is afraid?" Sudha slithered toward her as her acolytes stepped back.

"Get her, Sudha!" one of the Westerners cried.

Before she could even think, Mattie was fending off those six arms. She thought of Eli's paper target, applying the same technique. Every time a hand came at her, she tried to strike it with her "lance."

"Pathetic," Sudha sniffed, opening her mouth wide to reveal those cobra fangs.

Stay away from them, Mattie thought, remembering Geetha's words. *The* nāga's *bite...so poisonous...*

Even though Mattie thought that snakes were kind of cool, she preferred just seeing them at the zoo—safely behind glass.

Sudha could smell her panic. She fastened all of her arms around a tree trunk, upending her lower half. Mattie stood mesmerized as those giant coils came toward her, ensnaring her in their football-patterned grip.

"Hey, you ever see *Jungle Book*?" Mattie asked, trying to make a last desperate connection. "Boy, that Kaa was something!"

She choked on the last sentence since Sudha was squeezing her tighter. One more minute, and she assumed she'd be swallowed whole.

"Geetha really likes you!" she cried, not knowing where this came from.

"What?" Sudha relaxed her grip slightly.

"Yeah, he said that he's in love with you—he just went for me 'cause he thought you didn't like him."

"Really?"

"Yup!" It was easy to be convincing when you were in a snake's coils. Mattie felt Sudha unclench her muscles.

"This I did not know."

Sudha flicked her with the end of her tail, causing Mattie to roll on the ground. The taste of earth was welcome after the taste of fear.

Sudha gave a sort of half-smile. "All right. As long as Geetha has regained his senses."

She let go of the tree, popping upright like a top. "But if you are not telling the truth, you are deader than the Raj."

"Thanks!" Mattie cried, as if Sudha had suddenly offered her a delicious slice of cake.

The *nāgī* and her mean-girl dragons slithered and crawled back to ASH. Mattie lay on the ground, relieved that she could see Lumen and hear the trickle of water. She just hoped that Geetha really *did* like Sudha.

Well, Sudha was beautiful, so there was a good chance. As for her personality...Mattie wondered how much gold it would take to convince Geetha to ask her out. Professor Avarus probably knew.

Chapter Thirteen

Squire with an Attitude

After she got up, Mattie dragged herself to the lot where Eli and Jimmy waited. She wondered if she should say anything, but finally decided not to. *No one* was a match for Sudha, not even Eli.

"You're ruining his break *too?*" she asked Eli, motioning toward Jimmy.

"It's okay, Mattie," Jimmy replied. "If I weren't here, I'd be studying. Courtesy of my dad. Comparatively, you could say this is even fun."

"I'm glad that *someone* enjoys it," she snarled. After her near-strangulation, she was not in a happy mood.

Jimmy stepped forward, obviously prepped.

"Eli says that for training, there will now be squats, swimming, and pull-ups."

"Have you mistaken me for a member of the President's Fitness Team?"

"Also, you will train on the quintain."

"The what? The quatrain?"

"*Quintain.* It's over there."

Mattie pivoted. At the far side of the field a real shield and white crash test dummy hung from a pole.

"Your last pupil?" she asked Eli.

He glared.

"This exercise requires the use of a horse. So we are bringing one in for you." Jimmy let out a sharp whistle.

An enormous black shire loped up, kitted out in a funny saddle and bridle. He stopped and bowed before Mattie.

"How do?" he greeted. "Name's Fortis—that means 'strong' in Latin. I've always wanted to serve a knight. This is *so* exciting!"

Eli made some signs.

"Calm down," Jimmy told Fortis.

"Right. Sorry."

Eli made some more gestures.

"Eli says, 'soft Mundani girl has probably never been on horseback. So first, we focus on getting on.'"

Mattie's temper flared. "You tell Sir Lancelot I happen to be a *great* rider. Better than him, I dare say."

Eli gave a smirk.

"He heard you," Jimmy said.

"Give a leg up?" Mattie asked.

Fortis must have been eighteen hands, so Jimmy made a "basket" with his paws and heaved her into the saddle.

"Watch this, Dragon Boy!" she shouted.

Mattie proceeded to put Fortis through his paces, literally: walk, trot, and lope. She repeatedly switched leads as if she were in a show.

Eli nodded grudgingly. In fact, he looked relieved. He pointed to the quintain, indicating she was to rush it.

She and Fortis started off from about a hundred paces, running down the target with her wood lance held in the couch. BAM! She hit the shield, but the dummy's arms hit *her*, knocking her to the ground.

"Damn dummy!" she yelled, getting up. From Fortis's back, it wasn't exactly a short way down.

"I think I broke my rear," she said, limping.

Eli erupted in silent laughter, even holding his stomach. Mattie wanted to grab his little wings and twist them.

He just made his customary gesture for "again."

Jimmy hoisted her up, and again she ran at the target. Again those damned swinging arms knocked her off her seat. After ten tries, Mattie went on strike. She refused to rise from the dirt.

"You all right?" Fortis asked.

"*You* could do a better job."

"I suppose I could use my muzzle. And I do weigh over a ton."

Mattie groaned, refusing to open her eyes though she felt the shadow of Eli. He must have been saying something to Jimmy.

"Eli says that's okay, it happens to everyone. For a first-timer, you're doing really well."

Mattie's eyes flew open. Was the scaly little taskmaster actually offering *praise?*

While Mattie was on the ground, she thought to ask him something—something that had been bugging her. "How in heck did *a dragon* learn to be a knight?"

Eli didn't smirk or sign, he just stood there with arms folded. It was clear to Mattie that he refused to answer.

"Okay, fine, keep your mystique. I guess it doesn't matter. What matters to me right now is applying ice to my butt."

Eli grinned as Mattie limped off, trying not to think about squats or future training. *It was funny,* she thought. In all those books about King Arthur, they never told you *how* those guys became knights. No wonder they needed a

Round Table with big cushy seats for rears that ached from falling!

Chapter Fourteen

The Belching Dragon

The second quarter was starting, and Mattie had to prepare. Despite her aching body, she chose another dress, this one inlaid with sapphires. Taking her trusty knife, she cheerfully sheared off the sleeves. She was getting to be an expert!

She and Artorius traipsed to a solitary cave at ASH. Once inside, Mattie was surprised to see how deep it was. They were in a huge amphitheater with tiered seating for students.

Like Dragonlore, this class had two instructors, Professors Drake and Ignis. The former was nondescript: a typical Western dragon, though his wings were large. The latter was beyond flamboyant as he was literally *made of flames.*

"Welcome to *Ignis et Fuga.* For you non-Latin speakers, that means Fire and Flight."

A palpable excitement swept over the students, but Mattie just felt depressed. She couldn't fly and she couldn't flame, so what was she doing here?

Professor Drake answered her question.

"For those of you without...assets—say wings—you may take this class for credit, but you'll *not* have to do the lab."

Mattie felt relieved. She imagined the same was true for Geetha, Jimmy, and her nemesis Sudha.

"We shall begin with *fuga*—flight. Why, you may ask, must a dragon be taught to fly when she is born with this ability? Anyone?" Professor Drake scanned high and low.

Jimmy raised his tiger's paw. "This class is to help us refine technique and maximize lift and thrust."

"How would *you* know?" some dragon shouted.

Professor Drake flapped his wings. "Quiet! No further outbursts."

Professor Ignis was bursting himself, though it was with flame.

"We need a volunteer." Professor Drake inspected the class. "How about you?"

He pointed to Eli, who slowly rose from his seat. Mattie almost felt bad for him, then remembered her rear.

"What's your name, son?"

Eli scribbled something on his tablet, then handed it up to the teacher.

"Very well." The professor motioned him onstage, which Eli took with reluctance. "Now, son, demonstrate your basic takeoff."

Mattie was in the rafters, but she could have sworn that Eli turned a paler shade of brown.

"Don't be shy—take off and fly!"

Eli stood up on his hind legs. He ran forward a few steps, shakily lifted his wings, and promptly went...nowhere. He skidded to a stop, lowering his head.

"That's all right," Professor Drake said. "I take it you haven't had a lot of practice."

Eli shook his head ruefully as Artorius's claw shot up.

"Good, a *real* volunteer. Come up here, young man."

Artorius helped Eli back to his seat, then stood beside the instructor.

"Ah, a wyvern. Roar n' soar!"

Without effort, Artorius took off and flew circles around the arena. The other students cheered and applauded. Mattie let out a shrill whistle.

"Nice! Who's next?"

First it was a bold gold dragon, who actually did spins and loops. Then it was Superbas, and it was instantly clear to the class that as a flyer, he *was* superb. His technique was smoothness itself and he landed without taking a single step.

"I think we've found our star," Professor Drake told the students.

"Don't worry," Artorius said to Eli as they all streamed out of the cave. The latter's face bore an expression of woe. "I'll help you with your flying. I'm sure you're just out of practice."

Eli sighed, his posture slumping. He looked as pathetic as Sid had in his frozen state.

"Hey, after Infectious Diseases you wanna go out and blow off some steam? We can study after."

Eli smiled, revealing two neat rows of teeth. Mattie stepped back, unused to this rare sight.

Artorius kept his word. After classes were over, he beckoned for Eli to join them. Mattie had never seen a dragon hangout, and she wondered what it was like.

They passed the painted caves of the Plat and stopped at a welcoming corner. As their group entered The Belching Dragon, Mattie saw a sizable crowd. Artorius led them to a tree trunk that acted as a bench and sat in front of another slab that served as an impromptu table.

"Three Dragon's Breath," he told the waiter—a brownie who wore a cork as a hat.

"Yes, sir."

Twenty of his men carried the drinks on a silver tray so pristine it would have made Professor Avarus weep. The brownies handed up priceless goblets, but the most amazing thing was that the liquid within them was on fire!

"Whoa!" said Mattie. "Is this like a Tiki bar?"

"No, no," Artorius laughed. "*This* is Dragonsmede—the finest label, I might add. Just blow on the flames to put them out."

It took her at least ten tries to extinguish the flames.

"Cheers!" Artorius toasted. "To Eli!"

He raised his silver goblet and drained the cup in one gulp. "One more," he told the waiter.

Eli looked confused, but, wanting to be like Artorius, he too raised his cup. After a cautious sip, his blue eyes widened to twice their size. He tried another, then another, finally raising a talon in the "Oh waiter" signal.

"He seems to like it," said Mattie. "You know, Artorius, I'm only seventeen, and I've had one…bad time with booze. So I think I'm gonna pass."

"No worries," he said, hoisting her cup and emptying it.

"What exactly *is* Dragonsmede?"

"The most wonderful drink in the world! Nectar of the gods."

"Really?"

"Tastes like it! The closest drink on Mundanis would be beer. We dragons use the brew to sooth our throats after flaming."

"And at all other times?"

"Exactly."

The waiter brought him another, and he barely waited for the flames to douse before pouring it down his throat.

Eli was clearly enjoying the Dragon's Breath. After his *fuga* disaster, he was willing to forget his troubles at the bottom of a goblet. What he didn't consider, though, was the stealthy strength of the brew.

His head started to bob as he swayed from side to side. Mattie felt that if he could speak, he would have burst into "Sweet Adeline." This was not, strictly speaking, good.

"Eli, take it easy," she warned. "I once did what you're doing, and I can *still* hear the Pied Piper."

In reply, Eli belched in her face. Immediately, Mattie was taken back to Yellowstone National Park, where she'd stood before steaming vents. *Sulphur.* This was one of those smells that stayed with you, like a thousand rotting eggs or a million matches all being struck at once.

Mattie gagged and covered her face. "Gross," she coughed. "No wonder ASH has zero tolerance."

Eli gave a beatific smile before falling back off the bench. He immediately started snoring.

"Shall we?" Mattie asked Artorius, pointing to the door.

Her friend looked a little sheepish as he hoisted Eli onto his back. *He* seemed unaffected.

"Do you have a hollow leg?" she asked as they headed back down the Plat.

"Nah. Dragons are brought up on this stuff."

"Not Eli."

"Yeah, lightweight. He has the tolerance of a hatchling."

Mattie blanched. "So did I."

"What were *you* doing drinking?"

She blushed. "Trying to fit in."

"And did you?"

"I guess you could say my head fit nicely in the toilet."

"Mattie! What else were you up to?"

"Cutting class. Dissing my mom. Making fun of a guy like Jimmy."

"When you get back to Mundanis, you need to make amends. I don't mean to sound preachy, but sometimes best friends are right."

Mattie looked down. "I know."

"Okay then."

Once they arrived at ASH, Artorius reached around and gently laid Eli on the ground at the foot of a giant gold statue. Of course, it was of Praeses.

"You're just going to...leave him?"

"I don't know where he lives, and even if he could speak, I doubt he could tell us right now."

"Fraxinus will ream his tail."

"Good thing he can't talk to tell her where he's been."

"That's mean, and I don't even like him. Can't we just take him home?"

Artorius sighed. "I suppose." He re-lifted his burden. It was a slow but steady walk to the middle of his cave. Artorius laid Eli on one side of the moss bed. He even covered him with a gold cloth, gently tucking him in.

To his and Mattie's surprise, someone was in the cave studying. It was the first time *they* had gone out while *Ripley* listened intently as Hob described Mayan dragons.

"—known for their square faces—"

Even though Mattie hadn't had a drink, her head felt a little woozy. Cavernis or Mundanis, it really didn't matter. Whatever world you were on, it was sure to be topsy-turvy.

Chapter Fifteen

Small but Mighty

The next morning, they had a hard time waking Eli but finally managed to rouse him. When they removed his "blanket," his brown scales were streaked with green and he kept putting his claws to his head. He gave a silent series of what Mattie took to be groans.

She and Artorius cleaned him up by throwing a pail of water on him. He seemed ready to fight, but Hob calmed him with a hot cup of cocoa.

They carefully steered him to ASH, where they entered their first class, Infectious Diseases. Out of courtesy to Eli, they sat in the last row, putting as much distance as possible between him and Professor Fraxinus.

Frax was definitely sporting more pearls this quarter. And the number of clubs on her tail actually seemed to have doubled. Mattie had to confess, she was terrified of the green dragon.

"*Bumblefoot*," Frax drawled, holding up a slate that displayed the condition. "It begins as a small dot at the base of the claw, but progresses to a staph infection that can eventually become fatal. I recommend applying a gentle topical cream until the flesh looks normal."

Mattie started to snigger.

"Something amuse you, Sharpe?"

"No, ma'am, it's just that...on Mundanis, lotions like that are used for hemorrhoids."

The entire class—even Sudha—broke into gales of laughter.

"Thanks for that nugget of wisdom. You will write a five-tablet essay on Bumblefoot, due first thing tomorrow."

Mattie groaned. That meant *hours* in the library. And how many stone tablets did one of her screens equal? She had never been good at math conversions.

"On to insect infestation—"

"Ech," said everyone.

Mattie tried to take notes, but slates of dragons being eaten by giant bugs didn't do much for her stomach.

Ding ding! Thank heaven for Miss Fang. Mattie's least favorite class was over, and so, oddly, was her punishment.

Cymru pushed into the cave, waving a red claw frantically. The Welsh dragon's baritone was a nice contrast to Frax's whine.

"Ay, Sharpe! You're wanted *now*. The big boys are done with weights and we need our cox in the boat. Down to the river, double-quick."

"I have to write a five-tablet—"

"Never mind that," said Fraxinus. "When it comes to the boat race, all else takes second place." She gave a wink to Cymru. "As long as we take *first*."

"Wise as Praeses," Cymru nodded, beckoning to Mattie, Artorius, and the other S&B crew. In a way, Mattie was glad to be free of Bumblefoot; in another, she feared what was coming since she had no idea how she—at five-foot-six—could steer a boatload of dragons.

Yes! It's time to start training hard since the contest with R&R is just two weeks away."

"R&R is Row and Roar," Artorius told her. "They're the other Varsity team. Winner gets to be in the race against Jötunheimr."

Cymru went airborne as he bounced on four red feet in front of his whole team, which included Mattie, Eli, Jimmy, Ripley, the dreaded Sudha, Superbas, the gold dragon who'd shown off in class, a two-headed one she didn't recognize, and an Asian who could've been Jimmy's twin.

"Okay, guys and girls, today we start training *for real.* We're bringing in our cox and her assistant." He pointed to Mattie and Ripley.

"Keep them away from snakes," Sudha hissed.

"Team," the coach continued, "let me introduce Alazon."

The gold dragon gave a wide, insincere smile. He was wearing an ASH jacket festooned with various letters.

"Hey, ladies," he nodded. His smoothness reminded Mattie of Geetha.

"This is Huáng."

The Chinese dragon bowed with a smile.

"My brother," Jimmy said with pride.

"And this is Fractious and Unctuous. Two heads, four hands. Couldn't ask for a better rower."

"I'm actually the best," said Fractious, a male.

"*Liar! I* am!" said Unctuous, his female half. "Twit!"

"Twitette!"

"Twit for brains!"

"Half-twit!"

"Okay then," Cymru said cheerfully. "I think everybody else knows everyone. Let's bring out the boat."

The eight oarsmen—different sizes, species, gender, number of arms and heads—disappeared into a cave. They re-emerged a short time later, hoisting a boat ten times as big as the pharaoh's in the quad.

"Whoa," Mattie said.

The rowers set it on the water, fastening on the oars.

The prow was—naturally—shaped like a dragon's head, with red and blue ribbons tied to its wooden skull. The seats within were *huge* and the oars, kitty-corner, had blades the size of a steam shovel!

Mattie knew exactly nothing, but weren't those boats on TV tiny and lightweight? This one looked more like a naval carrier.

"All right, everybody in," Cymru ordered.

The crew took their positions: the strongest—Alazon, Fractious/Unctuous, Sudha, and Superbas—in the middle, Jimmy and Huáng in the bow, and Artorius and Eli in the stern.

"C'mon, coxswain," Cymru urged.

Artorius motioned for Mattie to sit in front of him, which she did. There was just one slight issue.

"You're facing the wrong way!" Cymru shouted.

Mattie cautiously turned about, belting herself to her seat. She was a little confused. There was one black string to her left and another to her right.

"Grab 'em!" said Coach. "That's how you steer the rudder."

The crew all sat there, poised, blades lifted out of the water. They seemed to be waiting for something.

"Send 'em out!" Coach yelled. He was pointing right at *her*.

"Uh, let's go," Mattie said softly. No one but Artorius heard. Ripley flew onto her shoulder, wearing two tiny boat shoes.

"*Move out!*" she yelled so loudly they probably heard her in Georgia.

The eight-dragon crew obeyed. As one, they dipped their blades in the water, throwing up an enormous splash.

"Count the strokes and yell praise," Artorius told her.

"Okay now, one—two—three, that's it, guys—four-five-six—stay together!—seven-eight-nine—doing fine!"

Hey, this was kind of fun!

As the crew really got going, sliding back and forth on their seats, they exhaled on the release. Normally this was fine, but these rowers were *dragons*, and each time they breathed out, they emitted a stream of fire.

"Watch it!" Mattie yelled. Eli and Artorius tried to point their heads up.

As she looked out of the boat, she saw the left bank coming up fast. At this speed, they'd be grounded before you could say 'bad cox.'"

"Mattie, steer the boat. Steer the boat!" Artorius shouted.

"I don't know how!"

"Pull the black strings beside you!"

Mattie stared at them, frozen.

"Oh, for Beowulf's sake!" Ripley said, grabbing the strings in her jaw while rapidly flapping her wings.

They just missed running ashore. All of the rowers cheered. Mattie decided that steering was something she'd better learn. Fast.

They swept through the whole practice course—two thousand meters—going with the bends of the river thanks to Ripley.

Finally, after a lifetime—really about ten minutes—they crossed what must have been the finish line.

"Hurrah!" the rowers shouted. "Three cheers for Ripley!"
Mattie joined in the hip-hip-hoorays.

All of the rowers got out, taking their oars with them. Mattie finally unstrapped herself and staggered onto the bank

"Not bad for your first time, missy," the coach encouraged her with a pat.

"I don't know what I'm doing. I'm sure that's more than clear. Also, a flameproof vest would be nice so I don't end up at a barbeque—as the main course."

"Right you are," Cymru boomed. "I'll make a note of it."

Mattie dragged after her teammates, who hoisted the boat on their shoulders, singing what must have been a pre-rehearsed song.

We are the Scull and Bones,
So much better than Row and Roar!
When we meet them two weeks from now,
We're going to drive them onshore.

We've got two Chows in the bow,
Six-armed Sudha won't have to scuttle.
Strong Superbas does us proud,
But our cox is a bit of a muddle.

Granted, she's small and light,
Just the right size for the job,
But she's a real mess on water,
Into which we think she'll soon bob!

That's all right, boys and girls,
We need to give her her due.
If she dumps us into the drink,
She's coming along with us too!

Artorius turned and winked. Mattie didn't know if she should be offended or flattered. Still, the song bolstered her spirits. She *knew* that she could learn. Hadn't she proved that with Eli? At that moment, she determined to master this sport, come you-know-what or high water!

Chapter Sixteen

The Boat Race

Two weeks on Cavernis slipped by like a boat on the Flavius.

Since her first sad attempt, Mattie had trained with the team up to three times a day, and she sort of felt like she was finally ready. Jimmy had helped tremendously, showing her how to steer, and she'd studied some old books, filled with fading drawings.

Their match against Row & Roar was actually *today,* and she was intent on being an asset, instead of a big fat handicap. But she remembered what Miss Evans—in a rare moment of lucidity—had said: "You can't say 'we tried real hard.' You have to do it right."

Already, the boats were on the water as Mattie fought through the crowd. Great. Every dragon on Cavernis must have converged for this race! She saw silvers, chameleons, and even a guy who shimmered! Not to mention all of her classmates...and teachers.

The competitors from both sides lined up inside the boat cave. R&R came out first, and Mattie heard Cymru say that

Agravaine was their captain. The rest were comprised of his set, including the hunky Geetha, who gave a low whistle to Sudha.

"Back to snake?" she scoffed, tossing her long black hair.

Mattie exhaled with relief. So Geetha *did* like Sudha!

S&B was next, with Superbas named as captain. They all waved to the cheering crowd, the rowers hefting their oars.

This time, Mattie came prepared. She wore a red fireman's hat, courtesy of Latro, and a matching flameproof jacket. Ripley looked sporting in a tiny sailor's hat.

R&R won the coin toss, which meant that they would row on the sunny side. An advantage, yes, but not a showstopper.

The two crews entered their boats and affixed their wooden oars. Mattie sat in the coxswain's seat with Ripley on her shoulder.

"On your mark—" Beowulf himself started them off.

"Get set—" Instead of firing a gun, he fired flame from his mouth.

"Go!"

The two giant crafts set off, absolutely dead even. Mattie thought she must be a sight: her sitting there in fireman's gear trying to handle eight dragons.

Now, she expertly played the black lines, keeping their boat to the center of the course.

"S&B! R&R!" the dragons onshore yelled, depending on their allegiance.

After the last two weeks, Mattie thought she knew what to say, and she yelled on every stroke.

"That's it, team! Push it! Keep pushing. That's the rhythm. Clear them! Nine-eight-seven-six...Send it! Don't sit. Don't freakin' sit!"

They rounded the first bend at two minutes, according to Ripley's watch. That wasn't bad, but they had to have something left for the final push.

Two ASH dragons flew overhead, playing referee. They made such a racket with their flapping of wings that Mattie had to scream like a fan at a rock concert:

"Hooooold baaack. That's it, Alazon! That's the stuff, Eli! Nice and long. Keep on it! Together!"

At four minutes, she was exhausted, and all she'd done was sit! Ripley flitted to each rower, repeating her cox's words.

Mattie stared at the R&R coxswain, an orange dragon no bigger than a hatchling. He'd been introduced as "Tiny." He also was shouting, willing his crew to win. The two boats were apart by a length, with S&B just ahead.

"Halfway mark. Halfway!" Mattie felt a shiver; she had never before been part of an actual team.

She saw Agravaine turn his head from the middle of the R&R "engine room." He shot her a dirty look.

"Call it!" he yelled to Tiny.

"St. George. *St. George!*" the small dragon screamed.

Mattie wondered what a saint had to do with Crew Eights, but R&R quickly showed her. Tiny steered his craft on a collision course with theirs, while Agravaine stuck out his blade.

BOOM! With a sickening splinter, Superbas' oar was shorn from its handle.

"Oops," Agravaine called, as his craft surged ahead by five lengths. Geetha winked at Sudha as he sped by.

"Cheaters!" Mattie yelled, practically in tears. She looked up at the sky, but the dragon refs were ahead of them. S&B was on its own.

"We won't let 'em get us!" she yelled, trying to stand up. "C'mon, Alazon! C'mon, Jimmy and Huáng! We can still make up the time. That's it. Tenacious. Everyone row as one. Press together! Together."

Despite the missing blade, they managed to make up two lengths. It was on this day of surprises that Mattie received one more.

Something shimmering rose from the water, swimming gracefully at portside. Mattie saw a water dragon, its body clear except for its lines, which were limned solely in liquid.

"That was a nasty move," it said, swimming with the aid of its tail. "I'll catch you up the three strokes you missed when you lost the blade. That's Yin and Yang, babe."

The creature stopped its forward motion and got behind their boat. Mattie saw it exhale a fountain of water, right by the stern. Just like that, they were back in the race!

"Go Eli. Go two-heads. Finish the stroke. Relentless! One more minute to go. We can catch them. We can beat them. We are the better crew." She made the gesture for "dragon" to Superbas.

The eight rowers pulled together as one. Jimmy and Huáng showed a strength that when united was the strongest in the boat. Mattie saw the shore fly by at fifteen miles-an-hour. Not fast by Mundanis standards, but from inside the boat it felt like NASCAR.

"Finish them. Finish them!" she yelled, as she turned and spotted a yellow tape strung across the Flavius. "Together. Press and set. We are friggin' Scull & Bones!"

Someone blew a whistle. The finish had been so close that Mattie didn't know who'd won. And she seriously doubted that ASH had instant replay.

Beowulf had arrived at this end of the river, either by foot or wing. He held a gorgeous trophy aloft, its gold striped with royal ermine and a King's bounty of rubies.

"Congratulations!" he boomed. He was so utterly massive that he nearly blocked Lumen. "The Crew Trophy for ASH Varsity eights is hereby awarded to last year's champion—"

Ripley's claws sunk into Mattie's jacket.

"—Scull & Bones!"

Mattie started screaming. She jumped up and down with such vigor that if she hadn't been belted in, she would have ended up in the water.

"We did it!" she yelled, throwing off her restraint and moving forward to embrace Artorius.

"Great job," he told her with pride. "You're the best cox S&B ever had!"

Somehow, they all got out of the boat, and Superbas accepted the trophy. Agravaine, Geetha, Tiny and their crew refused to shake hands and stomped off in a huff.

"Nice sportsmanship," said Sudha.

Mattie shook her head. Before she knew what was happening, she felt herself being lifted by Artorius and Eli. They moved perilously close to the Flavius's edge.

"Hey, what the—?"

"ASH tradition!" Artorius said.

They swung her back and forth.

"One. Two. Three!"

Mattie went flying through the air, then into the cold water of the Flavius.

"Thanks a lot," she sputtered, held down by her fireman's gear.

Artorius waded in beside her, putting her on his shoulders as he walked onto the bank.

"Three cheers for Mattie!" he told the crew.

"Hip Hip Hooray! Hip Hip Hooray! Hip Hip Hooray!"

Mattie stripped off her jacket and threw a towel over her head. She tried to absorb the fact that people—well, dragons—were cheering for *her*.

Then her crewmates started a song:

We are the S&B, so much better than Row and Roar,
With our new cox Mattie, we've managed to even the score.
She might be from Mundanis, and wear a coat to repel fire,
But without her shouting and skill, our standing would be dire.

So all hail Mattie, who looks and feels *mah-ve-lous,*
From a noob she has become our beloved Queen of the Flavius!

Mattie liked this song much better than the first. She threw off the towel and put it around her neck. Besides the day she'd found Artorius, this was—by far—the best day of her life.

Chapter Seventeen

A Sore Scaly Loser

U ntil she was walking back home...

Most of S&B—including Cymru—decided to go to The Belching Dragon. Mattie thought she knew what lay ahead, so she opted out, saying she was exhausted. This wasn't far from the truth, and besides, Jimmy stayed with her, a fellow non-fan of having sulfur burped in your face.

"I can't believe we won," she said, as he slithered by her side on the dirt path home. Everyone had gone. The spectators had dispersed and from the sound of things, they had carried their celebration to the plat.

"I know," Jimmy answered. "It almost doesn't seem real. Especially after they cheated. Thank Buddha for Unda!"

"Who?"

"The water dragon."

"Yeah. We should make up a song for *her*."

"Hey."

None other than the cheater himself—Agravaine—appeared from behind a boulder. Mattie felt the stab of poles topped with red flags poking into her brain.

"No hard feelings?" the chameleon asked, offering a huge purple claw to Jimmy.

"Of course not," Jimmy said. "Very decent of you." He stuck out one tiger paw.

Agravaine was more than happy to take it. Then, in a martial arts move, he lifted Jimmy's whole body, flipped him over his head, and smacked him to the ground.

"Hey!" Mattie yelled, the blood in her veins displaced by anger. "Isn't it enough you cheated? Now you have to be a dick?"

"Shut it, Mundani," said Agravaine, turning red as her fireman's coat. "I hate you almost as much as him." He thrust a black talon at the prone Jimmy.

"What'd he ever do to you?" Mattie asked, standing over her friend defensively.

"He's a Slant," Agravaine spat, "and I hate them all." In an obnoxious Chinese accent, he added, "Wanna eat some pig's feet, coolie?"

"*You're* the pig, pigswill!"

Mattie lost all sense of regard for her own well-being. She was practically screaming, "You're nothing but an ignorant racist!" Then her mind flashed back to Pico—and her treatment of David Wang. She must have flushed redder than Agravaine.

"I was once like you," she said softly. "And I hate myself for it. If there's anything I could take back in my life, that would be it."

"How dare a Mundani compare herself to *me?*"

Agravaine lowered his head, enabling her to get a close-up of his jagged, foot-long horns.

"You clearly haven't taken Our Diverse World of Dragons."

Mattie was stalling for time. She saw that the R&R captain was prepping for a massive head butt.

"Your time at ASH is over! I'm doing all dragons a favor."

Agravaine charged her like a purple rhino, and all she could see were cutting horns and massive teeth, until they faded to...nothing.

There was no sign of Agravaine. He had literally vanished from view. What she did notice was Jimmy, off the ground, and smacking his paws together.

"What happened?" she asked as he helped her up from her knees.

"As a martial artist, that guy was a total *chǔn dàn*. I managed to take him down with my best Tai Chi move. I can demonstrate, if you like."

"*No.* I mean, I already have enough adrenaline to start orbiting Lumen."

Jimmy smiled. They walked along in silence, Mattie glancing around warily, expecting Agravaine at every corner.

"Where is he?" she asked.

"Let's just say he has gone on a long, productive journey."

Mattie laughed.

"Listen, Mattie, I really want to thank you for standing up for me. That took a whole lot of guts."

"Not really. I hate that kind of ignorance, because I've acted that way myself." She looked away, ashamed.

"I should have kicked his tail years ago. In the name of all Chinese dragons, I absolve you of your sins. Consider yourself forgiven." Jimmy touched her forehead with a soft paw.

"Thanks, Jimmy. You don't know how much that means to me. Now I just have to ask forgiveness from a Chinese guy I know."

Mattie let out her breath now that the threat was over.

"Wanna come by? We can have soft drinks and just chill."

"Sure!" he said, and the two friends, bonded even closer, continued along their path.

Chapter Eighteen

Second Quarter Break

Mattie noticed that after the boat race, she suddenly became more popular, at least with everyone but R&R and Sudha.

Dragons who'd previously shunned her now said hi in the quad. Even Eli, small and plain, had become a Big Man on Campus. Superbas was swamped with fans, some even learning DSL so he could sign the entire race. Artorius, of course, let none of this go to his head, nor did the Chow brothers. Sudha remained aloof, which to Mattie was a good thing.

Still, she was surprised when, after midterms, she was rushed by a few sororities. She had done her best to ignore them as they sat in their booths on the quad, shouting to prospective pledges. But now, it seemed the Weirdo From Mundanis was actually being fought over!

"Mattie Sharpe! Over here."

A petite yellow "sister" beckoned her to Epsilon Kappa Kappa.

Mattie stopped reluctantly. "Hey."

"We would so love for you to pledge! We have an annual picnic and a really cool house."

"Thanks but—"

"Mattie, don't mind her. You need to come to Delta Sigma Chi. We give the best parties!"

"Lambda Sigma Nu!"

"Alpha Beta Gamma!"

Mattie found herself surrounded by sorority dragons, each wearing a knit sweater with their house's Greek initials.

"Thanks, everyone. Thanks, but I live with my friend Artorius, and there's no place I'd rather be."

Disappointed, the sisters returned to their booths as Jimmy slithered up to her.

"Delta Phi Sis Boom Bah!" he said, with a wink.

"Ugh, they're like parasites. Like the ones Frax is always talking about."

He laughed. "Don't think I'm cut out for a fraternity. I'm not into binge-drinking, ogling lady dragons, or thinking I'm all that."

"Thank God!" Mattie told him. "I like you just the way you are."

"Ditto."

They both walked to the dirt lot where Eli was waiting with a new torture device.

"What is *that?*" she cried.

Jimmy translated his signs. "*That* is for something called Running at the Rings."

"I saw this at Dark Ages Park! The knight gallops up and tries to put a lance through those teeny tiny rings. You have got to be kidding!"

Despite their camaraderie during the boat race, Eli was back to Master mode. He pointed to Fortis' back, then to a wooden lance, and finally at the rings.

This was the worst one yet. A person had to have a hand as steady as a surgeon's and aim as good as a sniper to even halfway succeed. Mattie tried time and time again—day after day—but always, she would miss. This one seemed hopeless.

"Did I mention that at fairs, when you throw balls into little bowls to try to win a fish, I never won a fish?"

Eli nodded and put her through her paces. There was the running, the squats—her thighs were always on fire—and sad attempts at doing a pull-up. Mattie figured she could do almost a fourth of one.

He made her go into the Flavius, strengthening her body by swimming. It wasn't exactly warm, and she always came out with teeth chattering.

"Did I mention that I hate you?"

Eli nodded, but obviously didn't care. He was going to make her a squire even if he killed her.

Mattie had done all right on her midterms—four Dragon Teeth—but she realized that Crew and Eli were dragging down her grades.

As the quarter unfolded, she tried to fit her training between bouts of study. In Julius—July—they would face the North in a boat race, and Cymru said they were amazing.

At last, the day came when she put down her tablet, handing it in to Miss Fang. The next day, final results were in: she had raised her marks to five-and-a-half Dragon Teeth!

"It's that damned Infectious Diseases," she told Artorius, Ripley, and Jimmy as they lounged in The Lazy Dragon, one of several student cafés. "Every time Frax says 'pus,' my mind just switches off. And oozing sores, yech."

She hoisted a cup of coffee, courtesy of Latro. "Guess I'll never be a vet."

"But you want to be a zoologist." Artorius looked confused.

"I did—I do."

Mattie felt a wave of depression. Even her cup's strong stimulant couldn't combat the feeling. How would she get to be anything stranded on another world? She'd been here for nearly six months and as much as she loved Artorius and coxing the S&B, there really *was* no place like home. She seriously missed her mom.

Artorius picked up on her mood. In some ways, he was as good a guesser as Praeses

"Hey, I've got an idea! Why don't we spend this break skiing the Dentes Mountains?"

"Cool!" said Jimmy.

"I am so in," chirped Ripley.

"Where are they?" Mattie asked.

"Over there." Artorius pointed up. "See those mountains in the distance? The ones with snow on their sides? They're an oasis for winter sports!"

He seemed really excited, and Mattie didn't want to be a wet snow blanket.

"Sure. Sounds great." She hoped she sounded convincing. Then for some reason, she decided to be nice. "What about Eli? Superbas is going home, but Eli will be by himself."

"He can come! The more the merrier."

"How exactly do we get there? Jimmy and I don't have wings."

Right." Artorius pondered the question. "Ripley and I will fly, Jimmy will slither, and I think it's best if you and Eli hike."

"How far is it?"

"Only twenty miles."

Mattie nearly fell off her bench. "Are you *serious?*" The farthest I walked in L.A. was from the carport to my room!"

"Perfect fitness opportunity."

This sucks," Mattie told Eli, about halfway through their trek.

They were somewhere in the high desert where it was scorching during the day and utterly freezing at night.

The winds blew without mercy, and Mattie spent most of the trip picking sand out of her teeth. She sensed that Eli was *not* having fun, since he carried their gear on his back.

"Eli, what's up with this dragon No Fly Zone? Is it really that big of a deal for you guys to carry a rider?"

Eli shrugged, spreading his front claws wide. He shook his head in disgust, then seemed to get an idea. With broad gestures, he crouched low and beckoned Mattie to climb on his back.

She remembered his not-great *Fuga* debut.

"Are you sure?"

Eli nodded vigorously. For some reason, Mattie trusted him. Not only had he come through in crew, but he was a serious Master, even when she was hopeless. With a bit of hesitation, she clambered onto his back, making sure to keep clear of his wings.

Eli spread them, then took a running leap and was airborne! Mattie felt his four feet leave the ground. Her hair swiped her face each time he flapped those brown wings. Artorius must have been training him since he was now smooth as a condor. Mattie tried to focus on his neck, as looking down didn't strike her as prudent.

She hadn't had this sense of freedom since she'd been on Spitfire's back, loping through Griffith Park. She tried to remember why she'd quit riding. All that pressure at school. But the real reason, she had to admit, was the wrenching away of Artorius.

Ten miles of dragon flight took what seemed like minutes. Eli soared to the side of Mt. Dentem, treating Mattie to the rare sight of snow. Before she could catch her breath, he landed gently beneath the summit.

"Thanks, Eli." Mattie slid off her relatively small mount.

"I won't give us away. The other dragons would freak."

Eli nodded, giving the okay sign as best he could with talons instead of fingers. He began hiking the south face and Mattie did the same, thinking that in the ranks of climbers, she was no Sir Edmund Hillary.

They finally made it to the top. There, she spotted their posse: Artorius, Ripley, and Jimmy.

"Wow, you made it in record time!" Artorius looked impressed. "Eli, did you carry her on your shoulders?"

Eli shook his head vehemently. After all, he hadn't.

"Let's have some fun!" Ripley shouted.

Mattie wanted to tell her she looked cute in a ski coat and hat, but she wished to retain all of her limbs.

Artorius had skis strapped to his front legs. Using his tail as a brake, he took off downhill like an Olympian. Ripley followed on skis the size of matchsticks: in fact, they probably *were*.

Eli removed his gear from their shared pack. He attached wood skis to his hind legs, grabbing poles in his front claws. Mattie was surprised to see him glide effortlessly, whooshing past Artorius. Guess he had hidden talents.

"Climb on!" Jimmy yelled to Mattie.

His orange-and-black scales served as an undulating sled, one that sped her downhill so fast she gave a little shriek. This was better than Space Mountain!

They all met at the bottom, sharing hot chocolate with marshmallows courtesy of Artorius. Mattie forgot her homesickness over the next two days as they skied, sledded, and threw snowballs (Artorius dropped them from the air like a blue bomber). He had also brought packs of hearty, delicious food.

When she wasn't covered in white, Mattie had time to think. Studying was fine in its place, but sometimes, you needed a break just to hang out with your friends, fill your head with nothing, or try something new. On break, Mattie felt like she could stay in Cavernis forever, maybe set up shop on the plat as a leading Dragonologist.

As always, with Artorius she felt content.

Wolf

Chapter Nineteen

Professor Ignis Lives Up to His Name

Third quarter, and it was time to learn the first part of *Ignis et Fuga*: how to properly breathe fire.

Again, the students trudged to the IEF cave to be greeted by an old friend. Mattie was now used to Professor Ignis, but there was still something strange about a guy made of fire. What if he lost his temper? Would they all become BBQ?

His upbeat, cheery tone, however, quickly put her at ease.

"Welcome, class. Welcome to Part Two of a dragon's favorite pastimes."

"Eating?" someone yelled.

Professor Ignis' face broke into an orange smile.

"Ha! Well, one nearly as key as that. *Fire.*"

All of the students leaned forward on their benches.

"Of course, as with flight, we—that is, most of us—are born with this gift. But to really control it, to know when and when not to use it, and at what volume, combines a bit of art and science. Let me ask a student to demonstrate."

His burning eyes scanned his class roster. "Mister...Alazon."

Mattie rolled her own eyes. Not that showoff again!

Alazon swaggered onstage to cheers from Agravaine and Geetha.

"I'm here," he announced, as if he were God's gift.

"Very well. I wish you to breathe fire. Start out full bore, then gradually dial back."

"Easy peasy," Alazon boasted.

He puffed out his golden chest, laying back his black-horned head.

With a heat that Mattie could feel, he expelled a torrent over his classmates' heads. The flames started out small, then gained breadth the farther they shot. To emphasize his fierceness, he roared like a T. Rex.

"Excellent. Now control, my boy. Dampen that flame to a trickle."

Alazon sucked in his chest, but this had no effect. His fire was just as volcanic, his heat just as searing.

"All right, you may stop."

Alazon did, and the temperature dropped about thirty degrees. He looked extremely self-satisfied.

"Thank you."

The gold dragon returned to his seat, air high-fiving his pals.

Professor Ignis remained impassive.

"Hmmm...how about...Mr. Superbas Visum?"

Eli motioned for his friend to take the stage.

"Very good. Please try the same exercise." Eli translated for him.

Superbas stood in the place Alazon had vacated. He produced the same mammoth blasts, but was able to reduce his flames by half, then a third, and finally to a barely visible thread.

"Yes!" Professor Ignis shouted, raising a fiery claw. "You never know if you might have to pull back. By Finals, I expect each of you to exhibit the skill of Superbas."

Alazon rolled his eyes while Geetha stuck out his forked tongue. Despite his being a different species, how had Mattie ever *liked* him?

The professor consulted his roster.

"I hereby make an exception for all Mundani, *nāga*s, and dragonets."

Mattie exhaled, but with relief instead of fire. Ripley looked dejected and Sudha just glared at Geetha.

Mattie was glad when it came time to leave the hot space. She and Artorius had the same next class: Dragonlore II. They returned to the main ASH campus, ducking into a cave that Mattie recognized.

"Good afternoon," Dr. Lung began. "I'd like to continue a theme I touched on in DL I. That is the nature of Power. Western dragons tend to use their gifts to subjugate: to hoard treasure and cause harm. We in the East try to influence the Elements for good and we are a symbol of protection. In other words, not a threat."

Sudha raised three hands.

"Yes?"

"We are also givers of life. Along with our power to destroy, we can sometimes raise the dead."

"An excellent point! Our cousins from India are indeed spiritual."

Mattie sighed. This was all getting a bit New Agey. What next? Were Dr. Lung and Sudha were going to bring out crystals?

"To continue. Even in a fight, one may maintain a Yin attitude and resolve without violence. Knowledge is stronger than force."

Mattie and Artorius exchanged a glance. *How?*

"Note this wisdom from the Dao—" And he looked straight at Mattie. "'We may be floating on Tao, but there is nothing wrong with steering. If Tao is like a river, it is certainly good to know where the rocks are.'"

Chapter Twenty

Georgia

Training continued. It never seemed to end.

Mattie was now at the point where she could do a whole *half* pull-up, avoid the stuffed arms of the dummy, and swim the equivalent of eight Olympic laps. She could feel muscles hardening where she'd never had them before.

The Running at the Rings, though, continued to be a farce. She was no closer to sticking that lance through the rings than she was to forcing Eli to yield his sword.

For a dragon, he had some serious skills. They struck at each other with wooden sticks and she could never get the best of him. Wherever he had learned his art, they had taught him well. *Why oh why couldn't she win just once? And hear him beg for mercy...*

The rest of that week passed peacefully: more IEF, more philosophy, mainly directed at *her*, more practice with S&B, and more—always more—training. On Freiday—Friday in Cavernis—Mattie was shocked when Sudha slid toward her in the quad.

"Sharpe," Sudha greeted her.

Mattie froze to the gold floor. Recalling the grip of the *nāgī's* coils, she didn't know whether to run or return the greeting.

"Guess I...well, I was wrong," Sudha said, not giving Mattie the chance to escape. "I tortured Geetha a little and he stands by his story. You really didn't know what he was."

Mattie exhaled. Would Sudha now burn her Burn Book?

"Plus, you were right. He really *does* like me. That means years—maybe decades—of more torture!"

Mattie managed a smile.

"What do you say to you and me taking a trip to Georgia?"

Now that Sudha wasn't trying to kill her, Mattie saw she was so breathtaking it was hard to refuse her anything.

"Um, isn't that kind of risky and against the rules?"

"Bah!" Sudha shook her long black hair. "The Mundani is afraid? They *are* your own kind."

"Well, yes—no. That is, I don't know."

"You humans are so capricious. Can't make up your minds."

Mattie wanted to defend her species, but she knew something that Sudha didn't. "Uh, it might not be a great idea to go to Georgia just now."

"I hear rumors too. That's all they are—rumors."

Not exactly, thought Mattie. "I think we better pass."

"Humph. So much for human 'bravery.'" Sudha gathered up those deadly coils.

"Okay, look, I'll go. Just don't tell Artorius."

Mattie felt a pang the minute she spoke. She'd never kept secrets from him—except for her adventure with Sid—and, oh yeah, the thing with Avarus's wife.

"Anyway, won't they kind of...notice you?" Her eyes focused on Sudha's snake half.

"You think Geetha's the only one who can change into a human?"

On an impulse, she did, becoming a red blur until her coils turned to legs.

"No way. It's just like *The Little Mermaid!*"

Sudha looked disgusted. She clearly wasn't a Disney fan. "Meet me on the Plat at tomorrow at nine. By the law office."

From her peripheral vision, Mattie saw something odd. She turned to see Eli, his tongue literally hanging out as he ogled Sudha.

"For God's sake, cover yourself," Mattie spat at her with annoyance.

Sudha let down her sari over perfectly shaped legs.

See you later," Mattie called to Artorius the next morning, her guilt weighing on her like a boulder. She'd told him that she and Sudha were having a "girls' day out," which wasn't really a lie.

Still, Ripley looked hurt at being left out and Hob shot a glance like a bolt to let her know he was onto her. This was worse than being back home. Instead of one mom, now she had three!

She found Sudha in front of the law firm Drakon, Drache, and Drakon. And it wasn't long before they passed The Belching Dragon. Mattie wrinkled her nose at the phantom smell of sulfur.

"So what's in Georgia?" she asked, as they stepped onto a trail she recognized from her first day. Sudha had kept her human shape and for once walked beside her.

"Not much." Sudha shrugged. "People. At least it's something different."

Mattie wondered if the *nāgī* longed for her own kind. To this she could wholly relate.

"What kind of people are Georgians?"

"They stopped coming from Mundanis around the 1500's, so basically medieval bores."

"Huh."

"Afternoon," a collie nodded from behind his sheep's enclosure. "Rather far from home, aren't we?"

"Mind your business, bow-wow, or I'll make you into a curry!"

"Woof!" the dog huffed, then went to gather its flock.

"Can't you try to be nicer?" Mattie asked her companion. "I'd rather *not* be put in the stocks the second we get there."

"I don't have to," Sudha said airily. "As a snake, my venom is toxic; as a woman, I am so beautiful that no one will ever cross me."

Mattie opened her mouth to argue, then realized she had a point.

"There it is."

Sudha pointed to the spot where Mattie had tumbled from the Cube. Thankfully, she only had two arms now. Beyond, they could see the thatched roofs of a village with a white cathedral at the center.

Mattie drew Sudha back behind some sturdy oaks.

"Careful," she whispered. "Remember, they hate dragons."

"Yet you and I are no such things." Sudha strode forward boldly.

"Wait—"

Mattie wanted to stop her, but she could really move on those legs. Reluctantly, she followed, taking heart that *she* at least would blend in with her medieval gown.

"Greetings, gentlewomen," a young farmer called, devouring Sudha with his eyes. "Care to linger for some milk?"

"You wish," Sudha said, tossing her hair over her sari and striding toward the town.

Mattie wished she would take it easy but somehow she felt powerless before the dynamic *nāgī*. What had Dr. Lung said? Something about a Yin attitude? She had to suppress her Yang.

PLINK!

Mattie heard a sound like rocks falling behind her. She was right: they *were* rocks, being thrown by Georgian boys—at Eli!

"Eli, what are you doing *here?*" she yelled, expecting an answer. "Are you *trying* to commit suicide?"

He was too busy dodging stones to even make a gesture.

"Get 'em!"

"Filthy wyrm!"

"In the name of St. George, slay the beast!"

Sudha stuck out her forked tongue, mesmerizing the kids. But they were soon back in action.

"Demon, abomination!" they shouted, directing their missiles at her.

Sudha opened her jaw and bared her fangs...

"No, Sudha, don't!" Mattie cried, trying to act as a human shield. "You'll only start a real war! Ow!" A sharp rock hit Mattie's arm, and she had to restrain an impulse to throttle the little brats. "Let's get out of here!"

Sudha nodded and Eli seemed game, but an obstacle had arisen in the middle of the path home. Swathed in opaque gray smoke, gradually the tall figure of a man appeared. He was wrapped in black robes, his features barely visible beneath a drooping black hood. He might have been twenty—he might have been a hundred. In any case, when the boys spotted his visage, they scampered off like squirrels.

One thing was for sure, he had met Eli before. The dragon cowered in the dirt, covering his face with his claws.

Sudha, vain but brave, stepped toward the man with bared fangs.

"I know what you are, *nāgī*," the wand-wielding figure announced. With a flick of his wrist, a blue bolt shot from the wood, dropping Sudha like a game bird.

"Bully!" Mattie shouted, running and kneeling over her prostrate form.

"You are known to me, Mundani," he said. "In fact, I know more about you than you do of yourself."

"Bullpucky!"

"Do you think that to someone like me, the prophecies are a mystery?"

Mattie saw that Eli still cowered on the path.

"What did you do to him?" she yelled.

"A bit of transformative magic."

That didn't bode well.

"Leave him alone!"

"Hmmm." The tall figure stood and considered for a moment. "There was a time, Mundani, when I would have crushed you like an ant." His tone was so affectless that Mattie tended to believe him.

"Happily for you, I have obtained what I need. You all are, so to speak, detritus." He pointed at the ASH threesome with a sweep of his cloak. "You." He addressed the cowering Eli. "You are no longer a threat to me."

He aimed his wand at Eli's head, striking him with what looked like a trio of bolts.

"Hey!" Mattie yelled.

"See you at the end of days," the man said calmly. "I'll say goodbye for now." He pivoted, leaving behind a wispy gray cloud.

"What—?" Sudha was coming to from her dust-eating posture.

"Eli, who was that guy?"

Mattie turned toward the brown dragon, but there was a human in his place! He was a little older than her, with long blond hair and an athlete's build. Though Mattie was shocked, she couldn't help but think he was cute.

She snapped herself out of it. "Eli? Is that you?"

"Yes."

For the first time, she heard his voice. It was hoarse from not speaking, but surprisingly deep.

"What is going on?" Sudha seemed groggy as she joined them. "Who is this person?"

"It's me, Eli."

Looking down, he seemed relieved that he wore clothes. Mattie and Sudha stared at him.

"Sarug turned me into a dragon," he said. "He thought that in the end days I would be some kind of threat. As you heard, he's changed his mind."

Eli turned to Mattie. "*You're* supposed to be even more of a danger...to Georgia."

"So you're Georgian?"

"Yes. I'm the squire to a knight, Sir Melliagraunce. I best return to my duties, if I haven't already been sacked."

"Why did Sarug make you mute?"

"So I couldn't tell what happened. At the time, I went to Cavernis, and Praeses kindly took me in. He knew who I really was and wanted to keep me safe." He stared at Mattie. "Like you."

"Then Sarug is a bad guy?"

135

"He helped found Georgia in the 300s at the side of St. George of Lydda. He's a sorcerer gone bad privy to the Old Magick."

"I think we could all see that."

"What now?" Sudha seemed stunned at her defeat.

"As I said, I must resume my duties—"

"No." Mattie's thoughts were speeding faster than their scull on water. "You stay in Georgia," she said, "and when the end times come, whatever they are, I guarantee you'll be slaughtered." She gave him a hard look. "Unless you're willing to kill dragons."

He stared down at the dirt.

"Your *friends*," she continued pointedly. "Could you plunge a sword through Praeses' heart? Fight Jimmy, Superbas, or Ripley? What about *us*?" She gestured to herself and Sudha.

Eli blinked several times. He seemed to be damping down some emotion. "No. I would never hurt my friends. They have been far too kind. Still..."

"Yes?"

"All my life, I've dreamed of being a knight. I've been a squire for five years now. That's a fourth of my life wasted."

He looked terribly sad. Mattie tried to cheer him up.

"You don't know that! Nothing in life is a waste—except maybe that time I got drunk. And all those days I spent ditching school. Anyway, you're using your skills to train *me*, right?"

Eli's features brightened.

"Hmmm. You're smart, Mattie. That's something I've admired, even though I couldn't speak. All right, I'll stay in Cavernis."

Mattie exhaled deeply. Even though no sparks were created, that didn't dampen her spirits. The good news was that Eli was a trained soldier. She should have figured as much. He could not only fight for *them*, but share Georgian secrets, like how they went about slaying dragons!

Her heart felt unburdened as she practically skipped down the road, Sudha to her left and Eli to her right. It might have been the perfect moment, if only Eli hadn't kept sighing at human-Sudha.

Chapter Twenty-One

Mundanis

Mrs. Sharpe had been frantic since the day her daughter ditched school, never to be seen again. When Mattie didn't come home, she'd assumed she was hanging with her new crowd and would appear—possibly hung over—the next morning.

But she didn't.

After that first day passed, she'd gone to the Burbank police to file a missing person report. They didn't seem that interested. "Do you know how many kids go missing?" they asked. In L.A., literally thousands. If she wanted to be found, she would be. Otherwise, good luck.

Mrs. Sharpe quickly realized she would get no help there. She took matters into her own hands, posting flyers at malls, on random telephone poles, and "Do Not Post" boards at construction sites around town.

She phoned Mrs. Rodriguez from her kitchen.

"Like I told you, that crowd she was hanging with is nothing but bad news."

Mrs. Sharpe gripped her cell phone. "How bad?"

"Drinking, partying, dropping out. They're like a lost generation."

Even though she didn't want to ask, Mrs. Sharp forced herself. "Do you think they're capable of kidnapping? Or...or worse?"

"Nah. They're just wannabe gangstas. I've never heard stuff like that. Only girls getting pregnant and boys busted for beer."

Mrs. Sharpe felt a flood of relief. It meant that there was hope.

She went to Pico Pico and talked to Miss B., the vice principal.

"Let me extend my sympathies," the—Mrs. Sharpe couldn't help it—battleaxe said from behind her desk. "All I can tell you is that the day your daughter vanished, she never showed up for P.E. After that, we have no record."

Mrs. Sharpe nodded sadly. She wasn't surprised that Mattie had ditched her least favorite class, but then to go missing completely? There had to be more to this story.

She left the 60s-style admin building and stationed herself by the school gates. Surely someone must have a clue.

After classes let out, she cornered that boy Peter, who'd once hung around their apartment. But he stated eloquently, "I swear, I don't know nothin'!"

When Mrs. Sharpe applied some more pressure—to the nub of his ear—he reluctantly identified two girls who might know more.

"Lana? Anna?"

"It's Lupe," one of the girls said, not bothering to hide her cigarette. "That's Lana. Aren't you a little old to go here?"

"Cute," said Mrs. Sharpe, trying to restrain her anger. *I am an adult,* she told herself. *Don't stoop to their high school level.* Still, there was no doubt in her mind that adults could stoop to murder.

"I'm Mattie's mom," she announced.

Lana and Lupe slunk back as if she'd said she was DEA.

"We don't know nothing," said Lana.

"Anything," Mrs. Sharpe corrected. What kind of education was this school providing? Really, it was shameful. Then she remembered why she was there.

"Please," she pleaded, and her maternal concern must have touched the girls a little.

"She said she wanted to cut and catch a show."

"Do you know at what theater?"

"Nah. But she liked to go to Hollyweird."

"Thanks, Lupe."

Thus began her strange odyssey in the land of tinsel and glitter. She met scores of runaways, many much younger than Mattie, inspected all the shelters, walked up and down Hollywood Boulevard. No, no one had seen anything. This town was teeming with people, all day and night, and a lone teenage girl could easily slip from sight.

She called her ex in New York and filled him in on the details.

"Mattie? Gone? That doesn't sound like her."

"I told you—she's changed. Hanging with Lupe and Poopy."

"Okay. I'm sure she'll turn up soon. I know you'll do everything to find her."

Mrs. Sharpe wanted to take her phone and yell, *And what about you?*

"Hey Miranda, gotta go. Boss's on the other line. Keep me in the loop."

Mrs. Sharpe stood in her kitchen, listening to a dead line. Boss, her *tuchis.* She knew what Steve was doing, readying to go on a raid with his guild in *World of Warcraft.*

He was more addicted to that game than a Hollywood star to Botox. Disgusted, she wrote him off as a resource.

Six terrible months passed. Mrs. Sharpe struggled at work. But her colleagues and friends were nice, trying to stay positive.

So did Mrs. Sharpe. She refused to give up hope. She would not sanction the thought that Mattie might be...gone. No, she was still out there—she could feel it as sure as she could feel her own pulse. As a mom, she simply *knew*.

One night, while lying awake, Mrs. Sharpe replayed the past, as she had every night. Where had she gone wrong? What had caused Mattie to turn?

"Dammit," she said to Felicia, wiping away her tears. "I should've let her keep that big lizard!"

Chapter Twenty-Two

The Fall of Avarus

For Mattie, ASH took on a whole other meaning.

It was hard to focus in class knowing that Sarug was out there, planning his own apocalypse. And it was painful to train with Eli now that he could speak.

"Again!" he yelled as they practiced and she fumbled her wooden "sword."

This unleashed a torrent of verbiage.

"God's blood, why did I ever say yes to this? Training a *girl* to be a knight? It's not even worth the accolade!"

"Huh?"

Mattie picked up her stick, wiping sweat from her eyes. She wished that Jimmy were here, but he had been dismissed, his services no longer needed.

"Praeses said he would dub me a knight *if* I train you properly. There's as much chance as flying to Lumen!"

"Which I'd rather do than hear you whine."

Eli brushed back his long blond hair, flexing his trim biceps. *Damn. Why did he have to be so cute?*

He started to recite a familiar litany to Mattie: "Women and girls should stay at home, preparing food and sewing clothes. They should only go out to shop or—"

"Don't tell me. Church."

"Exactly."

"Let's get something straight. You're from a place where women can't leave the house and I'm from one where they *build* them. We need to reach some kind of compromise."

Eli stared at her with his light blue eyes. She had to admit that, despite his warped views, he had a nice face.

"What would you suggest?"

"Just treat me like Sir What's-His-Face treated you. Pretend I don't have breasts."

Eli blushed. "Very well. I'll try. But it's hard making the adjustment from my world to—"

"Mine? Put that in reverse and you're me."

Eli sighed. Mattie knew this was hard, so she made the peace sign.

"Let's go to The Thirsty Dragon. I'm parched."

"Very well."

They tentatively shook hands.

Mattie led the way as they entered the quad. She was startled to see a circle of dragons since classes were already over. In the center, she spotted Professor Avarus, his bling blinding as always.

"It *will* work," he was saying.

Most of his acolytes—like Agravaine and Geetha—nodded. Others, whom Mattie didn't recognize, seemed to be more tentative.

Mattie grabbed Eli's hand, ducking with him behind a gold pillar.

"Not exactly broken up over Mrs. A.," she whispered.

He nodded.

"The Great Peace is over. It is time for dragons and men to do what comes naturally—fight! Over the only thing that matters." Avarus smiled. "Treasure."

"How do we know we'll get our share?" the always charming Agravaine asked.

"Relax, my boy. No time to be greedy."

But the professor's eyes sparkled as if he'd found a vein of silver.

"Night has fallen. Time to fly. Fly as we were meant to and be rich beyond our dreams!"

The dragons burst out of the quad. Mattie and Eli followed on tiptoe, peering out the yawning entrance.

What they saw next shocked them. Against ASH's rules, the flock of dragons took wing, Avarus in the lead. They flew in a V formation, silhouetted by torchlight.

"I...I can't believe this," Mattie gasped, watching the group arc east. "How did *Geetha* get caught up on this? He's really a super nice guy—I mean, dragon."

"You're clearly not filled with gold lust."

Mattie tossed her hair. "Well, I should hope not."

"Dragons have it in spades. To tell the truth, so do Georgians."

"*And* Mundani. But I would never double-cross my school! Or my team or good friends."

"Me neither. They must have put great pressure on Geetha. But as far as that snake Agravaine—he would turn against his own nest mates."

"He is like the biggest jerk on Cavernis."

"Don't forget Professor Avarus."

"That little Midas!" Mattie stomped her foot. "We need to let Praeses know."

Eli pointed over her head. "I think he already does."

Moving up beside them, the president stood on all fours, watching distant black shapes morph into what looked like witches on brooms.

Chapter Twenty-Three

Concilio Prius Dracones

During her time in Cavernis, Mattie had never entered the biggest cave on the Plat. Artorius said it was some kind of courtroom, and Mattie, fearful of lawyers since her parents' divorce, had never ventured in.

Now, as she, Artorius, and Ripley marched into the cave, she thought she had never seen so many dragons. Not just students from ASH but the elite from the Plat were joined by families and even solitaries emerging for a rare glimpse.

She and her friends took a seat by Jimmy, Eli, and Superbas. Mattie blinked her eyes against the flash of so many colors.

On the podium stood Praeses, flanked by Dr. Lung and Beowulf. They all seemed especially grave and more than a little depressed.

"Thank you. Take your seats. Could we have *quiet* please?"

Miss Fang scurried among the crowd. Those who had studied at ASH remembered her and fell silent.

"It is indeed unfortunate we must hold this council," Praeses said. "We haven't had to meet for at least the past five years."

The dragons in the audience all turned to one another. It was clear they had no idea what had happened.

"I am sorry—very sorry—to report that one of our own has turned. Professor Avarus, long a trusted teacher, has shown us his back and joined forces with Georgia. I fear he was involved in the death of his own wife."

A shocked outcry could be heard from hundreds of dragon throats. Praeses waited for it to subside.

"My colleague, Chancellor Beowulf, has used the magick at his disposal to unveil the Avarus scheme. To him I now yield the floor."

"Yes, thank you, Mr. President," Beowulf intoned, his steam-shovel head looming over the crowd. "It seems that twelve ASH students have also been seduced. Avarus has promised them battle and the divvying up of our gold."

The assemblage gave a collective gasp.

"Traitors!" someone shouted.

Beowulf raised a claw for silence.

"On their own, they are nothing—we could easily crush them. However, we believe they are in Georgia, where they will report to the sorcerer Sarug."

A near-riot broke out in the cave. Mattie looked around, feeling a stab of anxiety.

"Do you see Sudha?" she whispered to Artorius.

He scanned the space with his sharp dragon eyes, then shook his blue head no.

Mattie closed her eyes. Why had she ever trusted that snake?

"Order! I will have order!" Miss Fang's red body shook.

"What can we do?" a concerned father asked, his brood huddled beneath his wings.

"Kill them!" came the bloodthirsty cry.

"Kill them, kill them all!" the crowd started to chant.

"Who are they? *We want names!*"

Praeses looked down sadly. "I'm sorry to report the list includes students Agravaine, Geetha, Alazon—"

"No way!" Artorius turned to Mattie. He couldn't believe that their own crewmate had turned.

"Huáng Chow—"

"This cannot be." An agonized Chinese dragon stood erect on his lower coils. "President Praeses, I deeply apologize for my son. Is there anything we can do?"

"Thank you, Mr. Chow. We'll certainly let you know."

Jimmy and his other brother Heng looked deeply shocked.

Praeses sought to placate the noisy crowd.

"Miss Fang has compiled a slate of names that is available by the entrance."

The dragons rocked with hostility.

"Be assured, we will defend ourselves. There is no other way. I am sad to see the Great Peace broken, but such a thing has been foretold."

He focused his soft hazel eyes on the bench where Mattie sat.

"We have among us a champion. In point of fact, we have two. I ask that they accelerate their training in order to fight the Thirteen."

Dragon necks of many colors craned to get a look at Mattie. Now she knew how it felt to be in a zoo.

"Historically, knights have had the best luck at killing dragons. If you'd like the precise statistics—"

"*No!*" everyone shouted.

"We must *all* prepare to fight. Professors Drake and Ignis will hold classes round the clock, and ASH will offer a new course, How To Raze A Village. Not something we wanted, but under the present threat, we cannot be too vigilant."

"What about the school treasure?" Professor Fraxinus asked.

"It will stay where it is, under the protection of spells. I don't believe Sarug can undo them."

"And our *personal* treasure?" the concerned father asked.

"As always, it is up to every dragon to guard his or her hoard. *Dracones,* we enter a world that hasn't been seen since Caesar. I wish you the best of luck, and will convene this Council again."

He and Beowulf left the podium as Miss Fang ushered everyone out.

Artorius turned to Mattie. "So the time has finally come. War or no, believe me—I won't let you come to harm."

"I know."

Mattie embraced one ribbed blue wing. This whole thing was surreal. One minute, she'd been a relatively carefree student. The next, she was expected to fight thirteen dragons with a guy who viewed women as housemaids.

That guy now addressed her.

"Very well, *squire,* you heard the president. We start at 6 a.m. tomorrow, sharp."

"Yes?" Mattie said, trying to diffuse the tension.

"You won't be making jokes when Alazon is spitting fire down your neck!"

This made Mattie feel sick. If she could have hitched a ride in the Cube, she would have been back in L.A. before you could say Cavernis.

Chapter Twenty-Four

The Reluctant Warrior

Eli hadn't been kidding about 6 a.m. sharp.

When Mattie ran up to him, breathless, at 6:04, he was already pacing the lot. His expression was as sour as if he'd had lemons for breakfast.

"You're late," he said without ceremony.

"I know. I'm sorry. I'm not a morning person."

"Do you think Sarug and Avarus care if it's morning, noon, or night? They will attack when they feel we are weakest, so we must *always* be at the ready."

"All right," Mattie mumbled. She was *so sick* of his lectures. "I liked you better when you couldn't talk."

"Humph. Today, we're going to switch tactics. Georgians can't be fought with sticks. Despite your lack of skill, we are going to use real swords."

"Oh no!" Mattie cried.

"Did you not hear Praeses yesterday? We are to *accelerate* our training."

He pressed into her hand a blade twice the size of Excalibur and hefted another for himself just as enormous.

"Now, just pretend these are made of wood."

"Except they have points. And edges. And weigh like a hundred pounds."

In fact, Mattie couldn't even lift the one he'd given her. She struggled with two hands around the hilt.

Eli just looked disgusted. He made a run toward her, instantly casting her downturned steel across the dirt.

"How can I teach you to fight if you cannot hold your own blade?"

"Did it ever occur to you," Mattie asked, her arms aching, "that I am *not* a giant Georgian? Giving me a Crusader sword is like giving you a tank."

"Huh?"

"Exactly. You need to find one that's right for *me*. The proper tools for the job."

Eli tied his hair into a ponytail, bent to pick up a different sword, and handed it to Mattie.

"I was permitted to go into the ASH treasury, supervised by Miss Fang."

"Naturally."

"I found this. I thought if the other didn't work, *this one* might be suitable."

Mattie hefted the light sword. It was truly ornate—the steel carved with runic figures, the handle festooned with rubies—yet she had a feeling it could sting if wielded by a proper swordsman.

"Thanks," Mattie told him, possibly for the first time.

"You're welcome," he said gloomily. "If you're going to fight like a girl, might as well use a girlie sword."

"I'll make you eat those words."

"If you're still alive to threaten me."

"Let's go."

The steel in Mattie's eyes matched the blade in her hand. She was going to show this misogynist that she was up to the task.

"First off, remember that we have two foes: Georgians and dragons. Let's deal with the former first."

"I thought that was Praeses's job."

"In order to get to the dragons, we have to go through the Georgians."

"Oh."

"You should know that my people have an army, and they've been trained by the best—St. George himself. These soldiers are highly accomplished with sword, lance, and axe. So must you be."

Mattie was starting to lose her bravado. "I can't even run the rings."

"That won't be called for in battle. Just remember, you couldn't steer a boat before you could."

That made Mattie feel better. It *was* true.

"Now grip your hilt like this." He demonstrated. "When I move in, you step back and thrust like so—"

The actual clang of metal echoed through the lot. Mattie could tell that Eli was taking it easy. Still, she managed to meet his advances without feeling like a dork.

Eli stepped up his fight. He brought his sword down—hard—on hers, causing her to fall on her rump. He aimed the point of his blade directly at her throat.

"What do you do now?"

"Offer a bribe?"

"You bring your blade up swiftly and try to knock me off balance."

She did, but all she managed to accomplish was a painful ringing in her hands. She threw up her arms.

"Okay, I give up."

"There is no surrender," Eli said with contempt. "True knights fight to the death. And *you* are currently dead."

With one swift move, he disarmed her. She could hear her blade skitter across the lot's hard ground.

"It's no use." Mattie's whole body was aching, adding to her despair. "I wasn't cut out for this. Even though I *am* related to my great-great-great-great grandmother Matilda or whatever."

"Look." Eli's manner softened. "Do not discount that fact. Sarug was afraid of you, and he must have had good reason. Of course, now that he has his dragons, we're just—"

"—chopped liver?"

"I beg pardon?"

"I think it's like...sautéed calf's liver?"

Eli made a face. "Disgusting. I prefer Humbles of a Deere."

"Gross," said Mattie.

"Enough about food! Let's get back to dragons," Eli said.

Eli slid onto the dirt, directly across from Mattie. He tucked in his loose white tunic. "As you know, dragons like Praeses are Elders, and impossible to kill. Fortunately, most of ours are less than ten feet."

"Fabulous."

"According to the list, all except the Asians are winged."

"I thought Dr. Lung said they could fly."

"Only if they're spiritually evolved."

"What about Huáng?"

"Too young."

"I guess I'll take that as *good* news."

"To get back to what I was saying, that means—including Avarus—about ten can strike from above. In our favor, Cavernis is a desert, with very little that burns."

"Except us."

"Right. Now here's the thing about dragons—" Eli raised himself on one elbow, looking straight at her. "As you and I saw with Mrs. Avarus, they *do* have their weak spots—their throats and underbellies. If you can plunge a blade *there*, chances are you've struck a fatal blow."

Mattie stared into his eyes, which were just as blue as Artorius's. "That works both ways."

Eli looked confused.

"I mean, if *we* can kill their dragons like that, they can do the same to ours."

Eli nodded. "It *is* a double-edged sword."

Mattie looked away. She had conflicting feelings. On one hand, she wanted to protect her dragon friends; on the other, she didn't know if she could kill the ones she knew, like Huáng, Jimmy's brother. It would be like killing Jimmy.

Eli sensed her emotions and grabbed her hand.

"It will be hard for me as well. I have trained all my life to kill dragons. Yet now that I've actually *been* one, I'm not sure I can do it."

Mattie nodded. She liked Eli better now than she ever had.

"All right, let's move onto riding. An essential part of knighthood."

Mattie sighed, using his hand to help her up. She was already tired of training.

He led her on the path out of town, the same one that ended at Georgia. They stopped after half a mile, where a herd of horses grazed behind a wood fence. A dappled gray loped up to meet them.

"Is it true?" he asked excitedly. "Are we really going to war?"

"I'm afraid so," Mattie said.

"Fortis told me everything! Name's Duke."

"Very well, you shall serve as my mount," Eli told him. "Please retrieve Fortis."

"Yes, sir."

Eli turned to Mattie.

"I had Superbas drop off our tack. Know how to fasten a bridle?"

She snorted. As Duke returned with Fortis, she grabbed one from the fence, leaping over the rails and buckling it on as if she were being timed. Then she slung on the saddle.

Eli raised his eyebrows. He more slowly prepped Duke. "Need a boost?"

"Please," she said. She finished tightening the cinch, stepping onto his outspread hands. "Thanks."

"Just wait till you're in full armor." Eli swung onto Duke. "Then we'll need winches to get in the saddle."

"It looks so easy in the movies."

"Where?"

"Never mind."

She and her "foe" faced off across the pasture, separated by a hundred yards. They both held wooden lances. At Eli's signal, they spurred their mounts to a lope, and Mattie remembered her training: lance held in the couch, seat firm but relaxed. They crashed together like two small saplings, with Mattie landing, as usual, rear-down in the dirt.

She looked up at the mounted Eli, who seemed tall as Praeses. "I liked the dummy better."

She actually got a grin out of him!

"You'll get used to it. Just pretend that *I'm* the dummy."

"Why pretend?"

Eli sighed. "Why couldn't I get a girl who was modest and demure?"

"Because she'd make a lousy knight."

As they kept practicing over the next few days, Mattie felt herself improve at what Eli called "the tilt." She wasn't ready to win a tournament, but at least she could thwack his lance.

"Hey, I'm ready for Dark Ages Park!" she told Eli one afternoon.

From Duke's back, he shook his head sadly.

"I think not. You would be burned as a witch for your blasphemy about wenches."

Mattie laughed. "Good."

Eli looked serious.

"No really. There was a mass witch burning in Georgia shortly before I left."

"Great to know your enemy. And they call *dragons* beasts."

Eli nodded. "I understand now how wrong their views are."

"Except about women."

Mattie saw his back stiffen. "I believe I referred to *dragons*."

"Uh-huh."

Praeses had Miss Fang announce that all regular classes were canceled. Everyone at ASH was to hone their battle skills.

Eli, stickler that he was, followed through with a vengeance. Between swordplay and mace-and-chain, Mattie felt like an extra in *Gladiator*. The only problem was that at this point she'd get the big *thumbs down* from Caesar.

In the midst of all this prep, there was only one light moment, and it involved, of all people, Latro. As she was dragging across the quad, off to endless training, she saw his futuristic form lounging by Praeses' statue.

"Hey." He nodded.

She had a weird feeling that'd he'd been waiting for her specifically.

"Brought you a few things." From his brown cloak, he freed the sweet fumes of an In-N-Out bag and a whole sampler of makeup. The case was actually marked "Dior."

"Know most gals like this stuff," he shrugged.

"Wow, Latro, thanks. That was really considerate."

"Figured you must be stressed—war and all that." He sighed. "Just wish you were a few years older."

Mattie blushed. "Again, I thank you."

She put away her precious hoard and extended a hand.

"So...think I could have a kiss? Designer stuff don't come easy."

Mattie stared at the space trader's scarred temple. Despite his many miles, he was still darkly attractive.

"Maybe in a few years," she smiled.

A week into "accelerated training," Eli solemnly turned to Mattie.

"The time has come. We must procure our armor."

Mattie groaned. The thought of being winched onto Fortis, a ton of metal on her back, was not exactly appealing.

"Let's ask Miss Fang to unlock the secret rooms."

Mattie's eyes widened.

In tandem, they trudged from the lot back to ASH. The whole feel of the campus had changed. Mattie nearly expected the statue of Praeses to speak, exhorting them to train more.

They found Miss Fang in her usual spot. The admin had acknowledged the coming war by donning a Spartan helmet.

Eli expressed his wish and Miss Fang, whose look changed from wanting to stomp him to recalling he was a "champion," led them up a flight of stairs to two familiar doors. Mattie cringed, recalling her adventure with Sid.

"Be careful," she warned Eli. "There's frost—"

"And fire for you two," Miss Fang said, as if she were ordering drinks.

Eli and Mattie stepped back. Miss Fang approached a closed door and, in a low voice, uttered:

Dracones celati
Desinite artes de igne et glacie!
Nolite uti magicis artibus
Dum ego revenio.
Magicae artes, venite!

"Wow!" Mattie exclaimed. She had never heard *real magic* before. She would have to tell Artorius!

"It should be safe to enter," Miss Fang drawled. "I'll wait for you out here."

Eli made a run through the door, and nothing bad happened. But Mattie, recalling Sid's impression of a fish stick, proceeded with much more caution.

She was through! She wondered if the room itself was protected by spells or booby traps. But she trusted the efficient Miss Fang.

As she walked farther in, Mattie had to cover her eyes against the glare of ASH's treasure. Compared to this, Artorius's was a mere droplet. She was surrounded by stacked mounds of gold and gleaming gold items: chalices, candlesticks, and crosses. She hadn't known there were such riches in *any* world.

"Where did this come from?" she asked Eli, who stood atop a pirate's chest.

"Mundanis. When Praeses created the portal—three hundred years after the death of Our Lord—the dragons started taking treasure with them. Then, as more and more came—through the 1600's—they kept adding to the pile."

"It's...incredible," Mattie breathed, slipping on a necklace with a six-inch-thick chain that was heavy with diamonds.

"Careful," Eli warned.

"Of what? Is the gold going to bite me?"

"In a way."

Eli kept moving forward, his eyes inspecting the booty.

"You can fall prey to gold fever. That's what happened to Avarus. You get so blinded you forget everything else."

Mattie nodded. She had seen people like that, people in L.A. They were so caught up in material things that that became their identity.

"What exactly are you looking for?"

"Armor. A full suit. One to fit me and one for you."

"Okay."

Mattie removed the handle of a flagon from the toe of her boot.

"Anything specific?"

"*Strong,*" Eli said. "Enough to repel dragon's breath."

Did such a thing even exist?

"This might be a possibility."

Eli bent down to examine a suit of what looked like solid gold. Nearby was a matching shield with a dragon's head coat-of-arms.

"Mind helping?"

Mattie struggled with the plate, strapping here and buckling there, according to Eli's instructions.

At last, he was in full panoply and shut the visor over his face.

"C-3PO!" Mattie called.

Eli opened his visor. "Is that a blessing?" He gestured for her to help him remove the suit. "This should work. A little long in the thighs, but overall, not bad. Let's find something for you."

They waded knee-deep in gold, silver, and gems. It was like trying to make your way through precious rubble.

"Finding your size might be tough, but people were small back then. I'm basing that on St. George."

"Is he short?"

"Tiny."

"Hey, look at this!"

Mattie had practically tumbled over a standing suit. This one was coated in silver. It had Latin carved into the breastplate, a helmet with a snappy red comb, and best of all, it looked like the last inhabitant had been about five-six!

"Excellent."

Eli helped her to buckle up. Once she was fully encased, she felt like R2-D2.

"It's hot in here."

"What did you expect? Some sort of cooling device?"

"It's called *air conditioning*," Mattie yelled, then lifted her visor. "Please free me."

He did, and Mattie stood there panting. She helped him bundle up the lighter pieces of armor.

"Hey, don't forget your shield!"

"Thanks." Mattie turned to accept it, gasping when she saw the insignia. It was of a wyvern, forked tongue distended, fiercely clawing the air. *If this isn't a sign,* she thought, *I don't know what is.*

Eli did some further rummaging, dragging huge pieces of armor in both gold and silver.

"Are those for us?" Mattie asked.

"Our mounts."

He scraped the massive metal over the foyer's marble.

Mattie turned and noticed something sticking out of a gold mound. She bent and brushed away a flurry of coins. This thing was pure steel, but even a single corner looked huge!

"Can we use this?" she asked Eli as he came back in.

He bent to examine the piece. "No. It's too big even for Fortis."

"Okay."

Mattie followed him out.

"Very well," Miss Fang said. *"Premat, resumere."*

The secret room door swung shut.

She hoisted most of the armor onto her sturdy red back. And with no more concern than if she were ringing her triangle, she led them back down the stairs.

Chapter Twenty-Five

You Want What?

The next day, Mattie and Eli went to the pasture to try out their new gear. Superbas, with his muscular build, carried the lion's share of armor.

"Okay, you buckle me and I buckle you," Eli told her, once their mounts were in place.

"But not at the same time?"

"Funny. You won't be laughing once Alazon's talons grip you."

Mattie swallowed hard. She was trying not to think about it. Still, war seemed as inevitable as a dragon laying eggs.

Mattie groaned as her silver coffin encased her. She could barely keep her feet.

"How much does this thing weigh?" she asked.

"About...thirty-five pounds—maybe fifty."

"What? That's like one of Lady Gaga's outfits!"

Eli looked puzzled.

"Trust me, you will become accustomed. Why don't you start by walking?"

Mattie tried. She lurched from side to side, probably looking like a drunk Tin Man. As a free encore, she crashed into a tree. "Ow!"

"Look where you're going."

"I can't. These visor slits are tiny!"

"Can you guess why?"

Mattie sighed. "So a weapon can't get through there."

"To quote yourself, no duh."

She tried to move again. This must be how Captain Nemo felt in his clunky diving suit. She opened her visor for air. She was sticky, she was cranky, and she wanted to go home.

Eli came bounding up to her, as if his plate weighed less than a hummingbird.

"Feeling better?" he asked.

"No. I need a portable fan. And the weight. Maybe I should just ask Praeses to sit on me."

Eli laughed. "You'll practice wearing the suit more and more each day. For today, five minutes is good."

Mattie clunked over to Superbas, uprooting a bush or two. He helped her to unbuckle.

"Superbas," she asked, making sure he could see her lips. "Do you think Eli forgot to pay his brain bill?"

Superbas laughed himself silly, giving a dismissive wave. Well, at least *someone* thought he was sane.

The inhuman torture continued, up to three times a day. Mattie got to a point where she could stand it for half an hour. But her movements were so slow, she felt like she was climbing Everest—without the benefit of oxygen.

Since the suit's heat was intense, Mattie tried a few tricks. First, she fastened a wet cloth around her forehead. Then, she took to wearing practically nothing underneath. If she were killed, and her body stripped of armor, at least she was wearing nice undies. This thought gave her some comfort.

Slowly, *very* slowly, she learned to cope with her new "weight," and the trees around her was safe.

"See, I told you that you could do it!" Eli said.

"Must. Rest. Now."

Looking like a second trunk, Mattie leaned stiffly against a maple. Eli came clanking over and removed his gold helmet.

"I know you must think me harsh—"

"We have another word for it."

Eli nodded. "But this is all I know. You see, my master, Sir Melliagraunce, never showed me any mercy. If I erred during training, I was whipped with a branch."

"What did your parents say?" Mattie cried.

"Alas, I never knew them. There was a plague in Georgia shortly after my birth, and it killed my whole family. Sir Melliagraunce took me in."

"That was nice." Mattie started to remove her armor.

"Yes, that was his one act of kindness. After that, it was just 'boy' this and 'boy' that, with plenty of whippings between."

"We don't allow corporal punishment." Mattie wanted to find this guy and thrash him till he yelled "Uncle."

"That's good—I think. I don't know. I don't know any other way."

He slid a hand on her hauberk and expertly undid the buckles.

"Well, I think his way sucks."

Eli sighed. "I guess that's why I'm such a horse's ass."

"Thank you God!" Mattie crowed, removing her heavy greaves.

Eli looked down. "I apologize. I so *want* you to be a good knight—but I know my methods are harsh. That is simply how I was taught."

"That's okay." Mattie patted his shoulder. "We don't have that much time, so you keep doing your worst. I can take it."

"Thanks." He smiled shyly. "I'll try to be more aware of my failings."

"I wish I could be," Mattie sighed.

"I am not ready for this. I am *so* not ready."

"We have to start sometime. Georgia won't wait forever."

"What are they waiting for now?"

"I honestly don't know. But every day they delay is like a gift to Cavernis."

They were back in the dreaded location—the dusty lot by ASH—for a new and dreaded exercise: tilting in full armor.

Mattie and Eli buckled each other up—she guessed he was used to the sight of her bra and undies by now. But without any impetus, he flew into a rage.

"Must you look like *that*?" he asked, pointing to her undergarments while averting his eyes.

"Like what?"

He had seen her this way so many times. What was different now?

"Like *that*. What are you trying to do? Drive me out of my mind?"

Mattie considered this. No, she was just trying to be practical. But now that he'd brought it up, an embarrassment overcame her, and she covered herself with her hands. Why did she care, she asked herself as her cheeks flamed. This guy was only her trainer, no different than Coach Cymru. Of course, Eli was human, and definitely pretty cute. But could he ever like someone who thought women were beneath him? *Especially her?* No, not gonna happen. She determined to shake it off.

Just then Superbas loped up, leading Fortis and Duke.

Eli turned to his friend and made a series of signs. The red-and-gold striped dragon heaved saddles onto the horses, then fastened breastplates to both.

"I'm so excited!" Fortis said.

Superbas armored the horses' heads and backsides. Stepping back, he seemed pleased with his work.

"Excellent," Eli signed, also speaking the word. "You'd make a great squire."

Superbas grinned as Mattie rolled her eyes. She and Eli completed their own panoply.

"Now, to get us onto our seats." Eli's gauntleted hands flashed some more DSL.

Mattie felt two claws lifting her from the back. To Superbas, she must have weighed no more than Ripley. With a heave, he placed her onto the saddle.

She signed her thanks.

He did the same for Eli, and at last, the gold and silver knights faced each other on horseback.

"Now, to lance!" Eli ordered.

He pointed to two poles with blunted points. Superbas handed them up as the knights left for the "field."

"Remember, try to hit me first."

Eli closed his visor and Mattie did the same. As she moved off, she wondered how painful it would be to hit the ground from five feet up—in fifty pounds of steel.

"One. Two. Three!" Eli counted off and the two steeds, now separated, began to run for each other.

Mattie's heart beat in time to the rhythm of Fortis's hooves. *Steady,* she told herself. *You can do this.* She tried to hold the lance straight in a hand stiffened by metal.

Something crashed together, but she wasn't sure just what. She only knew that when she came to, Superbas was stripping off her hauberk and Eli was checking her pulse.

"What happened?" she asked. The last thing she remembered was her feet lifting from the stirrups.

"You were vanquished," Eli said. Remembering his new vow, he struggled to say something nice. "But it was good for a first attempt."

He started to remove his own armor.

"This is insane," Mattie groaned. "I can barely *walk* in this thing."

"You'll get there."

The sound of giant wings echoed from above. They all looked up to see a flight of three dragons, streaking low over the field.

"Guess the 'No Fly' ban has been lifted."

"Yes. That's an ASH patrol."

They continued gazing upward, toward wings that flapped and then glided. Flames that spewed gracefully from each dragon's throat.

"And we have to fight *eleven* of those?" Mattie heard her own near-hysteria. "On flesh-and-blood horses. Which can be burnt to a crisp. Like *us.*"

Duke and Fortis flinched. Mattie rose painfully, facing Superbas so that he could read her lips.

"This isn't going to work. Maybe two knights can fight two dragons, but *thirteen?* Even with Cavernis behind us, *you and I* are going to be killed."

"Such is the lot of a warrior. If we die, it will be with honor."

"Honor, *shmonor!* Look, Eli, we're smart. Let's *think.*"

Mattie started to pace. Was there *anything* she could come up with? She didn't want to end her life as a rack of barbequed ribs.

Horses were definitely out. Against the fire of dragons, they were as useless as she was. And Cavernis wasn't exactly stocked with tanks, Humvees, or planes.

Mattie did have a passing thought, but it was a definite longshot. She turned to Eli.

"How good are you at being a salesman?"

He looked confused.

"Um...someone who sells things, like a shopkeeper or merchant."

Eli looked offended. "Well, certainly *I* am not of that rank."

"Even so, it's gonna take hella persuasion to make a convincing case."

"For what?"

"My idea."

Mattie gestured for Superbas to strip their mounts of armor. Once he was done, hoisting the burden on his back, she led a determined march straight back to her cave.

"Hey Mattie," Artorius said as he ripped into a leg of lamb. "Anyone want some?"

"No thanks. We're kind of here on business."

She and Eli gladly dumped their heavy gear.

"I see. How's it going?"

"We have as much chance of fighting those dragons as I do of becoming Miss World."

"How about me?"

"You have an outside chance. How do you look in a swimsuit?" She switched gears. "What have *you* been doing?"

"Flying, flaming, getting in shape. This is the first break I've had all day."

"Sure it is 'at Mr. Artorius has bin workin' his heart it!" Hob affirmed.

"Good. Where's Ripley?"

"Acting as Praeses' sergeant."

"God help ASH."

Mattie then stood there dumbly, staring at her feet. She was afraid to ask her question, but the fate of all Cavernis might actually hinge upon it.

"Artorius, remember when I first came here, you told me dragons don't take riders?"

"Of course not! It's demeaning. Do we look like beasts of burden?"

He stood up to his full nine feet, using his tail as ballast, his yellow pupils dangerously slit.

"Calm down. Please hear me out."

Artorius put down his food.

"Eli and I are toast if we ride out on horses. No knight has ever fought this many dragons and won. I doubt the whole Round Table could."

"It's true," Eli said.

Artorius shrugged in tacit admission.

"If, however, we could ride on dragonback, our chance of survival would go from negative one to one."

Artorius merely stood there like a giant figurine.

Mattie tried another tactic.

"Look, I'm your friend right? Do you want to see me incinerated? And *him?*" She pointed to Eli.

Artorius' head whipped back and forth as if he were watching Wimbledon.

"Of course not! But I thought that as an heir of Matilda— you might have special gifts..."

"All I have is right here." Mattie pointed to her head. "And so far, this is the best it's come up with."

"You know this completely smashes our Code. Not since the age of St. George have we accepted a rider! I have only seen such nonsense on Mundanis TV."

"Excuse me, sir, but this is war," Eli spoke up forcefully. "I am a Georgian and know their ways. They not only have an army, but weapons like catapults and siege engines—"

"Not to mention a buttload of dragons!"

Artorius stared at the ground as Eli continued.

"Let us not forget Sarug. Who knows of what he is capable? I can tell you this: he is able to conjure demons. That's how he transformed *me.*"

Artorius considered this gravely. "I never doubted his strength. Still..." He sighed deeply. "I don't know. It's such a break with protocol. Yet..." He closed his eyes, shading his yellow pupils. "I'm sure you can appreciate...I must consult Praeses first. I take it you mean to ride me, Mattie, but what about Eli?"

Eli exchanged some signs with Superbas, then turned back to Artorius.

"He says he will do it for ASH."

"It is a grave day indeed when dragons must be ridden. But I believe we have no choice. Against such a powerful host, we must employ every means, no matter how…distasteful."

"The right tools for the job," said Mattie.

"All right, friend," Artorius said, taking her under a wing. "I will not stand by to see you turned into toast."

"Thanks, Artorius." Mattie threw her arms around his stomach. "You're the best."

"I'll seek out Praeses after dinner. In the meantime, let's do what dragons do best. Let's eat!"

Chapter Twenty-Six

Dragonrider

After dinner, which Mattie had to admit was sumptuous, topped off by everyone's favorite—gelato—Artorius flew to ASH.

An hour later, Ripley came in, sporting a small beret. She looked like a pint-sized version of Che Guevara.

"Wassup, troops?" she yelled, clearly in high spirits. "Frax and I drilled those blue-heads till they had nothing left. They were flying straighter than they did at the Battle of Lydda. Dragon comeback, you say? Folks, *we never left!*"

Hob shook his small head. "Calm yerself, Ripley, ur yoo're gonnae gie an aneurysm."

"Man, I love this war prep!" Ripley seized a small piece of meat.

"We couldn't tell," said Mattie, wondering what was keeping Artorius.

"What else occurs at ASH?" Eli asked the dragonet.

"Besides *me* kicking butt? Beowulf used his hocus pocus to work out why Georgia hasn't attacked. Seems Sarug is waiting for some kind of 'transformation.'"

"I hate those," Eli said, shuddering.

"Wulfie thinks it has something to do with the traitors. We're calling them *malum autem dracones*: bad dragons. MAD for short."

"Cute," Mattie said. She turned to Eli. "He wouldn't make them all human, would he?"

Eli spread his hands. "Who knows?"

There was a succession of thumps as Artorius came into view.

"Well?" Mattie hadn't been this nervous since the Infectious Diseases final.

"We're good to go," said Artorius, patting her on the head. "Praeses thinks your plan is a grand one. He says that's why you're here, to think of the things we don't."

"Yeah!" Mattie grabbed both Hob and Ripley, placing them on each shoulder. "We won!"

"Not yet," Eli said grimly. "We haven't even begun."

The next morning, after a breakfast of poached eggs, kippers, boiled tomatoes, and German chocolate cake, Artorius set out for the airport, his three charges in tow. Superbas and Eli had spent the night and signed to each other excitedly almost the whole way there.

Mattie saw that Artorius reluctantly led them past Restaurant Row to a wide field tarmacked not in asphalt but pebbles. He spread his claws wide.

"Welcome to CIA: Cavernis International Airport."

"International?" Mattie asked.

"It could be."

He led them to a rocky runway, already filled with six dragons who grumbled among themselves.

"I am *so* sick of delays," a small silver one said to his friend.

"It took nearly an hour to clear me for takeoff on Thorsday!"

"Can't someone tell these clowns it's wartime?"

The two presumed "clowns" were seated on a rock tower, megaphones poised to their snouts.

"Zyxxyx, cleared for takeoff on Runway Two. Alphacore, there will be a five-minute delay."

"More like five hours," said Silver Two, presumably Alphacore.

"You mean...you guys can't take off when you want?" Mattie asked Artorius.

"Not in Cavernis. There would be too many crashes. We try to make flying safe."

"At least you don't charge for carry-ons."

Her friend looked at her strangely.

"Hey Artorius, where's our gear?" she suddenly thought.

"Gear?"

"You know, like saddles and bridles and stuff."

His yellow pupils began to retract to slits.

"I mean, on TV, all those riders have cool stuff."

"During my brief time on Mundanis, the one thing I learned is this: television has no bearing on reality."

Mattie had to agree.

"As I recall, in the old days, dragonriders required no gear. They simply *held on.*"

"Can't we make up some new rules?"

"Nope. You will have to rely on skill."

Eli nodded, completely up for the challenge. Mattie made the "cutting your own throat" sign to Superbas, but he just grinned and patted her on the back.

"We're almost there," Eli said.

They watched the next few dragons take off in an orderly line.

"This is us!" Eli shouted.

They stood unimpeded on the tarmac. Superbas bent down and Artorius—grudgingly, Mattie thought—did likewise.

She clambered aboard his back as she'd once done with Eli, but now, she was truly afraid. Eli had been a good flyer, but Artorius was world-class. He and Superbas could execute moves that Eli had never heard of.

"Hang on to the back of my neck," Artorius told her.

"I don't want to lose mine."

"Here we go!" He took a few running steps with his front feet, then extended his wings, rising. Mattie felt the disturbed air pushing back, causing her to eat her own hair. She clung on fiercely, digging her nails into Artorius's back.

"Ouch!" he said. "Ease up, will ya? I'm not Spitfire here."

"Spitfire couldn't fly," Mattie moaned.

"Now listen to me carefully." He craned his head back, nearly unloosing her grip. "This is really no different than riding a horse—"

"Named Pegasus!"

"Just relax, and try to flow with my movement. We are a team, remember? Just like S&B. I have my job, and you have yours."

"Not to fall!" she yelled, as they continued to ascend. She saw Eli on Superbas' back, grinning like he'd just been made a knight. *He was born for this,* she thought.

"Today, we're going to get the general feel. Take a deep breath and remember: *you're flying*."

This was something Mattie couldn't forget. Unlike her first time with Eli, she made the mistake of looking down and saw the yawning desert below. She adjusted her gaze quickly, trying to focus on the now eye-level Dentes Mountains.

"*Yes!*" Eli yelled. He was completely in his element. Give him a suit of armor and he'd be flying into Georgia to take on Sarug and his army.

"C'mon Mattie—let go," Artorius said.

"Not literally, right?"

She tried to heed his advice, relaxing into his flight, which was as effortless as an eagle's. The only sound she heard was the flapping of surprisingly strong wings. The only sight the smooth scales of his blue head.

"Ready for some fun stuff?" he asked.

"No!"

Like a plunging jet, he dropped altitude quickly, then proceeded to make slow, ever-widening circles.

"I don't like to rotate," she told him.

Mattie glanced at Eli and Superbas. They were actually *upside down,* Eli whooping with glee. Just the mere sight of them made her physically ill.

"Can we go down?" she asked.

"Sure. We can start up again later."

"Goody," Mattie said sarcastically.

Artorius descended slowly, circling close above CIA.

"Blue Wyvern, cleared for landing. Please use Runway Four."

Artorius complied, pushing out his claws and extending his tail as he dropped softly onto the stones. Mattie was so relieved by the sight of land that she tumbled off his back and actually kissed the ground.

177

"That wasn't so bad, was it?"

"Bargyle," Mattie said. She was unable to form real words.

"You'll get used to it." He gently rubbed her head. "Just like you did with crew. Remember: you and I are a team. When we fly, we fly as one."

"You sound like Dr. Lung."

True to his word as always, Artorius made Mattie trudge back to CIA.

By this time, Lumen beat down on her flesh with the force of two Earth suns. Although she was from a warm climate, she had to keep drinking water so she didn't shrivel and die.

"Where're Eli and Superbas?" she asked. She didn't see them anywhere on the rocky tarmac.

"You'll see," Artorius said, and to her ears, that sounded scary. "We're going to stage an attack—on the Georgian knights." He handed her her sword.

"We're not actually *going* there?"

"No, no. Eli will pretend to be one of them."

"Which he is."

"Humph."

They waited their turn on the runway, sandwiched behind two burly dragons trading gossip about a friend.

"Did you hear about the sulfur?"

"No!"

"And the 'misplaced eggs'?"

"Tell me!"

Some things never change, Mattie thought. Even on Cavernis, gossip was king.

"Ready?" Artorius crouched, letting her slide onto his back. "This should be fun."

"Yippee," Mattie said flatly.

Artorius took off, departing CIA to head back to where they'd just come from.

Mattie felt him lose height in a few easy glides, felt his scales through her breeches as they made for the tilting field. There, panoplied in gold and mounted on Duke, sat Eli. Superbas stood on the sidelines, a one-dragon cheering section.

"All right, when I swoop in, you take your sword and try to bash his shield." Artorius craned his blue head to address her.

"O...kay," Mattie said, not so sure about this plan.

"Go!" Artorius yelled.

He was falling like a downed bird, pivoting at the last moment to give her a clear shot.

"Strike a blow!"

Mattie tried to concentrate, recalling the endless training she'd received at her "foe's" hands.

"Filthy Georgian!" she yelled, really trying to get into it. She pulled back her arm, then thrust her blade forward, scoring a direct hit on Eli's shield's gold dragon!

"Yay!" Artorius yelled.

"Huzzah!" said Eli, his cheer muffled behind his helm.

Superbas did an excited handstand.

"Again."

They did. Again and again. By the end of the practice session, Mattie was almost bored since her aim was true every time.

"Okay, Eli!" Artorius called, prior to taking off. "See you guys at the cave."

Eli saluted with one gauntleted hand, then trotted off on Duke. He and Superbas met them back home within the hour.

"How'd it gang?" Hob asked.

"Brilliant!" Eli crowed. "Mattie's a match for the Georgians."

"I don't know," she said, collapsing onto the bed. "You're just one and they have a whole army."

"But you'll have me," Eli assured her, plopping down beside her. "And every dragon in Cavernis."

"Right."

Mattie half-closed her eyes. Even though Hob had brought out prime rib, she felt too tired to eat. Eli had other plans.

"Here." He peeled off a giant slab. "A good knight knows not to fight on an empty stomach."

"I thought I was a squire," Mattie said sleepily.

"Good squires are apprentice knights."

This made Mattie fully open her eyes. "So you acknowledge that I'm good?"

"Yes."

"For a girl?"

He gave this some serious thought. "For anyone."

"Ha!"

Before she fell asleep, Mattie felt that she had already scored a victory.

This is *insane*," she told Artorius as she struggled to get on his back in her clunky silver armor.

Once again, they were poised for takeoff at CIA.

"I might as well be in a spacesuit!"

"Luckily, I'm the one dragon on Cavernis who actually knows what you mean."

"Come on, Artorius, I told you—I suck when I'm in this thing. I can't even stay on a *horse*, much less a dragon."

"Trust me," he said, and because it was him, she did.

She managed to get her right leg over his bulk. She sat on his back like a ramrod, praying that steel didn't slip.

"Ready?"

"No, not reall—"

It didn't matter, since they were off. Artorius sought out Eli on the tilting field. He swooped over the gold knight, curving away sharply to let her sword strike.

"Argh!" she said, tumbling off as she tried to extend her blade. In a heap, she landed at Duke's feet.

"Pity," the horse said.

Eli raised his visor. "You all right, Mattie?"

She groaned, raising hers. "P.S., this hurts. I think I sprained my rear."

Eli tried not to laugh. "Again? Good thing there's adequate padding."

"I beg your pardon?"

His words spurred Mattie to rise—with the considerable help of Superbas.

"Let's go again."

Artorius touched down on the dirt.

"Do we *have* to?"

"Think of Sarug."

She did, which got her to mount again. Artorius set off for the air, diving in at their mounted "foe."

"I can do this!" Mattie yelled. She wasn't sure if she was telling the others or herself. This time, she really tried to keep her seat, squeezing her steel-clad legs into Artorius' sides. When she lifted her blade, she actually made contact with Eli's, and managed *not* to eat dirt.

"Brava!" Artorius yelled.

"Well done," said Eli and Duke.

Superbas bowed deeply.

The next few days were mostly devoted to practice. Mattie got to a point where she could not only engage Eli, but actually *unseat* him, using Artorius' momentum to sweep him from Duke.

On those rare occasions when she could get away, she went to visit ASH. It seemed to her that the whole place burned with war fever. No one knew when Georgia would strike, so they spent all their time training. Mattie felt—after so many ups and downs—that she was maybe kind of ready. Her dual goal was simple: she didn't want to disgrace Eli nor her distant relative Matilda.

Chapter Twenty-Seven

Ignis et Fuga!

In between practices, Mattie saw Dr. Lung at his office on the Prat. As a rider of dragons, she had acquired so many bruises she looked like Rocky after a fight.

Dr. Lung preferred ancient remedies to the pills prescribed in L.A. His herbs did their work well, and she was 100% in no time.

"We treat the whole body," Dr. Lung proclaimed.

He did, and practiced his art on many: Eli, Ripley, even Professor Fraxinus. Mattie wondered how he'd keep up once the fighting started.

A few weeks after the Council, Eli was the guest speaker at *"Ignis et Fuga."* Professors Drake and Ignis yielded the stage as dragons from all walks of life filled the benches of the amphitheater.

"Um, hello," Eli started.

Mattie could tell he wasn't used to public speaking. His lower lip trembled slightly.

"You can do it," she whispered up to where he stood. He seemed to relax a little.

"As you know, I am by birth a Georgian, and am intimate with their ways." He went on to describe how knights aimed for a dragon's underbelly or their vulnerable throat.

From the back of the stage, Professor Ignis frowned.

"We of course suspected as much, especially after Helen, uh...Mrs. Avarus. How then to protect ourselves?" His concern was reflected in his body's heightened flame.

"I—I don't know," Eli said. "When I was a dragon, I'm not sure what I would have done."

Professor Drake looked grim. "Well, this is a sorry scale."

In the very back of the cave, where Praeses could barely fit, the president heaved a sigh. This seemed to be a classic no-win.

A hundred rows in front of him, Mattie tried to think. She thought of everything she'd seen on Cavernis, which unspooled in her mind like a filmstrip: portals, Latro, caves, Rex, secret rooms, and spells...

"Wait." Mattie's voice echoed in the giant space. She approached the stage where Eli stood, taking a place beside him. "I saw something."

All the dragons there went silent.

"In the secret rooms, buried in school treasure, I saw something unusual while we were looking for armor."

Eli's expression told her that he was drawing a blank.

"It was plate, enormous. Much bigger than a horse's. I saw armor designed for a dragon."

The cave exploded with sound, most of it derisive.

"And what, pray tell, would a dragon do with armor?" one lively gray asked. "You might have noticed we have *scales* which are our natural defense."

Most of the seated dragons nodded and shouted, "That's right!"

"Let the girl speak!" The thundering words belonged to Praeses, who could have silenced the Hollywood Bowl without raising his voice.

"Thank you, Mr. President." Mattie tried to assemble her thoughts. "I know that you guys have scales, and claws, and tails, and teeth. But those still didn't help poor Helen."

Eli nodded, encouraging her to go on.

"Master Eliwlod of Georgia has told you that you have two chinks in your natural armor. Cover those in the real thing, and you're one-up on the Georgians."

"And where is such a quantity of plate to be found *for all of us?*" the gray asked.

"In the secret rooms. Melt down the enormous pieces and have the brownies rework them. You should have more than enough."

"Brilliant!" Praeses cried. "This is why we must always embrace new minds. We are so caught up in the old ways, it takes an outsider to devise something fresh!"

"Hear, hear," the assembled dragons roared.

Mattie turned to Eli and showed him how to work a high five.

"Amazing," he said. "I saw the same thing as you, but gave it no more thought. From now on, I should be *your* squire."

"Don't be silly," Mattie blushed. "Thinking and fighting are two very different skills."

"Good thing that I can do one—"

"—and I can do the other!"

This led to a second—much higher—high five. Mattie thought that between Eli's time as a dragon and as her human instructor, he'd developed into someone she was actually glad to know.

The next two days saw a frenzy of activity with the onus on the brownies.

Hob had taken charge and assembled his troop and all others in front of the secret rooms. Miss Fang watched carefully as helmets, breastplates, and tail covers were lugged out to a new forge. There, they were refashioned into sensible dragon armor.

"This rocks," Mattie told Hob, watching his huge smithy, which flared like dragon's breath. "You guys are better than dwarves."

"Who?" the brownie asked, wrinkling his leathery nose.

"Never mind."

"Missy, ah hae somethin' fur ye."

"Really?" Mattie couldn't imagine what.

"Aye. When Ah was schoolin' Miss Ripley, Ah reid abit hoo knights-errant used tae wear a sleeve in their helmets. As a token ay favur."

"Right."

"Weel—here's a body fur ye."

He shyly presented her with a red pennant, etched in black with the sign of a dragon.

"Thanks, Hob. This is...the nicest present I've ever gotten."

She bent nearly in two to deliver a kiss to the brownie's hat.

"Guid day noo—gonnae—no 'at!" he protested, his face turning several shades of red.

"I will proudly wear this in battle so that the brownies are with us in spirit."

Hob sputtered, then pretended to be *very* engrossed in his work.

Mattie was truly touched. Everyone in Cavernis seemed to want to do his or her part. That reminded her of something, something that had been nagging her since the Council.

In Artorius's cave that night, she approached her circle of friends.

"Hey guys. Anyone seen Sudha lately?"

"Nope." The response was unanimous.

"Hmmm."

"Was her name on the list?" she asked Eli.

"Honestly, I don't remember. I was so shocked by the others."

"I haven't seen her at ASH," Ripley chirped. "Would anyone be surprised if she's part of the MAD? That snake is *not* to be trusted."

Mattie nodded in agreement.

"Come on, girls," Artorius said. "We don't *know* for sure. Here's one thing I learned on Mundanis: 'Innocent till proven guilty.' Right, Mattie?"

She sighed. "I guess."

Artorius could think what he liked, and he liked to think the best of everyone. As for her, she could easily see Sudha as Sarug's disciple, turning human, snake, or half of each to inflict maximum damage. On them.

Chapter Twenty-Eight

First Assault

A few more days passed filled with heroic effort—at least from Hob and the brownies. Mattie had come up with what she thought was another good idea.

"President Praeses." She addressed the gold Elder as he watched a flight of dragons belching fire from the morning sky. He and Mattie were—somewhat eerily—on the quad beside his statue.

"Something came to me last night."

"Yes?" As always, he seemed genuinely interested in what she had to say.

"Well, there was this thing the Russians used—it was called a Pot—a Potam—a a—"

"A Potemkin village. Yes. When Westerners wanted to glimpse Soviet life, they were taken to fake villages constructed to deceive them. After the visitors left, the villages were usually torn down."

"Exactly! So I was thinking...what if we build a 'Georgian' town right here at ASH? Then our dragons can practice what they learned from Razing a Village."

Praeses clapped a claw to his head. "Yes! Inspired, as always. I will see that it's done right away."

He gestured Miss Fang over and began to recite his orders.

"Another day, another brainstorm," Mattie told Eli, who had descended on Superbas in full gold regalia.

Superbas signed something to Eli, pointing a black talon to his head.

Eli lifted his visor, crouching so Superbas could read his lips. "I know. That's why we keep her around."

Mattie didn't feel like training again that day, but she knew Artorius. He never made an unneeded request, so she resolved not to whine. Still...

"I'm worried," she said to Eli.

"About what?" He clanked over to her side.

"All of this delay. How long will it take Sarug to do his 'transformation'? He's not exactly a slouch."

"No one knows that better than I," Eli said with a shudder. "It must be very important for him to wait so long."

"You think they'll show up here?"

"Absolutely. This is where the enemy is, but most important, this is where the treasure lies."

"They'll never get their filthy claws on it!"

Mattie took Hob's red sleeve out of her tunic pocket.

"Do me a favor," she asked.

"Of course."

"If I'm killed in battle, please ask Latro—provided he can get still here—to give this to my mom. And tell her everything that's happened."

It wasn't so much the thought of her own death but the image of her mom, standing silently in the kitchen, worried about her daughter, that brought the quick-flowing tears to her eyes.

"Don't think like that," said Eli. He gave her a gauntleted pat.

"Sorry, I know apprentice knights shouldn't cry. I just haven't been one that long."

"You're doing better than I did."

"You were seven. But thanks." After all the training, falls, and bruises, that meant a lot to her.

By the side of his statue, Praeses stiffened, rising to full height.

"They're coming," he said, his voice strong and fearless. "*Dracones* of Cavernis, I bid you fight nobly. Remember our ancient war cry: *Ignis et Fuga!*"

Miss Fang set off a deafening siren that sounded like the Blitz. Dragons arrived from all quarters to assemble on the quad. They came from their homes, from ASH, and offices on the Plat. Some took positions on the ground while others rose rapidly, forming tightly bunched flights. After all their preparation, the time to act had arrived.

Artorius loped up to Mattie, armor protecting his belly and throat. He and Superbas began to gird her in silver.

Mattie hoped they couldn't tell that she shook. The wildest thing she'd done at home was to get drunk at a party. Now she was supposed to ride a wyvern against a troop of treasure-mad dragons who had behind them not just a saint, but a crazed sorcerer!

"Artorius, I'm scared," she said as he fastened her hauberk's buckles.

"So am I," he admitted, closing her cuirass. "I don't want you to come to harm. After all, you're my person! You raised me from an egg."

Then he did something he'd never done before. He applied his forked tongue directly to her cheek. *This*, Mattie thought, *must be a dragon kiss.*

191

She stood stiffly in her armor and planted her own on his snout.

"I would rather die than have anything happen to you," she said.

"I feel the same."

Mattie didn't know if grown dragons cried, but something like liquid was filling his yellow pupils. She could feel her own tears streaming down her cheeks.

"None of that," Artorius told her, "or you'll have to be polished."

"Come on, you two," Eli chided from Superbas' back. "They'll be here any second."

Artorius closed Mattie's helm, then fastened Hob's sleeve to the top. He knelt on his front feet and tail and she mounted with a clunk. This was it. The first—maybe last—battle for a new age.

Mattie heard them before she saw them. The steady tramp of steel shaking the desert floor, the distinctive whir of wings as the MAD prepared to assault.

"There they are!" Praeses bellowed.

A cluster of black dots silhouetted by midday Lumen dropped like unloosed arrows.

"*Ignis et Fuga!*" Artorius yelled, taking a running start until he and Mattie were airborne. She saw two shapes at his shoulder: Eli and Superbas.

The MAD continued to plunge as the ASH dragons rose to meet them. Now the enemy came into focus. Mattie still couldn't believe she was up against her own teammates. She saw Agravaine change from orange to magenta while Alazon's bulky muscles looked even bigger in flight. Bringing up the rear was Professor Avarus, still sporting all his bling.

I'd like to cut those chains right off his yellow neck! Mattie thought.

Mattie then spotted Fractious and Unctuous, but where the others were and what they were doing was unknown. One thing they had in common, per Eli: they were driven by pure greed.

"*Follow me!*" Artorius yelled to Eli.

Superbas knew what to do. "Knights—lances at the ready!"

Mattie and Eli complied. Artorius wheeled toward the oncoming dragons, his small wings able to generate blistering speed. Superbas, the superb flyer, was able to turn in tandem in a graceful dragon ballet.

Both mounts gave a stupendous roar—louder than Rex if he'd been able—then belched streams of fire from their gaping mouths.

Mattie put up her shield, expecting a searing counterblast; but instead of an inferno, she found herself assaulted with firehose streams of frost!

Artorius's flames were instantly rendered harmless. The substance coming from the MAD's jaws was blinding in its paleness, contoured around the edges by dripping icicles!

"*Retreat!*" Artorius yelled, following his own advice. Superbas obeyed, and the two dragons landed on the quad, shaking off a thin sheet of ice.

"*Frost!*" Artorius shouted to Praeses, who had his own claws full with a battalion of Georgians. He was doing an excellent job, the ironworks of flame he spewed keeping most of them at bay.

"This must be the transformation," Beowulf announced, alighting by his fellow Elder. "Since frost has always trumped flame, we are helpless against them."

Mattie lifted her visor. "We can't fight the MAD," she told Eli. "But we *can* harass the knights."

He nodded and the riders took off again. Artorius flew low enough to impede the Georgians' progress with steady blasts of flame. He and Superbas were targeted by darts, most of which bounced harmlessly off their new plate.

Mattie had a perfect view of the war on the ground. It was clear that Cavernis dragons could stave off the knights with fire. Also clear was that whenever the MAD struck, they took out at least one dragon, causing it to morph into an icy block.

Mattie could see Geetha whirling with swords in all six hands. Huáng Chow used frost against fire as he slithered across the quad.

She watched as he ambushed a Chinese dragon, the spitting image of himself. The assaulted one clunked to the ground, his body covered with frost. Mattie couldn't tell if it was Jimmy or Heng.

She scanned the entire field, looking for a distinctive shape. There she was, easy to spot in her blazing red sari.

Sudha! *Another traitor!* She was in her *nāgī* form, her upper half wielding six kinds of blades, her lower cobra scales giving her speed and height. Mattie stared as she spun like a dervish, at last teaming with Geetha to repel a squadron from ASH.

Right! Mattie thought. The guy she wanted to torture.

Geetha's icy breath—toxic at the best of times—felled dragon after dragon. He barely had to use his weapons.

In contrast, Sudha was a wreck. She kept missing her targets, but, being a dragon, was impervious to ASH's flames.

Finally, she turned to Geetha and said something. He nodded. Mattie gasped as Sudha aimed her frost *at* her fellow *nāga,* causing him to topple. She whirled in a blur of red over to an ASH squad, whose ranks she proudly joined.

Whoa, Mattie thought. Talk about your double-cross!

Yet even with the addition of *one* frost-breathing dragon, things were not going well for their side. The twelve MAD were freezing their foe so often that the quad resembled a graveyard, white tombs littering the dirt.

Ripley, now completely in uniform, flew onto Mattie's shoulder.

"*Retreat!*" she yelled into her helm. "Praeses says fall back to the quad!"

Ripley delivered the message to Eli. Artorius, giving a parting blast, motioned for his wingman to land on the quad.

Many of their classmates were there. Some were riddled with arrows and being treated by Dr. Lung while others were too exhausted to stand. They lay back on the gold floor, exhaling tendrils of smoke.

"Are you all right?" Mattie asked Artorius, who was plucking darts from his tail.

"Fine," he said, looking with concern at Superbas. "Everyone okay?"

"Yes," said Eli, shaking off his helm. "But what does that matter when the MAD have handed us our tails?"

The foursome leaned against a wall, still clad in heavy plate. They saw Praeses and Beowulf enter—at the head of a noxious cloud.

Everyone inside tensed as they listened for sounds outside. They heard the fall of hooves and the clank of armor receding, the faint flap of wings as the MAD turned to the east. It seemed that the enemy, content with their first triumph, would not press their advantage this day, at least until they resolved how to withstand a stench that brought grown men to their knees.

"I fear we've broken a school rule," Praeses said to Beowulf, but he didn't look ashamed.

Beowulf gave a chuckle, though one else joined him.

"The Georgians may have frost, but we dragons have sulfur. By the by, I did see Frost as an option when I looked to the Old Magick."

"As did I," Praeses nodded.

"Now that it's a reality, I'm not quite sure what to do."

"We must regroup and strategize. Use our minds to create a better defense." The president shot a look at Mattie.

"I can't think of anything," she told Eli. They helped each other to remove their armor. "Can you?"

"No," he answered, throwing her a full-length towel. As he had been doing recently, he was sure to avert his eyes. "We can repel the Georgians, as long as we have dragons. But if most of them freeze, then surely we will fall."

The lethality of the enemy's weapon struck Mattie as faculty dragged in the stricken. She saw that among them was a Chinese dragon. Running over and peering through the frosty veil, she exhaled in relief. It wasn't her friend.

"Fang," someone said sadly, and Mattie looked up to find Jimmy. Despite his sharp talons and coils, she managed to give him a hug.

"Jimmy! I was afraid it was you."

"No, but to lose a brother is worse than losing yourself."

"I'm so sorry." Mattie didn't know what else to say.

Jimmy sighed. "Our shock was great when Huáng joined the MAD. Now that he's killed his nest mate, I don't know what Father will do."

"He has to go on! To fight!" Mattie exhorted herself as much as Mr. Chow.

"Yes. So must we all."

Jimmy bent his head over the fallen Fang, and Mattie left him to mourn in privacy.

She walked over to where Sudha coiled before the ice-entombed Geetha. This was not going to be easy.

"Sudha, I owe you a huge apology. The biggest one of my life."

The *nāgī* looked up from under her hood. "Oh?"

"I thought you were one of them. That you were swayed by Sarug. Now I know you're a total goddess. Like...like Krishna or something!"

Sudha smiled, her green eyes shining. "Thanks for that, Sharpe—Mattie. I see you've come a long way. You're pretty kickass yourself."

Mattie blushed, changing the subject. "How did you fool Sarug?"

"We *nāga* have our own magic. I simply masked my true intentions."

"Sweet."

"So that leaves us with one frost dragon. Too bad I'm not big as Praeses."

"Yeah." Mattie reached out to touch one of Sudha's hands. To her surprise, she wasn't repelled.

Sudha extended two arms and clasped Mattie's shoulders. It was a far cry from the last time she'd touched her. Now, in one silent moment, the two had become real friends.

Chapter Twenty-Nine

Take the War to Them!

So the dragons that got frozen, they won't recover?"

"No. Frost kills, and there's no way back."

Mattie and Artorius were still huddled inside the quad. It seemed safer than going home.

And all this treasure can't do a thing, Mattie thought, surveying the ornate hall and its priceless artifacts. She leaned against her friend as Praeses walked slowly by. The president looked shaken, but tried to dispel this with his words. "*Dracones* of Cavernis, we have fought a single battle. It was darker than we thought, but we lost only eighteen. Hundreds of us still live."

No one—not even Miss Fang in her helmet—seemed cheered by this booming speech.

"Our foe is evil and cunning. Who knows what more he might hurl at us? I only ask that you remain strong."

"What about the frost?" Jimmy asked. His brother's sudden death seemed to have emboldened him.

"Yes, it is a significant threat. We Elders are reflecting on the matter."

"What about Jötunheimr? Aren't there frost dragons there?" The thought had occurred to Mattie so fast it went right from her brain to her mouth. "Maybe *they* would be willing to help us."

Praeses shook his head. "From the beginning, fire and frost have fought. They will rejoice in our fall."

Eli looked crestfallen.

"Do not despair, *dracones*! We have secret weapons of our own. And we are going to use them tomorrow, in Georgia."

The cave echoed with murmured excitement. *This was more like it.* If they were going to lose, it might as well be on the attack, tails up and teeth bared. In a moment, the morale in the quad. shot up like the desert temperature.

"What secret weapon?" Mattie asked her friends.

"Ice cannons," Ripley blurted.

"A Son of Heaven descending from the clouds!" That was Jimmy.

"The goddess Kali exacting revenge," countered Sudha.

"*I* hope it's Sir Lancelot, summoned from beneath the lake!" Eli sounded enthused.

Superbas signed frantically, Eli acting as his interpreter. "He says he wants a Sir Beethoven."

Mattie nodded. "And *I* wouldn't mind a couple of tanks and bombers."

There was complete silence.

"Just forget I said anything."

It was a sleepless night for everyone in the quad. Praeses conferred with Ripley, etching out battle plans, while Dr. Lung huddled with Jimmy and the Asians.

"Now, this might not be common knowledge, but I am able to fly," Dr. Lung told his troops. "However, since there are just a handful of us that can, we are going to stay with you and attack on foot."

"Do you think we have a prayer?" Mattie whispered to Eli, who reclined by his armor beside her.

"Always there is a prayer, but...Georgia can become a fortress. And now, with the MAD and their killing frost..." His voice trailed off. Mattie translated this to mean, *The odds aren't exactly great.*

Still, Eli reached over and patted her arm. She felt her gooseflesh rise.

"We must trust Praeses, for he has put his trust in us."

Just before sunrise, Ripley flew into view and hovered, her martial outfit crisp.

"Orders from the prez-slash-general."

"Shoot," Mattie said.

Ripley gave her a strange look. "You two dragonriders are to *wait* for my signal. Once it's given, you're to distract the MAD with flying maneuvers and tricks."

"Okay." Artorius nodded.

Eli translated to Superbas, who gleefully clapped his claws.

"So we're a distraction," Mattie told Eli. "Like some kind of flying circus."

"We must put our faith in the Elders and their skill in warfare. They did fight the Battle of Lydda."

"And won?"

"Oh yes. There wasn't a Mundani left."

"Fab."

They both started to don their armor and helped their mounts with theirs. Eli turned his back while she undressed.

Mattie affixed Hob's sleeve and gripped the ruby hilt of her sword. She exited the quad, watching as dragons around her split into two factions: the Western ones heading for the statue, the Asians making for the tall grass adjacent to the quad.

She wondered what the secret weapon was as she and Artorius, followed by their wingmen, joined the cluster of color comprised of hundreds of flying dragons.

On dragonback, Georgia was not very far. Within a few minutes, she spied the spot where the Cube had landed, then looked down upon the village and cathedral.

Even in a helmet, she sensed something above her head, turning the morning to evening. It was Praeses, gold wings outspread, but unarmored, which really disturbed her. *Why in Cavernis would he take that kind of chance?*

The Georgians were ready for their arrival. Sarug must have foreseen it, for they formed a border of steel more impregnable than a wall.

In the tower of a ruined stone castle, Mattie saw a black-robed figure—Sarug—leaning out the open window. He seemed to delight in their coming, yelling down to his troops.

"Shields! Use shields to repel the beasts' flames!"

Clattering shields formed a "turtle" with the speed of a Roman legion, sheltering Georgian flesh.

"Abominations! Slay them before they pollute the holy ground of St. George!"

A low cry went up from the knights. They managed to hold their ground, even as the dragons above unloosed their spigots of flame.

Despite their armor, many were charred, for dragon's breath could melt steel. Mattie cringed as she saw them go down, rolling to quench the flames, only then to cease all movement. Their screams of pain were hard for her to hear. These were people after all. Yet she thought of eighteen corpses lying in state at the quad. and tried to steel her heart so that it matched her blade.

Sarug shouted from his tower, waving his wand three times.

"Dragons of frost, dragons of ice, come forth and vanquish your foe!"

Over the cathedral spire came the MAD eleven, crazed with greed and bloodlust. Their object was almost in their talons.

"*I summon Quetzalcoatl!*" Praeses shouted, winging toward the cathedral. "I beg him to descend from the realm of the gods!"

With a crash like two sonic booms, an apparition popped over the Georgians' heads so bizarre, so exotic, that Mattie almost stopped breathing.

Quetzalcoatl was a dragon, but differed from all the others. His body was vibrant green, with yellow scales stretching across the belly. His jaw was actually square—almost stone-like—and behind his skull waved red and green feathers, each shaped like a leaf. Quetzalcoatl was not a guy to be taken lightly. Clearly, *he* was the secret weapon.

"I am Quetzalcoatl!" the beast roared. "Revered by the Maya and Aztecs. As the dragon said, *I am a god!* Who among you dares to oppose me?"

If the Georgians weren't wearing armor, their knees would have been visibly shaking. This was reinforced when Quetzalcoatl dove, grabbing a knight in his jaw. All assembled could see—and hear—the victim being eaten alive.

"Gross!" Mattie cried.

"Go Quetzalcoatl!" enthused Artorius.

Quetzalcoatl darted upward, hovering over the Georgians.

"I created you and all mankind. I brought you maize and time. I am a patron of the arts, but ignore this warning at your peril: *do not make me angry!*"

As if to emphasize his point, he opened his mouth and spewed forth a rain of lava.

The Georgians screamed in terror and a few ran for their lives.

"Cowards!" Sarug shouted. "Try to stop him with darts!"

A company of archers fired swarm after swarm of arrows into the dragon's hide. In response, Quetzalcoatl gave a laugh that shook the whole village.

"Idiots!" he roared, picking arrows out of his scales. "Did I not say that I am a god and therefore immortal?"

"Cool," Mattie said.

"Avarus, freeze him!" Sarug commanded as the frost dragons rose from behind the spire. Avarus did as he was told. To Mattie's surprise, Quetzalcoatl dropped to the ground, unable to withstand frost.

"Damnit!"

Yet within minutes, the ice around the god's body melted, and he was once again skyborne.

"What part of immortal *don't* you understand?"

This went on like an endless loop: Quetzalcoatl would take out some Georgians, the MAD dragons would freeze him, and then he would resuscitate.

This is could go on all day, Mattie thought with alarm.

She sat back in reserve, waiting for Ripley's cue. Before it could be issued, ASH unleashed another wave. From the pastures surrounding Georgia emerged a slithering army, Asian dragons of every sort, moving more quickly on coils than any human could run.

"Snakes! Snakes!" ran the terrified cry up and down the enemy lines.

"Fools," Dr. Lung snapped. "We are dragons. *Anyone* can see that."

It didn't matter to the Georgians. They dreaded these serpentine creatures with their forked tongues and carp scales.

"Fight them!" Sarug screamed. "*They* are not immortal."

Some of the Georgians did and were successful. Their swords, lances, and darts often found their mark. As did some of the dragons. Sudha used her fangs to advantage, as well as her freezing breath. Dr. Lung hurled his flaming pearl and bowled down a line of soldiers.

"Freeze them all!" Sarug commanded.

The MAD spread their chilling effect. Dragons—both Western and Asian, airborne and on the ground—tumbled onto the main square, encased in icy tombs.

"Where's Ripley?" Mattie hissed.

"Patience," counseled Artorius. "We have to wait for the signal."

From her vantage point in the sky, it didn't look good to Mattie. Each time Quetzalcoatl was knocked out, the MAD froze even more dragons. As the hours passed, the ranks of Cavernis thinned.

Praeses, perched on the spire, looked increasingly grim.

"*Retreat!*" he finally called, and though the MAD succeeded in knocking him off the cathedral, he rose again like Quetzalcoatl to continue leading his troops.

At last, Ripley landed on Mattie's helm.

"*Now!*" the dragonet ordered, and Artorius and Superbas issued one last blast of flame to cover the Asians below.

They feinted and dodged the MAD with an arsenal of moves. At one point, Mattie could have sworn that the cathedral was upside down, then she realized it was *she* who was upside down!

As Artorius righted, she saw the Asians slither back across the grass and the Westerners wheel and fly west. When all had dispersed, Artorius prepared to follow. Then— *screech!*—a thundering like a split glacier sounded at his left wing. Mattie watched as their wingmen fell like weights, bodies engulfed in frost.

She twisted her head in its helmet and caught Agravaine and Alazon cheering.

"*No!*" she yelled. "Artorius, we've got to go after them!"

"Can't," he replied sternly, winging west at top speed. "We'd just get killed too."

Chapter Thirty

Desperate Times

M attie tumbled from his back the minute they hit the ground. She stomped rigidly into the quad, throwing down her helm.

"I can't believe you just *left them!*" she cried. "Can't we at least go back for the bodies?"

Artorius shook his head. "Too dangerous."

As he approached, she had to repress a shudder.

"Mattie, you're still young—so am I, in dragon years—but I want you to understand. If we had followed Eli and Superbas, we'd have been frozen too. If we fly back to Georgia now, we'll surely be killed by the guard."

"But I want to do...*something*," Mattie whispered, and a jolt hit her. She would never see her friends again. She started to sob as she never had before, convulsions wrenching her insides.

"Eli," she barely got out. "And Superbas. They were so brave and good. Eli fought his own people for us."

She cried so hard that tears bounced off her hauberk.

"I never got to tell him," Mattie sobbed out when she could.

"What?" Artorius folded a wing around her, gently squeezing her to him.

"How much I admired him. Eli. We fought a lot but..."

"Deep down, you loved him."

"Yes."

"And I'm sure he returned the feeling."

They both fell silent amid the bustle of the quad. Dr. Lung attended to the wounded, barking orders to the nurses he'd just deputized.

Sudha slithered up to them. "I froze that traitor Huáng. Jimmy was pretty upset, but he said I did the right thing."

Mattie nodded.

"We lost Miyabi."

"Sorry, I didn't know her."

"She was a Japanese dragon. A total kick-ass."

"I'm sorry." Mattie wiped away her own tears.

"Hey." Sudha looked around. "Where's Eli and Superbas?"

Mattie answered with a sob. Artorius looked at the floor.

"No." Sudha glided back a few paces. "Those bastards! I'll bet it was an ASH student."

"Two," Mattie whispered.

"Don't tell me. Agravaine and Alazon."

Mattie bit her lip and nodded.

Sudha straightened in her saree, looking regal as a princess.

"They shall be avenged," she said quietly. She saw Jimmy come in and hurried over to talk to him.

"How?" Mattie half-cried to Artorius.

Her friend drew her in closer. "I'm afraid I don't really know."

In a corner, Praeses sat solemnly with Beowulf and Quetzalcoatl. Miss Fang and Professor Fraxinus rounded out their Council.

"I fear it's the only way," Mattie heard Fraxinus saying. "What choice do we have? Sarug might let us stay."

"No." Beowulf stood, his jagged teeth gleaming. "We have never suffered a defeat. We will be expelled from Cavernis— I know these *Europeans*." He spat out the last word like a curse.

"What do you think, Mr. President?" Miss Fang asked, turning her gold helmet toward her boss.

"I agree with Beowulf. At this rate, our rout is certain, and we must find another world. Again build up our treasure. Conversely, I wish to stall as long as possible. No sense hastening the end."

The other Elders nodded. All of them looked grim. Praeses summoned Ripley with a black talon.

"Twinkletoes, I wish you to take a message to Sarug."

Ripley blanched at the use of her real name.

"Tell him we are willing to meet his terms. Our only request is that we need time to prepare."

"What if he asks how long?" Ripley hung in the air, her uniform still spotless.

"Don't commit to specifics. Tell him you need to ask me."

"Yes, sir." For once, Ripley seemed deflated. "So we're throwing in our eggs, General?"

Praeses dropped his head. "I'm afraid there's no alternative. For us, this is truly the end of days."

That night, back in their cave for the first time in days, Mattie and Artorius just stared at Hob's banquet.

Artorius made a small fire using a nest of twigs and they watched the orange flames dance, casting shadows on the cave walls. Mattie took up a stick, drawing aimless circles in the dirt.

"I wish Eli were here," she blurted. "And Superbas."

"I'll miss th' wee laddie an' 'at bampot lizard," Hob added sadly.

The three friends—different species but all united in feeling—sat and watched the fire spark.

"Sae yoo'll be givin' up aw thes?" Hob gestured at the piles of gold and silver.

"It doesn't matter," Artorius mumbled.

Mattie clutched her head, which ached at both temples from the sheer power of grief.

"I'd give all the gold in Cavernis just to have our friends back."

Artorius and Hob nodded.

"I heard we lost thirty-six dragons today," Artorius said grimly. "And they lost fifty-two men and one MAD: Huáng."

"May he burn in the flames of Hell!"

Artorius looked puzzled at the negative reference to fire.

Mattie choked. "Don't forget, we lost a man too. The best."

Artorius blinked his eyes as she continued.

"I wonder if Praeses will still make him knight. Posthumously, I mean." As the word left her lips, she could hardly believe it was real.

"We will request it," said Artorius. "It is only right."

"Even though we don't have the bodies, maybe we can still hold a service."

"Yes." Artorius gave a bitter laugh. "Perhaps St. George can lead it."

"Coward! He didn't even fight."

"He doesn't have to. He has Sarug."

Mattie bowed her head, using the small fire as a kind of votive candle. *May God bless Eli and Superbas,* she thought. *May they always ride together in the next world.* They died as they had lived: bravely, and honorably. No shame would stain their memory.

Mattie cried herself to sleep that night, clutching Eli's tunic, which still bore a trace of his smell. She could almost feel him there, watching. She saw his trim yet muscular frame, blond hair streaming as he told her, *Mattie, don't give up! Never give up!*

"I won't," she whispered to the nighttime phantom. In her mind, she was forming a desperate plan.

Chapter Thirty-One

Preamble

Mattie hated to deceive Artorius, but she didn't want him to stop her. And if he knew what she was up to, he would.

She stealthily packed some supplies. Food that wouldn't spoil, heavy cloth that could serve as a blanket. She rummaged around the cave until she found a very nice brocade jacket and a very thick pair of trousers. She slipped on her old blue boots, which had come through for her so far.

Mattie searched around for a map. There were many at ASH, but she didn't want to risk the detour. Artorius must know his world well since there wasn't one to be found. No matter. She knew the general direction she had to go in.

"Missy?"

"Shhhh!" Mattie cautioned Hob with a finger to her lips. He looked especially disapproving, tapping a pointed shoe. "Don't say anything to Artorius. Please?"

"Ah can't. He is mah master."

"Can't you make *one* exception? For *me*?" She gave him a too-bright smile.

He pursed his lips, scowling. "Humph."

"Thanks, Hob."

Mattie fastened on her sword, eyeing her armor sadly. No doubt it would come in handy, but the weight was too much to bear.

"Goodbye," she said to Artorius, who snored away in his bed. Was this yet another friend she would never see after tonight?

Mattie tiptoed to the cave entrance. She was so numb from today that she didn't even feel anxious. She took a final look back.

"Bye, Artorius," she whispered.

"Bye."

She heard a familiar voice. When its owner stepped from the shadows, she saw it came from a familiar blue wyvern.

"Going somewhere?"

"But—you were just—I mean—"

"Forgot what you learned in Dragonlore? 'Dragons have acute senses in the physical and mental realms.' Remember?"

Mattie set down her pack. "Yes."

"And where do you think you are off to in the middle of the night?"

"Um..." She really didn't want to tell him. When she did, she got the expected response.

"Have you completely lost it? That's *the dumbest thing* I've ever heard!"

"Thanks, Artorius." She stared moodily out at Cavernis. "Unlike you—and the others—I can't just sit around while Praeses hoists the white flag. I'm a person—a, a *human*—and I've got to do *something*."

She searched for a hint of approval in his yellow eyes. She wasn't sure what she saw there.

"Believe me, I get it. I don't want to give up either. But sometimes...you have to accept things the way they are. I commend you for your bravery, but your plan will never work."

"What if it does?"

Mattie stood straight up, giving her a bird's-eye view of his stomach.

"You've got to try, don't you? Eli told me, 'You couldn't steer the boat before you could.' Well, I did, and we won! I've learned to fight, and ride a dragon, even to be friends with Sudha. If you just stop trying and don't do anything new, you might as well be dead!"

Her words echoed back through the cave. Mattie thought she had never said so much in her life. But her speech had a hidden listener, who popped his head around a crevice.

"Th' lass is reit, ye ken," Hob said. "Ask yoorself whit woods Rob Roy dae?"

Mattie didn't know much about the Scot, but of one thing she was certain. "He'd kick some serious tail!"

"Damn straecht," Hob agreed.

"Mother of Quetzalcoatl! I can't fight you both. All right, Mattie, you win. We'll give your plan a whirl. If we die trying, I guess it'll be no worse than when Sarug takes over."

"*You're* coming with me?"

"Like I'm going to let you leave while *I* hide in my cave?"

"Thanks, Artorius!" She put her arms around his belly, squeezing the blue scales tightly. "You *always* come through for me."

"That's just the meaning of the word friend."

Chapter Thirty-Two

The Frost Dragons

Mattie picked up her pack and tied it around Artorius. Without any words spoken, he crouched on his front legs and tail and she swung aboard. This time, they weren't headed for battle, but maybe something scarier since they didn't know what they'd find.

Artorius headed due north, toward a star he called Septentriones. There was no sign of knights on the ground, no ominous flap of wings before the MAD swooped.

"Here's a question," Artorius called, shortly into their flight. "How exactly did you plan to do this without me?"

"Hang around CIA?" Mattie asked sheepishly.

"I don't mean to be rude—but sometimes, humans are just dumb."

"Point taken," she answered.

As they flew through the night, leaving the desert behind, the air grew chillier, and the silence of space more eerie.

"How much longer do you think?" Mattie asked the back of Artorius' head.

"No one's actually been there, not for centuries anyway. I estimate five more hours."

"Phew!"

"Hey, *I'm* the one being ridden."

"I know. Thanks."

Septentriones seemed to come closer, and Mattie wondered if its planets were seeded with life, like Mundanis, Cavernis, or the other ten worlds frequented by Latro.

Two hours in, it *really* began to get cold. Mattie was glad she was wearing the heavy gold coat. She put her hand on her sword. Just a little more time and they would know what awaited—stumbling folly or glory.

"Artorius, do you want to stop?" she asked, after another hour.

"No, our mission is far too crucial."

They flew on in silence, over a landscape so dark that Mattie could make out nothing. Once, she thought she saw a blue lake, but that might have been a mirage. As the air became more biting and the scenery below pale, she had a feeling they were close.

Finally, Lumen rose faintly in the west, revealing the terrain below. It wasn't really that striking, consisting of snow, snow, and snow. As Artorius descended, she saw imposing mountains and huge icefalls with broken crevasses. Not a speck of color broke through. No trees, no brush, no sign of life on the ground. *Maybe everyone left,* Mattie thought. *And we've come here for nothing.*

Artorius flexed his front claws and tail, braking to a halt on a field of sheer ice. Relieved, Mattie dismounted. If there was such a thing as "dragonsore," she was—and had the aching rear to prove it.

The two of them stood and looked in every direction. The ground was absolutely frigid, the wind chill decreasing the temperature by half. Snow and sleet assaulted Mattie's extremities. She slipped on a pair of wool mittens, the best she'd been able to scavenge. Artorius, a desert native wrapped his arms around his body and his wings around his arms. He looked like a big blue ball.

"See anything?" she yelled to him over the wind.

"Nope." Even his dragon vision was useless.

"Do you think everyone's gone? Maybe they went to Miami."

A tremendous cracking sounded nearby. Mattie and Artorius froze as an avalanche fell, cascading down a white face. This was followed by the emergence of a great white head. What's more, it possessed more teeth than Mattie had ever seen, along with a trail of spikes from its snout to its frosty antlers!

"*Who are you?*" it roared, causing several more avalanches.

"Would you mind keeping your voice down?" Mattie whispered.

"*Silence!* I asked who you are."

"Uh, sir...my name is Mattie Sharpe. From...from Mundanis. And this is my friend Artorius."

The wyvern made a short bow.

"Why have you come to Jötunheimr?"

Snow tumbled from every direction. Mattie feared they might not survive this inquiry.

"Mighty Frost Dragon, we have come to seek your aid. The Georgians have attacked Cavernis, and they have a fleet of *you*—"

"Created by black magick," Artorius added.

The frost dragon turned its white neck to stare down with pale eyes. Mattie shivered as she continued.

"If we can't fight frost with frost, there won't be good dragons at ASH, and the Georgians will seize all the treasure."

Mattie hoped she had appealed to the beast's basic nature. They all loved treasure, right?

"*Ignorant girl*," the frost dragon thundered. "Know you not that Frost and Fire are opposed, and have been for all time? Wyvern, have you forgotten your history?" He cast a contemptuous glance at his diminutive cousin.

"No, but—"

"Lemminkäinen!"

The frost dragon's cry echoed from all the mountains and Mattie covered her ears. She tried to hope for the best. Maybe he was calling for snacks?

"What is it, Hrossþjófr?"

A near-identical dragon jutted his head from out an adjoining cave.

"We have visitors," Hrossþjófr said. "Shall we show them some Norse hospitality?"

"Of course, brother."

The two of them burst out from their white confines. Mattie took a step back. They were as big as Praeses!

"Can't we talk this ov—?"

Diplomacy wasn't going to happen. The two frost dragons circled them, talons stomping and huge jaws opening. Mattie knew what to expect: a fire truck full of frost!

"*Wait!*" she cried. "*Beowulf.*"

"*What?*" Lemminkäinen halted his movements. "How dare you mention that dragonslayer's name to *us*?"

"He is despised by our kind. How can you show such disrespect?" Hrossþjófr slammed one frost-covered claw in the snow.

"Listen, guys—can I call you Hoss and Lemmy?— Beowulf isn't only a man. He's a *dragon*. He's the one who killed the man, and he lives right in Cavernis!"

"He helped found our school," Artorius chimed in.

220

"Impossible!" Lemmy roared.

He and Hoss conferred in low voices.

"Is this true?" the latter asked.

"It is," Artorius swore. "Consult your own Norse gods."

Lemmy closed his eyes, releasing a tendril of frost from one nostril. He seemed to be communing with an unseen force. Then, his white eyelids popped open.

"True," he verified.

Mattie exhaled visibly. Maybe they wouldn't end up in somebody's drink after all!

"Well, this *is* news," Hoss exclaimed. "We really had no idea. But if a hero of the Norse is about to be stripped of treasure, we frost dragons can't just sit by."

"Hallelujah!" Mattie cried.

"Megi Odin blessi þig!" Lemmy said.

"Well, let's all relax," Hoss declared. "Why not be our guests?"

"Thanks but we really have to—"

"*Já, já*. Sit and have some *ludenhosen*. They're wonderfully delicious."

"That's what I've heard." Mattie turned to Artorius. "Should we?"

"Well, we really should eat before heading back..."

"Thank you," she said to the dragons. "We appreciate your hospitality."

"Such a sweet *fífla*," Lemmy beamed to Hoss. They seemed to be oblivious that just moments ago they were trying to kill her.

"Come in, come in. Please, enter our *heim*."

The frost dragons motioned their guests into a deep snow cave.

"Nice place," Artorius said. "Where's the gold and silver?"

"We bury it in the snow. Can't be too careful these days."

Hoss brought out a diamond platter filled with what Mattie assumed was *ludenhosen,* an apple strudel generously doused with frosting.

"I take it Latro comes here?"

"Oh yes. We are his Frieday morning stop."

"That guy gets around," Mattie told Artorius.

After taking a bite of the scrumptious treat, she tried to direct their hosts back to pressing matters.

"I don't mean to be rude, but—how do you think you can help us? Could you fly with us back to Cavernis?"

"But of course." Lemmy was all smiles.

Mattie breathed out near-icicles. Her plan—the one Artorius called dumb—might just rescue ASH.

"Told you so." She poked her friend in the ribs.

Lemmy cleared his throat. "There is just one minor detail."

Oh no, Mattie thought. Isn't there always?

"No one can leave Jötunheimr without first fighting the frost giants."

"The what?" Mattie put down her pastry, which for her said a lot.

"The frost giants: Fafryd and Siggaard. If they even have a hunch that anyone wants to leave, they kill them."

"Can they be reasoned with?" Mattie asked.

After all, it had worked with the two of *them.*

"Oh *nei,*" Lemmy laughed. "These are not civilized creatures. They are, to put it plainly, bloodthirsty barbarians."

"With no love of gold?"

"They'd rather rip your heart out."

Hoss finished a plateful of *ludenhosen.* "You're not eating, my *dȳrr.* Are you ill?"

Mattie looked at Artorius and slowly shook her head. "Yes, I think that I am."

Chapter Thirty-Three

The Frost Giants

S o...where can we find these giants?" Mattie asked. She tried to stay focused on Cavernis.

"No worries—they will find *you*," Lemmy said. "The minute you try to leave—*poof!*—there they'll be."

"Why won't they let anyone go?"

"They love Jötunheimr," said Hoss. "They take wanting to leave as a personal insult."

"But *they* are not where they live."

"Barbarians might not know that," Artorius noted wisely.

"Right." Mattie turned to their hosts with hope.

"Can *you* help us defeat them? I'll bet that you could take them—with one claw tied behind your back!"

"No, no," said the two frost dragons, shaking their shaggy white heads. "*We* are not the ones who expressly wish to be off. Besides, we are your judges."

"What is this, my family?" Mattie cried.

"No. You might describe it as a Viking death games."

"Huh?"

"It's a real *atburuðr,* but the loser is of course killed."

223

"Of course," Mattie said, turning toward Artorius. "What do we do?"

"Hmmm." He put a claw to his head. "Well, if that's the only way out, I guess we have to take it."

"But frost—"

"I know, trumps flame. Remember though, they're not dragons, so they can't blast us with it."

"Great. We just have to fight two giants who make Bigfoot look like a wimp."

"It could be worse?" Artorius asked.

"Yeah, it could be snowing. What's our strategy?"

"I'm not sure until we see them. We should call them by their names: Fafryd and Siggaard. Kind of warms things up."

"There is *nothing* warm about Jötunheimr." Mattie shivered. "Okay, let's get it over with."

Artorius nodded and crawled out of the ice cave. Mattie was at his tail, firmly clutching her sword, while Lemmy and Hoss, their judges, flew to a high serac.

"This is fun," Lemmy said to Hoss. "We so seldom get visitors."

"That's because we usually kill them."

Mattie strode to the ice field they'd landed on.

"Hey, Fafryd and Siggaard! We want to leave. What are you going to do about it?" She tried to summon some of Ripley's pluck.

"*Bikkjas! Bua andask!*" A guttural growl bounced from peak to peak.

"Huh?"

"They said, 'Dogs! Prepare to die'!" Hoss explained.

"Oh. Thanks." Mattie unsheathed her sword while Artorius scanned the horizon. They saw, over the tumble of an icefall, two behemoths striding toward them, both clad in what looked like fur togas, despite the sub-zero temps, with steel helmets crowned by horns, and leather sandals strapped to the knee. But most notable were their axes, huge blades dripping with frost.

"Hey!" Mattie yelled. "Can we talk?"

One of the giants—who must have been thirty feet tall—gave a roar that reminded her of Agravaine, nasty and aggressive.

"*Bana!*" he yelled to his brother. They both looked like twins, with red hair flowing down their backs and red beards obscuring their throats. Their expressions were probably unpleasant. One strode toward Mattie with a force that shook the ice. The other stalked Artorius.

Mattie waved her sword left to right, looking for an opening. The giant hefted his axe, preparing to cleave her in two.

Wham! The ax came down just inches from Mattie's head. For big guys, they sure had excellent aim.

But they wore no armor. *Mistake*, Mattie told herself.

She tried to ignore the bone-snapping cold as she skated across the ice, delivering a thrust to the giant's calf.

"*Grrrrrrr!*" he screamed in pain. Now he seemed really mad.

At her side, Mattie saw Artorius hold off *his* giant with flame. Their foes didn't even have shields, so they ripped off part of a glacier.

Barbarians, Mattie thought. But she was wrong to dismiss them so soon.

Her giant hefted his ax, poising it above her. He shook it back and forth, unloosing a chunk of ice directly onto her head. She instantly felt a cold sting that put the air to shame. As the feeling crept down her body, her lungs began to freeze.

"Artorius!" she gasped with her last bit of air.

He wheeled from his own opponent, lying down a line of fire to her right and then to her left. For the first time, fire fought frost, and fire actually won!

"Thanks," Mattie told him, struggling to get up.

Her giant stomped his great foot, giving her the opportunity to slice it with her sword.

"*Ahhhhhhhh!*" he yelled, bringing up his now-bleeding foot and hopping up and down. If things hadn't been so dire, it would have almost been comical.

"Let's join forces!" she yelled to Artorius, ducking like a student in a drop drill as she powered her way to his side. He crouched, and in one swift motion, they were off!

"I think that was a good move," Lemmy said to Hoss.

"I'm not sure. Fafryd seems very angry."

From her vantage point above, Mattie could see the tips of the Frost Giants' horns. She also noted idly that their togas needed a wash.

"Divide and conquer?" she asked.

"No," Artorius said. "I think it's best if get them together. Two bodies—one blast."

"Okay."

This part hadn't been covered in *Ignis et Fuga*. She made a mental note to tell Ignis when they got back to ASH.

Fafryd and Siggaard were highly displeased to see their foes in the air. They shook their mighty axes and stomped the snow like toddlers. Artorius wheeled and dropped altitude, coming at them straight on. He let loose a firehose-worth of flame, moving his head back and forth to target both of the brothers.

All the frost in Jötunheimr couldn't withstand Artorius. The giants used their great strength, but were unable to strike a blow, and their togas were starting to smoke. Mattie got in a great hit when she knocked the helmet off one of their heads. Artorius aimed for an ax, whose wood handle became as charred as a stick at a weenie roast.

"It's over!" Lemmy shouted.

But the brothers had one more trick up their cut-off sleeves. They removed long ropes from their tunics, one lashing his toward Artorius' left wing, the other throwing to the right. In a spectacular snowy crash, Artorius—and Mattie—were brought down to Jötunheimr in a tangled mass.

"Artorius, get off me," Mattie groaned.

Her friend had landed on his backside, pinning her beneath a wing. But the pressure of the ropes held him down.

"*I don't like you!*" Mattie yelled at the giants, who were moving in for the kill.

She still held her sword tightly. Gauging the giants' steps, she moved her arm back as best as she could and hurled her sword, striking one of the Giants in the...let's just say that even they had frail bits.

"Fafryd!" Siggaard yelled, watching his brother drop to the snow, then greet it with his face.

The standing giant ran full tilt at his foes. Handle gone, all he had was the blade of his ax, which he hurled at Artorius' throat. Thankfully, he wore his dragon armor, and the blade bounced like a boomerang directly back at Siggaard, slashing him in the belly.

"*Ooof!*" the giant yelled as he too hit the snow. The two brothers lay side by side like patients in an ER.

"Hooray!" Mattie shouted, rolling out from beneath her friend. She hastily cut his ropes, which freed him to sit up.

"What happened?" Artorius asked, shaking his head groggily. He looked at the pure white landscape. "Did we go to Valhalla?"

"Nope," Mattie said, checking him over for bruises. "But I think that before too long, we're going to be in Cavernis."

Chapter Thirty-Four

Sarug

The black-robed, hooded sorcerer stood inside his Magic Circle. Its area was chalked with pentagrams and at the four points of its compass stood a lit black candle. Etched at the circle's center was a triangle. On its three sides was the chalked word "Tetragrammaton." Sarug had all of his talismans—an altar, a dagger, incense of pinewood, and a book, his dark grimoire.

How many years had it been since he'd found *The Book of Thoth*? How many Mundani were killed before he wrenched away its secrets? Yet all that he had endured, the battles with ancient gods, the endless hunt through Luxor, had been eminently worth it, for the spell book provided his Power.

There had been a time when he practiced the White Arts only. What a naive young man he was then, trembling before the Circulus! That had been when he still worshipped George and valued the saint's people. It was so many centuries past he could barely recall himself clad in white robes. But he did remember his weakness—the weakness of mortality.

In his Circle's center, he held a small folded paper scrawled with a seal. He faced a second triangle adjacent to his own and pronounced the following words while unwrapping the note:

Zi kia kanpa
Zi anna kanpa
Zi dingir kia kanpa
Zi anna kanpa
Hear me, O Thou Duke Vual
Come to Me by the Powers of the Word Vual
And answer my urgent prayer!
Zi kia kanpa
Zi anna kanpa

A foul stench announced his presence as the Duke of Hell appeared. He was monstrous to look upon. He had the face of a handsome man, though his pupils were red and goat horns jutted from his skull. His body was that of a dromedary, yet he stood upright on two cloven hooves. His forked red tail could barely fit in his three-sided prison.

"Who dares disturb my peace?" he asked. "I must attend to my legions in Hell."

"I am aware, mighty Duke, and promise not to keep you. It is I, Sarug, keeper of ancient magick."

"*Black*," the demon spat.

"The blackest."

Duke Vual smiled. "Tarry not. What is thy bidding?"

"O Duke, you have the power to divine so much better than my weak self. Tell me, what lies ahead for Georgia? Will we succeed in putting down the puling beasts of Praeses?"

"No concern have I for dragons. We have sufficient beasts to amuse us Down Below."

"Perhaps this will pique your interest."

Sarug drew forth his wand, blasting his guest with a storm of electric current.

"Enough, enough!" Vual yelled. "Truly you are powerful, and I will tell you all."

Sarug kept his wand at the ready.

Vual closed his eyes. "I see...frost, cold, death."

"Those are *our* dragons," Sarug cried with impatience.

"No."

Vual opened his eyes and fixed his red pupils on Sarug.

"These are from the north. Two are frost *dracones*, and the others...are fierce creatures of old."

"What?"

Sarug was so disturbed that he nearly stepped out of his circle. But he knew if he did so, Vual would tear him to pieces. It had happened to Dr. Faustus, one of the greats, and it could easily happen to him. Sarug knew from long experience that demons held no loyalties, except to themselves, of course, and to the Master who kept them in thrall through fear.

The sorcerer gripped his wand tighter.

"How were such creatures summoned?"

"By the girl, Matilda's progeny. You should have killed her on the road to Georgia."

"Damn!" Sarug slammed his fist against the wood altar. "This I did not foresee. How is such a threat to be countered?"

"How can I predict your own actions? That is up to you."

"Quiet, or I'll blast you again!"

Duke Vual gave a low chuckle. "I have answered in good faith. Now remand me back to the Black Realm."

"Very well."

Sarug muttered a Release spell and Vual vanished from sight.

"Avarus!" the sorcerer cried.

"What is it, My Lord?" The yellow dragon panted as he entered the high tower. His gold chains weighed him down.

"There is danger lurking. It could destroy our Cause."

"What is it?"

Avarus began to shake. He thought they had matters sewn up, like the hundred-carat diamond he'd hidden in his cloak.

"That cursed girl! At least we got the boy. She is bringing four creatures of Jötunheimr: and two are *real* frost dragons!"

"I did not think it possible—"

"If you knew how little I cared for your thoughts, you would not trouble to present them!"

Avarus shut his snout.

"We must persuade Praeses to surrender—*now*, before the girl arrives from the north," Sarug said.

"Uh..."

"What is it, fool? Get it out, quickly!"

"We just received a scroll from Cavernis."

"Why wasn't I told?"

"You were um, busy with...your friend—"

"No matter!" the sorcerer snapped. "What does it say?" Sarug stepped outside his circle.

"Well, rather oddly," Avarus told him, "Praeses wants a one-on-one challenge."

"With *me?* Surely he understands that is utterly pointless."

"No, Lordship." Avarus had the cheek to look straight at him. "With St. George."

Sarug's eyes widened. *"What?"*

"I fear he was quite specific."

Sarug made a dismissive gesture. "Leave me."

As Avarus took the stairs, the sorcerer strode to his window, looking out at what he'd hoped would be a sliver of his empire. Now Cavernis was slipping through his hands like gold dust through a sieve! How could this happen to *him*, the eternal keeper of the Tetragrammaton? Centuries-old defender of the holy name of St. George?

Sarug groaned, gripping the window casing. George, that pathetic fool. His people must *never* learn the truth. Sarug strove to prevent this by freeing a lance from its bindings and hurling it into the Circle.

Zip kea kappa
Zip Anna kappa

He intoned, flicking his wand like a conductor.

Let this sacred lance, Escalon,
Be impervious to all fire.
And let it perform
What it should have
In the holy place of Lydda.
Teresita!

The lance rose above the four pentagrams and above the dimly lit candles. Blue bolts consumed its length as it spun wildly. Then, it clanked to the stone, looking just as before.

Chapter Thirty-Five

A Terrible Fraud

Praeses flew east to Georgia, flanked by Beowulf and Quetzalcoatl. They made a formidable trio, flying wing-to-wing. Only Immortals made the trip in light of Sarug's dark powers and the MAD at his command.

The dragons landed before St. George's Cathedral, their triple bulk barely contained in the square. The dragons folded their wings, and the cathedral's namesake—a tiny man in black armor mounted on a pure white steed—rode out alone amidst spectating Georgians.

Sarug stood on the topmost cathedral step, and if his face could have been spied, the people would have seen a confident smile.

St. George raised his visor. His first words were hardly saint-like.

"Beast," he addressed Praeses, in a clear voice used to command. "I defeated you once, in Lydda, but the dark dominion of serpents saw fit to resurrect you. Now, I shall deal you your final death blow!"

The Georgians—knights, merchants, and peasants—sent up a rousing cheer. Many flew their leader's pennant: a red cross on a white background.

Praeses addressed the king.

"Dear 'St.' George, we did meet once, but the outcome wasn't quite what you've described. I am confident that today you will be vanquished. If so, I want you to promise—here before your people—that you will quit all claims to Cavernis."

St. George glanced at his lance and smiled. "I agree readily, for I know I shall send you to Hell where all your kind belong!"

The Georgian crowd roared as Quetzalcoatl and Beowulf retreated. Praeses and St. George faced off in the square, the gold of the dragon's scales and that of Ascalon's spear reflecting Lumen's rays. Praeses's crest stood up. George pointed his lance directly at the dragon's heart.

"We have a few basic rules," Sarug drawled from his perch. "One: No coming back from the dead. Once you are down, St. George will claim victory. Two: No flying. Let's keep it on the ground, shall we? Three: No fire. Hardly sporting, is it? Four: No use of magick. Let's have a fair fight."

Quetzalcoatl tried to protest as Sarug extended his wand. "This is absurd—" he started to say.

"*Commence,*" Sarug cried, his wand emitting sparks and a crack like a pistol.

"I commend myself to God!" George said, spurring his white mount forward.

"And I to the power of Truth," Praeses replied calmly.

The two combatants circled each other, looking for an opening. George stabbed at Praeses's underbelly, but was repelled by dragon armor.

"No fair!" someone shouted.

Praeses shook his head. What was good for a man should also be good for a dragon.

George tried another tactic. He galloped full-tilt at his foe, hurling Ascalon so that it speared the dragon's leg. Praeses let out a roar as he felt a strange tingling. This was no ordinary lance!

The rumor had been for centuries that he'd been slain by Ascalon. Praeses knew better, but it was clear that the blade was now bewitched, enhanced by Sarug with a magickal sting.

Praeses gathered his strength. He tried to resist the numbness working its way upward. Just a few more seconds and he would be immobilized!

"The Truth will prevail," he roared, lifting a giant claw and seizing George in his talons. He brought him up to his mouth.

"I could devour you in one bite, but I daresay your flesh is tough."

"No, please!" George removed his helm, his words resounding through the square.

"Humph," said Praeses, shaking off the effects of the lance. He willed himself to combat it until his mind was clear.

"Perhaps you'd like to tell these good people what actually happened in Lydda."

"Yes, um…" George addressed the crowd from the center of Praeses' palm. He looked especially small.

"Fellow Georgians," he began, "you know me as the saint who slew the dragon. In fact, I've been honored just about everywhere. There's a sculpture of me at Westminster and Raphael, for example—"

"Get on with it!" Beowulf growled.

"Yes, I'm afraid that story is more...uh, myth than fact. You see, when I first fought this dragon, he in fact defeated *me*. Narrowly, I might add."

The crowd fell silent, shocked to its very core.

"Narrowly," Beowulf snorted. "He handed you your butt on a plate!"

"And how did you survive?" a knight shouted to his king.

"Yes, uh, you see...Praeses here spared me. That's when he founded Cavernis and I claimed this land for Georgia seventeen centuries ago." He made a dismissive motion.

"Fraud!"

The chant started with the peasants, then gravitated outward to the merchants and knights.

"Liar!" The knights bellowed. "This whole kingdom is built on a lie!"

Some unsheathed their swords and waved them above their heads.

"Georgians, calm yourself," Sarug shouted from above them. "What matters this ancient dispute? We must engage with *the future*. A future filled with Cavernis' treasure!"

"According to the rules, St. George promised—" Quetzalcoatl began heatedly.

"He is a coward and weakling. *I* am king now," Sarug smiled. "Those who would stand with me will receive their measure in gold."

Praeses addressed the crowd. "Sarug just broke one promise. Who's to say he won't break another? The sweet phrases of those who practice the Black Arts are generally meant to deceive."

Still, the Georgians, so used to their hatred of dragons, so filled with visions of gold, applauded and cheered their new king.

"Arrest him!" Sarug pointed to George. "Put him in my dungeon."

His guards—formerly George's—did as they were told, binding the old king's hands with rope and marching him off between them.

"Sarug—can't we arrive at a compromise?" George cried as he left.

"It is now time to end this," Sarug sad coolly to the dragons. "I know you three are Immortal, but most in Cavernis are not. I shall unleash my dragons until all of yours are frozen."

Praeses, Beowulf, and Quetzalcoatl lifted off for the west. So much for rules, for fighting *mano-a-claw*. As long as Sarug held power, as long as the MAD eleven used frost to combat their fire, they were all but lost.

The Elder dragons let Praeses voice their thoughts.

"Even if Cavernis is doomed, we must continue to fight. Let future minstrels sing that Beowulf was bold and Quetzalcoatl magnificent!"

"With Praeses mightiest of all."

The gold dragon smiled. At least they would be remembered.

Chapter Thirty-Six

The Last Battle

M attie found herself re-fighting the same war, and frankly, she was sick of it.

"How else are Fafryd and Siggaard going to get to Cavernis?"

Hoss and Lemmy, from their judge's serac, firmly folded their arms.

"We've never heard anything so gauche!"

"An insult to frost dragons everywhere."

"Please. Our world is at stake."

Mattie turned to the two frost giants. "Think how *you'd* feel if Jötunheimr were razed."

Hoss translated into Old Norse and the hirsute brothers roared.

"Exactly. Please, Hrossþjófr & Lemminkäinen—" Mattie knew she was mangling their names "—just this once. If we win, you'll be more honored than Siegfried!"

"Ugh, a dragonslayer."

"You know what I mean."

Hoss and Lemmy looked at each other.

"A dragon—as a Norse hero! Brother, that would be a first."

"Well, there *is* Beowulf."

"Besides him. You and I would get the respect we deserve."

Lemmy put a claw to his breast like Napoleon. "And be celebrated in the sagas."

Hoss was practically in tears.

"No offense, guys, but we really need to get going." Mattie turned to Artorius for help.

"Last one on is a rotten *ludenhosen!*" he said, crouching in the snow so Mattie could leap on his back.

"*Hvarfa!*" said Fafryd.

"He's right," Mattie agreed, though she had no idea what that meant.

Lemmy and Hoss glided down to the ice and assumed Artorius' stance. The two frost giants easily mounted, their sinewy legs dangling.

"*Sæll,*" they agreed.

"Let's go!"

Artorius gave the command, and within seconds, they were off. As mountains and icefalls receded, giving way to dust-colored hills, Fafryd let out a roar.

"What's wrong with him?" Mattie asked Lemmy.

"He misses home."

Wow, Mattie thought, he so wouldn't want to be me.

They flew on in the heat of midday, the scenery below devoid life. Lemmy and Hoss, with their prehistoric wingspans, frequently had to glide so that Artorius could catch up.

"It's like trying to pace Praeses," he panted.

"Don't worry. You're doing great."

Secretly, Mattie felt nothing *but* worry. After all they'd been through in Jötunheimr, would they arrive too late? Miss Fang might be opening the secret rooms right now...

Artorius picked up his speed. He was like a tiny Cessna buzzing a 747, but his effort as always was valiant.

"I wonder what's happening at home." Mattie surprised herself by referring to Cavernis this way.

"Hard to say. I've known Praeses most of my life, and it's just not like him to quit."

"Right." Mattie hoped so. There were enough icy tombs sitting in the quad.

The trip back took a little more time since they were battling headwinds. It'd been eleven hours since they'd left Artorius' cave. It was likely that when they arrived, there would *be* no more Cavernis, just a bunch of vacant caves with Avarus dancing on treasure.

"How much longer?" she asked Artorius.

"Only about an *hora*."

"Okay." She turned to survey the frost dragons, their huge white bodies imposing. And their riders, whose appearance could inspire fear even in the heart of Conan! But would these four be enough to go up against the MAD?

They were getting closer. Mattie could see the peak of Mt. Dentem. At last, they flew over the mountains and the familiar desert.

Cavernis, Mattie thought. "*Ignis et Fuga!*" she shouted.

"And *Gelu,*" Lemmy roared.

"*Glaciem,*" Hoss added.

Artorius translated for her. "They said frost and ice."

Mattie nodded. They would need every claw in dragondom to defeat Sarug and his army.

The Frost Dragons, slightly ahead, saw the ASH battlefield first.

"Bad news!" Lemmy shouted back.

Artorius caught up to them. He and Mattie looked down and saw a raging fight. Unda the water dragon was fully raised from the Flavius, spurting torrents at Georgian soldiers. Dr. Lung and the Asian dragons were aiming their breath at the sky, creating not fire but wind, which batted the MAD about but did not disable them.

"Let the frost giants off!" Mattie yelled, assuming the role of leader.

Lemmy and Hoss hovered above the quad as their supersized riders crashed down.

The Georgian knights stepped back from what to them was a horror. Fafryd and Siggaard loved it, hefting their ice-dripping axes.

"Arggh!" A Georgian knight fell, followed by ten of his fellows who tumbled like wooden soldiers. They had no real defense against these two goliaths, since their puny swords and lances were tossed aside like toys.

One Georgian captain quickly came to this conclusion. *"Retreat!"* he cried.

His men wheeled and obeyed, some mounted and some on foot, while the giants lumbered behind, waving their axes and roaring. The two brothers seemed truly angry that most of their fun was on the run.

From Artorius' back, Mattie eyed the sky, searching for the MAD. She saw them swooping low, aiming for a small black dragon who bravely stood alone.

Sid!

"Oh no," Mattie groaned, watching him tumble backward, a permanent block of ice. It was so unfair! He was just an awkward kid.

"They'll pay," she told Artorius.

"Look at Cymru!" The Welsh dragon was like a race car, dashing back and forth so fast he was a blur of red. As

Avarus and company made a run on the Asian line, Cymru got in his own by clawing Agravaine's belly.

"Ahhhhh!" the chameleon screamed, blood streaming from his wound. "You'll die for that!" he told his ex-coach, teaming up with Alazon to blast him into ice.

Cymru fell, but before he did, Mattie could have sworn he flashed an extended middle talon.

The chief dragons—Praeses, Quetzalcoatl, and Beowulf—watched from the center of the quad. The MAD must have tired of seeing them resurrect since they basically left them alone. Georgians who hadn't fled occasionally made a run for them, but were rewarded with triple fire. When the three Elders heard the whoosh of huge wings, they looked up and saw the two frost dragons.

"Okay guys, it's all you," Mattie told them. "Remember, you promised to save Cavernis."

Lemmy and Hoss nodded, sweating a bit from the heat. Hoss flew right and Lemmy flew left, ensnaring Avarus and three of the MAD between them.

The frost that flew from their mouths made the MAD's look like a portable fridge's. The storm of ice they generated was enough to entomb all Georgia!

The three captive MAD plunged, their enchanted breath no match for the real thing. Avarus soon followed, his gold chains frozen to his neck as he hit the ground in a block.

"Yes!" Mattie cried, pumping her fist. "That's for Mrs. Avarus!"

Only six MAD remained, led by Agravaine and Alazon. If they were affected by their leader's loss, they certainly didn't show it.

Looking very small, they darted away from the frost dragons...directly toward Mattie.

"You think you're so smart?" Agravaine roared. "Won't matter when you're dead."

"That goes double!" Mattie yelled, not sure if that made sense.

Artorius let them get close—almost in frost-shooting range—before he drew in his wings and shot down like an arrow.

"What's the plan?" she asked, barely able to hold on. The wind whipped her face and hair.

"We give the frosties time to regroup."

If Mattie could have nodded, she would have, but the centrifugal force of their plunge pinned her head straight back.

Artorius pulled out of his dive so close to the ground that he actually raised a dust storm.

Agravaine and Alazon, momentarily blinded, didn't realize that their single-minded pursuit had distracted them from the *real* threat—Lemmy and Hoss, diving with them, then gliding to track them from behind.

Alazon turned his head. This was the pose he'd hold forever, since Lemmy shot a gale at him. He fell, a frozen Icarus, and Mattie felt nothing but joy.

"Coach killer!" she yelled.

That left Agravaine in Hoss' sights.

"Malum autem Dracones!" the MAD yelled to the remaining four. "Help me."

"Are you kidding?" Fractious asked.

"Get real!" said Unctuous.

All four flew upside down, the sign of dragon surrender, and gave themselves up to Praeses.

"Cowards! Yellow necks!" Agravaine screamed, turning a bruise-like purple and black. "You disgrace the name of Avarus!"

"He's dead!" another yelled back.

The chameleon clearly intended to go out in flames. He spun up to evade the frosties, then set after Mattie, trying to bite her arm!

"I don't taste that great," she said, lifting her sword to hack the underside of his throat. Without the benefit of armor, he spurted blood as he fell, dislodging the dust with his back. Mattie watched in fascination as he turned whiter than the Frost Dragons.

"That's for you, Eli!"

"Good riddance," Artorius said, landing neatly on the quad. Lemmy and Hoss did likewise while the giants loped up from where they'd been torturing Georgians.

"Thank Quetzalcoatl, it's over," said Beowulf, half-nodding at Quetzalcoatl.

"We did this for you, great Beowulf." Hoss seemed rather shy. "You're our best-est hero."

Beowulf dropped his mighty head.

"We have kept our word to the *fifla*," said Lemmy. "Let there be no more enmity between dragons of fire and frost."

Quetzalcoatl nodded regally, his red and green feathers ruffling. "Thanks to you, Cavernis is safe. You have performed like gods."

Praeses extended a claw. "I thank the dwellers of Jötunheimr for their indispensable aid. It goes without saying you will receive your weight in gold."

He looked at the four displaced Northerners, sweat dripping from their snouts and beards.

"I imagine our Cavernin climate must be hard for you to weather. If you wish to return to your homeland, please feel free to do so."

"May Odin always favor you."

Lemmy and Hoss bowed, translating for the Giants, who roared.

"Please come back and visit," Hoss said to Mattie. "We haven't had so much fun since we slew Sigfried!"

"Of course! I'll stop by for some *ludenhosen.*"

She watched as the fur-clad giants hoisted themselves on dragonback. They flew off until four distinct shapes became white specks in the sky.

"We should start assessing our losses," Beowulf announced.

"Not so fast. We are not out of the cave just yet."

The Elders stepped back, but Mattie knew what he meant.

"There is still a usurper in Georgia, the self-proclaimed 'King Sarug.' Until his reign is put down, we may never live in peace."

Mattie leaned wearily against Artorius' wing. *Would the war and killing ever stop?*

Chapter Thirty-Seven

Sarug Goes On a Journey

It was a small contingent that flew to Georgia next morning: Praeses, Artorius, and Mattie. They alighted before the cathedral, unchallenged by ragtag troops.

"*Dracones,* leave us be," one bloodied knight begged from a stretcher. "You have defeated our ranks. What more do you want?"

"Be at peace, soldier," said Praeses. "We have no quarrel with *you*. Only with your self-crowned 'king.'"

"He is blacker than death," the knight whispered. "If you unseat him, all of Georgia will bow to the dragon king."

"I am merely a president." Praeses smiled. "But we will do our best to relieve you of this scourge."

The knight held up a hand. "Please God that you succeed."

Mattie and Artorius trailed Praeses as he stopped by a nearby tower.

"I must ask you to go in," he said. "As you see, I cannot fit. But I will be right here to help."

"Yes, sir."

Mattie approached the door. It was locked with a rusty bolt.

"It's all you," she told Artorius.

He backed up a few steps and assaulted the door with flame. It crumbled into red splinters.

"After you," he bowed.

They ran up the tower steps, winding their way to the top. Oddly, the door to the topmost room was cracked open.

"Enter," said a voice, and they did, only to find Sarug in his Magic Circle. But he was not alone. Vual was contained in the triangle, his human face distended.

"Why must you always disturb me?" he asked his jailer, stomping a cloven hoof. "Find another demon to annoy!"

"Quiet."

With his wand, Sarug blasted him, causing the Duke to roar with pain.

"So you plague even Satan's spawn?" Praeses's giant gold head could be partially seen through the window.

"Which *you* are among, *dracon!*"

"*I'm* not the one summoning Hell to Cavernis."

"No matter. Since we are both Immortal, I take it you're not here to kill me. Why then have you come?"

"I want you to abdicate."

"Ha!"

Sarug threw back his hood, revealing his gray-flecked beard and hair. Mattie thought he looked to be about sixty, though she knew he was much older.

"We shall do you no harm, Sarug, provided you go with Latro and settle on another world. One of your own choosing."

Mattie thought Praeses's terms were more than fair.

"*Never*, beast. It is *you* who will do the leaving!"

He brought up his black wand, shooting a volley of sparks at his foe. Praeses didn't even flinch. He stuck one gold claw through the window, deflecting the magic harmlessly.

"What?"

Sarug had clearly never seen anything like this. He thrust out his whole arm, intent as his wand's blast intensified.

Praeses answered, gold sparks flowing from his outstretched talons. Sarug cried out, his wand hitting the floor.

"What is this?" he cried. "*Wandless* magic? I thought that was only a legend!"

"We dragons are possessors of a magick more subtle than yours. Admit it—you are bested."

Mattie felt the force of Praeses' breath as he spoke. She was even blown back a few steps.

"Hardly." Sarug smiled. "You forget my friend here. Duke Vual, I command by the spell that binds you to drag this beast to Hell!"

"Yes, Master," Vual said reluctantly, opening his mouth to reveal black fangs. He shot a noxious green fluid at Praeses. Praeses barely stirred as he countered the goo with fire, dissolving it in mid-air.

Sarug became livid as he turned to Vual. "Can you not summon your legions?"

"No, Master." Vual seemed happy to contradict him. "Only *I* am caught in the Triangle of Art."

"Have you no other powers?"

"I torment damned souls in Hell by eating their flesh and blasting them with fire. But I must be *beside* my victims, not forbidden to tread beyond chalk." He gestured with contempt at his three-sided cell.

"Very well, I release you from the Triangle. Now kill the beast and its allies!"

Mattie watched as the demon, now freed, stepped inside the Magic Circle. For the first time, she saw his handsome man's face smile.

"You forget your art, sorcerer," the Duke said with a smirk. "As long as I am trapped in the Triangle, I belong to you. Outside, I am no longer captive."

"But our bargain—"

"Ha! In truth, I owe you nothing. I feel nothing but hate for your kind. You drag us from our warm home and force us to become vassals. Do you know how it feels to be made to crawl like a worm?"

"I—"

Vual stomped his cloven hoof. "*This time*, I am going to be nice. I won't rip you into pieces."

"Even if you did, I would just return."

"Yes. That's the reason for my benevolence. However, you and I are going on a journey. I trust you'll enjoy Hell. No doubt you have many friends there."

The demon approached his former Master. Sarug looked desperately at Praeses.

"*Dracon!* Help me!"

But it was too late.

Sarug threw up his arms as Vual half-swallowed him, then plunged through the floor of stone as if it were a lake.

"See you in Hell!" Mattie heard the demon shriek as— joined by Sarug's cries—his words faded the farther he fell.

"Whoa," Mattie said, putting away her sword. "That must be a long way down."

"I hope Sarug likes a dry heat," said Artorius.

From outside the window, Praeses relaxed visibly. Mattie stepped toward him.

"I can't believe Sarug asked *you* for help! Anyway, that was cool—the way you did that wandless thing! Got any other tricks up your claw?"

"A few. But for now, we must find a new king for Georgia."

Chapter Thirty-Eight

The Elixir of Life

It took just a few minutes to fly back to ASH, something that Mattie dreaded.

She knew that upon landing, she would remember those who were gone, especially one Georgian who used to be a dragon.

When they arrived, ASH students were lining up ice blocks in a field near the quad. They were preparing them for burial.

"I can't," Mattie told Artorius, wiping away her tears. "What good is being the winner when you have to pay this price?"

Artorius sighed. "Believe me, I feel the losses as much as you do. But I know if we hadn't fought back, there would be no Cavernis. And, knowing Sarug, no dragons either."

"So we had to do it?"

"Yeah. War sucks, but if you're forced to go there, the best you can do is fight on the side of Right."

Mattie enfolded herself in his wing so the others wouldn't see her cry. He bent it around her, and for one brief, joyous moment, she was lost in her old blue world.

When she emerged, Miss Fang—now without a helmet—was ringing her golden triangle at the side of Praeses' statue. The students had finished moving the blocks, each of which faced a deep hole cut directly in front of it.

Praeses stood on the far side of the graves, his massive head bowed.

Dragons streamed in from all over, taking a respectful place behind the frosty tombs.

"We are gathered here today to pay tribute to our fallen." Praeses raised his head. "And to ensure they enjoy their final rest with all honors due."

The attendees listened in silence.

"First, we commit to the earth Professor Cymru. Always upbeat, a firebrand of energy, he steered Scull & Bones and its crew toward continued achievement."

"Except for Alazon, Huáng, and Two Heads," Mattie whispered to Artorius. She felt her anger flame at the thought of those four traitors.

With ceremony, Professors Fraxinus and Drake lifted Cymru's block and dropped it into its hole.

"Next, Heng Chow. Always an exemplary student, he died protecting those he loved."

Jimmy, who stood close to Mattie, shed a single tear. Beside him, Mr. Chow could barely stand.

"I next commend Sidney Levine, who showed astonishing courage as he took on the MAD by himself."

Mattie looked away as the professors lifted his block.

Praeses hesitated slightly before moving on to the next.

"Our own Professor Avarus."

Fraxinus looked disgusted.

"Alas, he allowed his love of treasure to consume his whole being. Let us hope he has learned and is wiser in the next world.

His pupils—Huáng Chow, Agravaine, Alazon, and Geetha. Let them know that we forgive them, for they were very young."

"Yet they killed Cymru, Heng, and Sid!" Mattie said to Artorius. She was actually shaking with rage. *Praeses* might forgive them, but the hell if she ever would!

"I come sadly to two great champions. Master Eliwlod of Georgia and Superbas Visum, the latter to be known henceforth as Superbas the Bold."

Mattie was so overcome she almost dropped to the ground, but Artorius held her up.

"You must be strong for them," he said.

"Where do I begin? Superbas the Bold excelled in all he attempted: rowing, flying, flaming. He never allowed his so-called disability to stand in his way. Smart, strong, and loyal, he was superb beyond all measure."

Praeses paused for a moment, looking down at his gold medallions.

"Now we come to Master Eliwlod, or Eli, as he was known. He first came to me as a dragon, one who had been silenced by Sarug. Though he'd been born a Georgian, I let him stay, for I sensed his innate goodness. As a man and as a dragon, he showed incredible bravery. He even fought against his own people for what he believed was right. And he leaves us with a champion, Matilda Sharpe of Mundanis."

Mattie took out Hob's red sleeve and used it as a handkerchief. All she saw was a sea of red.

"In accord with my promise and his own wishes, I hereby pronounce Eli *Sir* Eliwlod of Cavernis, member of the Order of the Wyrm. It is thus that we honor Eli by proclaiming him knight."

An appreciative murmur broke out, with many dragons nodding in approval. Mattie had no idea what happened then, since her next memory was Artorius and Jimmy leaning over her, and her face dripping with water.

"Please. Leave me," she said, and they honored her request.

She sat up on her knees, not bothering to brush away dirt. She saw Fraxinus and Drake, each wielding a golden shovel, start to fill in Cymru's grave.

Mattie felt lower than she ever had in her life. It was worse than the thought of her own death. That at least had a finite end, but this would go on forever.

"Hey."

Mattie turned to see Sudha, stunning as always in her sari. Ripley sat on her shoulder, dressed in solemn black.

Mattie nodded, since she couldn't speak. Each clang of the golden shovel was like a personal blow.

"You lost two who were very close," Sudha said. "I'm sorry."

"Me too," Ripley piped in, without her usual sass.

Mattie wiped her eyes. "The only thing I ever lost on Mundanis was a cat."

Sudha helped her to her feet. "But you still have your great friend Artorius."

"Yes. I couldn't go on without him."

Thump. There went Professor Avarus.

"Mattie, did you know that Indian *nāga* are more than just cobras with legs?"

"Huh?" Mattie wondered if she'd heard right. This seemed to come out of nowhere.

"Our bite contains deadly venom, yes. But, thanks to Garuda, we carry the elixir of life."

"I don't—"

"Remember what I said in Dragonlore? Garuda bequeathed it to us in a cup, but Indra took it away. Still, we managed to lick up enough from the kusha."

Mattie *didn't* remember, but she did catch one phrase. "'Elixir of life'?"

"*Hām.* Since we transform into humans or snakes, it only works on them. Not, I am sorry to say, on dragons."

"Humans?" Is that what Sudha had said?

"I have never used it before. But—"

"Please Sudha, try. I beg you." Mattie went back on her knees.

"Come, I am not Vishnu. I too admired your friend, and am prepared to make the attempt."

"Thanks, Sudha! Thanks!"

Mattie rose and gave her a hug, dislodging Ripley from her shoulder. She looked down the line of holes, spotting Fraxinus and Drake coming closer.

"Hurry!" she implored.

Sudha nodded, standing on human legs before Eli's block. They could see his vague outline, hands held up to shield his face.

Sudha focused on the ground, spreading out her hands. She closed her eyes and recited:

Garuda
Giver of the elixir
To the nāgas of old
I beg you for your aid!
Let me use my power
To revive and not to kill
Let me breathe life into another
And suppress my snake self
Aba!

A red mist smelling sweetly of flowers escaped from Sudha's lips. She directed it toward the block. The mist grew opaque until the block was no longer visible.

"What's happening?" Mattie asked.

Sudha finally stopped exhaling. "Patience."

The three of them stood motionless as the mist dispersed. What they saw was not an icy tomb, but the body of Eli himself! He blinked in the glare of Lumen and removed his helm shakily.

"Where are we?" he asked Mattie. "You look like you've been to a funeral."

Mattie threw herself across him, assaulting his cheeks with kisses.

"Whoa!" Eli said, struggling to his feet.

"Oh Eli," Mattie said tearfully, "I'm sorry for every bad thing I thought about you!"

Eli looked puzzled, until he turned to survey the field.

"Ah." He lowered his head for a moment. "I remember. I was dead. I saw my folks and cranky Aunt Myrtle."

"Yes. Sudha brought you back. Thanks again, Sudha! You are an Indian goddess."

Mattie rose to kiss her atop her red-hooded head.

"You Westerners. So effusive." But Sudha still smiled widely.

"Way to go, girlfriend!" Ripley offered her tiny claw. "From now on, I go wherever you do."

"Such happiness," Sudha said, walking back to the quad with her new fan perched on her shoulder.

Mattie helped Eli strip off his gold plate. He glanced to his right, seeing the large block beside him.

"Superbas," he said softly.

"Now Superbas the Bold." Mattie hung her head. "I'm sorry, Eli. Sudha can't bring back dragons of any sort."

He nodded, his blue eyes filling with tears. Before the gold shovels clanged, he placed a handful of dirt in the grave.

"Superbas," Eli said, "you were my best friend, whatever form I took. I pray you are in a place where there's no war or sorrow. Goodbye, my friend."

Now the tears streamed freely from his eyes. Mattie stepped forward and without even thinking, embraced him. They stood that way for a while.

"Well, all is not death and sadness," she finally managed to say.

Eli stepped back a few paces.

"You have been made a knight! Of the Order of the Wyrm. And, I'm happy to say, *not* posthumously."

Eli attempted a smile, but his grief was too great. "I'm sure I'll appreciate that. For now, I can only think of Superbas."

Mattie nodded, and the two of them walked hand-in-hand back toward the quad.

Chapter Thirty-Nine

How It All Turned Out

For the second time that year, Praeses called the *Concilio Prius Dracones*.

All the dragons of Cavernis—even the most anti-social—jostled to enter the council cave so they could get a good seat.

After dressing in what she considered her best outfit—a white dress with *tons* of gold—Mattie, accompanied by Artorius, Eli, and Ripley, met Sudha and Jimmy at the entrance, then took a bench in the middle of the hall.

All those dragons crowded together created a noticeable heat. Miss Fang stood at Praeses' side, fanning him with feathers. The president looked abashed, but leaned into his podium.

"*Dracones!* I don't have to tell you how pleased we are at having defeated Sarug, and how stricken we remain by having to bury our dead. Now, however, we meet not for mourning but voting. The Elders and I—" he directed a claw toward Beowulf, Quetzalcoatl, and Dr. Lung, all seated behind him, "—have decided on a way to govern Georgia. We would very much like your approval."

The listening dragons sat rapt.

"First, we decree that the so-called members of MAD be required to repeat their years at ASH, regardless of their standing."

"This is *your* fault!" Unctuous hissed.

"No, yours," said Fractious.

"Shut it!"

The two heads glared at each other.

"However, before they return to ASH, they will perform a duty. Each will bear as much treasure as he or she can hold and fly it up to Jötunheimr, under the eye of Beowulf."

The assembled dragons cheered. Beowulf rose, his yellow eyes fixed on his charges.

"Come," he commanded. "The *real* frost dragons are waiting." He frog-marched them down the aisle.

Mattie applauded along with the others, then turned to Artorius. "Here's hoping that Hoss and Lemmy give them a 'proper' welcome."

"And the giants."

"Second, we propose that a wise and judicious leader be appointed to oversee Georgia. We can think of no better candidate than our own Dr. Lung."

Mattie put her fingers in her mouth and whistled. Eli did the same.

"To aid him, we propose that Jimmy Chow be made his General Secretary."

"*Go, Jimmy!*" Mattie yelled over to him. His whiskers were frozen in place.

"Are we all in agreement?" Praeses asked.

"*Aye,*" every dragon there shouted, plus two humans.

"Anyone opposed?"

Silence.

"Good. After our dragons have righted things, we declare that Sir Eliwlod will be made King of Georgia."

Eli's eyes widened as the room broke into cheers.

"Nice to have you back, son," Praeses told him gently.

"Thank you, sir." Eli threw him a sharp salute.

Mattie slapped him with a high five, feeling a flood of pride. *Her* special friend was going to be a king! Back home, she'd never even known her councilperson!

"Now, we come to honors delayed."

Miss Fang motioned for the crowd to quiet. She held a slate in her claws, fully prepared to take names.

"Artorius Wyvernis, rise!"

Artorius seemed shaken, but did as he was told.

"There is a legend among us that a wyvern will earn his back legs if he slays a knight in battle. Mr. Wyvernis has done this, and so much more. I hereby grant him his due."

Praeses extended a claw. Gold sparks shot from his talons, encircling Artorius. When they faded, he was standing on his tail—plus two sturdy back legs!

"I can't believe it," he breathed.

"Oh Artorius, no one deserves it more than you." Mattie gave him a kiss on his snout, not caring who was looking.

Praeses flashed a rare smile. "One thing more. Matilda Sharpe and Sir Eliwlod, approach."

Mattie's heart started to thump, but she made it to the stage courtesy of Eli's arm.

"Kneel, Eliwlod."

Eli dropped to one knee as Miss Fang handed her boss a sword.

"Since I was prevented from doing this, I hereby do so now." Praeses touched Eli on both shoulders. "Rise, Sir Knight."

Mattie thought she heard Sudha and Ripley cheering.

"Matilda Sharpe. I have thought long about this. Your service to Cavernis is equal to your co-champion. How often your quick thinking has saved us is really quite remarkable."

Mattie blushed at such lavish praise.

"Kneel, Matilda."

Mattie tucked her dress beneath her as she sank to the floor. She felt the cold kiss of steel on both shoulders.

"Arise, Sir Matilda of Cavernis. You are the second living member of the Order of the Wyrm."

There was so much partying that night—so much hopping from the Thirsty Dragon to the Belching Dragon and back again—that Mattie didn't remember much. She only knew that she was happy, happier than she'd ever been.

Artorius practiced walking on his new back legs. He did fine, but six goblets of Dragonsmede made his gait—and *him*—slightly tipsy.

Sudha danced with Jimmy, gliding around the pub, while Ripley sang pop tunes along with her radio. Even Latro stopped by, accompanied by his crew. He gave a wink to Mattie, then sat at the bar, no doubt dreaming of future profits.

Mattie smiled as Professor Fraxinus let her antlers down, even flirting with Professor Drake! And Ignis set off some fireworks, using himself as the lighter.

Mattie and Eli found a table in a—relatively—quiet corner of The Belching Dragon.

"I can't believe I'm a knight," Mattie said.

"Me neither. And the future King of Georgia!"

"It all seems so unreal."

"I wonder if knights here get land, like they do in Georgia. We could build a real stone castle and invite our friends over for tourneys!"

"'We'?"

Eli blushed. "I mean...*in principle.*"

"Right." Mattie took a sip from a silver chalice. It was good old water. "I wonder what happens now. Do we just go back to ASH?"

Eli gestured for a brownie. "I have no idea, but there is one thing of which I'm certain."

Mattie stared at him intently.

"I'm going to have some Dragonsmede. Waiter, bring me as big a fiery goblet as if I were a dragon!"

Chapter Forty

A Request

The ensuing days were filled with more festivities. There was even a dragon parade on the plat, led by Praeses and Quetzalcoatl. Gradually, things quieted. The quad was swept clean of rubble and Praeses had Miss Fang announce that the quarter would resume shortly.

Through all of this cheer, Mattie felt herself torn. Of course, she was thrilled Cavernis had won, and that Sarug was *exactly* where he should be. But she had a nagging feeling that now that the prophecy was fulfilled, she had no reason to stay.

As always, Artorius sensed her unease.

"You want to leave, don't you?" he asked her one night at home.

"No way!" Ripley shouted, digging her claws into Mattie's shoulder.

"Ow! And yes...I do, Artorius. I've been away for eight months. My mom probably thinks I'm dead."

Mattie started to tear up imagining her mom, alone in that small apartment, not knowing what'd happened to her, never achieving closure. She saw Mom's sad, thin face, more worried and lined than usual. That was it. She *had* to get home—now.

"Artorius, can you help me?"

He sighed, flexing his new back legs. "Only Praeses controls the portals. You'll have to talk to him."

Mattie nodded. The next morning, she made the trek to ASH, where she found Praeses beside his statue, surveying the newly-clean quad.

"Sir Mattie," he hailed as he saw her, giving a slight bow. "I trust you've recovered from all the excitement?"

He bent down to see her face.

"Yes, sir."

Mattie looked at the ground, the site of so much conflict. This was going to be hard.

Praeses closed his eyes and breathed deeply. "You wish to leave," he said, his pupils again visible.

"Yes, sir. My mom must be frantic."

Mattie thought her own voice reflected the same emotion.

"Of course. It was not my intent to keep you here forever. You must return to Mundanis."

"Thanks." Mattie forced a tight smile.

"I can't thank you enough for what you've done for us. You've shown exemplary courage, and everyone here loves you. Some perhaps more than others."

Mattie blushed. She pretended not to understand. "The hardest part is saying goodbye to Artorius. Again."

"Nothing is forever. I promise, if Cavernis needs you in future, you will hear from me."

Mattie, now incapable of speech, nodded.

"I will open the Georgian portal when Lumen is at its height. Since the window is short, you must be sure not to miss it."

Mattie nodded again, stepping away from the quad. She knew it was unseemly for a Knight of the Order to cry, but in this case she couldn't help it.

She tramped back to Artorius' cave.

"Well?" he asked, approaching her on all fours. She still couldn't get used to it.

"It's all set. For noon today."

Artorius tried to look happy, but Mattie knew the truth.

"You'll see me off?"

"Think I wouldn't?"

She spent some time getting into her old clothes. As if no time had passed, she was back in her skinny jeans, animal-print top, and thigh-high blue suede boots. What stories those shoes could tell, of cracked glaciers in Jötunheimr, the thick fertile dirt of Georgia. For Quetzalcoatl's sake, they'd hung off a dragon! Good thing they couldn't talk.

Mattie wanted to take something with her—kind of like a souvenir—so she chose Hob's red sleeve. She crammed it into a pocket, then stood before Artorius.

"I guess it's time to go."

He nodded sadly, crouching to let her swing onto his back. His takeoff was powerful, aided by extra limbs, and before Mattie knew it, they were in the air, leaving Cavernis behind. This desolate desert—a land of rocks and caves— seemed more beautiful at that moment than the beach at Malibu.

It didn't take much longer to alight at the Georgian border, where Mattie was amazed to see all her friends! There was Hob, looking large next to Ripley, Sudha and Jimmy on their coils, and, standing apart, Eli.

Sudha broke the sad mood. "So, Mundanis girl is going. She doesn't love us anymore." She feigned a lovely pout.

"It's not that, Sudha. I'll never forget you. But my mom—"

"Of course I am pulling your tail! Cavernis is *our* home, but yours is on Mundanis."

Mattie approached the *nāgī*, hugging her human half. She whispered into her ear. "Sudha, I apologize again. I misjudged you, and that was wrong."

"That's all right, Mattie. Even *I* know I can be a bit of a bitch."

She returned the hug with six arms, giving Mattie a kiss on both cheeks.

"Come back to us," she said.

Mattie, her eyes welling like Mrs. Wyvernis, nodded.

Jimmy slithered over.

"Oh Jimmy! I know you're going to rock as Dr. Lung's go-to guy."

"Thanks, Mattie," he said shyly, and she thought she saw his eyes glisten. "I'll never forget our time together. In S&B. And with Eli."

She gave him a huge hug, feeling his whiskers caress her shoulders.

"Don't start thes blubberin' wi' me," Hob exhorted, folding his small arms. "I wish ye luck, lassie. Ye weren't tay big a pain in mah erse."

"Thanks, Hob."

Mattie leaned down and stuck out a hand. To her absolute amazement, he seized it and bestowed upon it a kiss!

"Naw be aff wi' ye," he said gruffly, turning his back. Mattie saw a tiny cloth make its way to his eyes.

"Girlfriend, it won't be the same without you." Ripley hovered before her. "Thanks for the kickass new name!" She held out a thumb-size claw and Mattie shook it gently.

Then she walked to Artorius. He was pretending to be *very engrossed* in a tree.

"Artorius," she said simply, "you're my best friend, on this world or any other. I know we'll meet again."

"We better," the ex-wyvern answered, his yellow pupils shining.

"You've saved me so many times," she said, throwing her arms around him. "I don't know how I'll ever repay you."

He placed his wings over her, and—for perhaps the last time—she dwelt in her cool blue world.

"Don't forget me," he whispered. "And always be my friend."

She didn't want to let go, but she knew that her time was short.

"*Ignis et Fuga,*" she mumbled into his neck.

"You did us all proud," he said. "You should have been born a dragon."

He lowered his wings and stepped back.

That left only Eli.

"Well."

Eli didn't move, trying to adopt the old air of his Master of Chivalry. He stuck out his right hand.

Mattie shook it, then threw her arms around his neck. She wasn't going to let him be distant—not when she was leaving.

"I guess the two Knights of the Order have to go their separate ways." Eli tried to keep his voice even.

"Yeah. But if there's future danger, Praeses says he's bringing me back."

"Good."

Eli's blue eyes were cryptic as he removed her arms and stepped back.

"Fare thee well, Sir Knight. You fought nobly and hard."

He gave a full bow, then, like Hob, turned his back.

Mattie gazed up at Lumen. The star was floating eastward, ready to attain its apex. Mattie didn't think she could stand there for one more minute.

"Goodbye, my friends," she said, looking at each in turn, and lingering on Artorius. "Believe me when I say you are more precious to me than life."

She ran toward the portal as she saw it distend the air. Again, there was the translucent Cube, the rainbow tail of light. She tumbled over and over, still hating the feeling. Stars flecked the blackness around her as she went completely weightless. Then, she popped out of a small stone wall.

Mattie got up—she hoped casually—from all fours. Hollywood was so weird that no one even noticed. She took a long look back at the carved Chinese dragon. On the movie marquee, something she'd never heard of was playing.

She walked to the Red Line station, relieved to find change in her pocket. Her head swam as she tried to adjust to Mund...*L.A.*, with its heat wafting from the sidewalks, its crowds of jostling tourists amid the blasé locals.

She stepped down to the train, boarding the next one to NoHo. She didn't feel too discouraged by the tired workers around her, the complete disaffection of one person for another.

Not when she was going home!

Chapter Forty-One

Home

Mattie fidgeted on the Orange Line, impatient to get to Burbank. At least this bus was an Express.

She practically leaped down the stairs when she reached her stop. She ran full out until she reached her corner complex and dashed into the elevator.

Finally, she reached her apartment and fumbled with her keys. No magic spells required here.

As she careened through the door, she saw Mom on the couch, looking sad—and next to her was Dad!

"*Mattie!*" Mom yelled, nearly flying off her seat to embrace her. "*Where. Have. You. Been?*"

Mom seemed both angry and happy as she showered Mattie with kisses.

"Mom, you'll never believe it, but I saw my old friend, the dragon!"

"I knew it!" Mom pressed a hand to her forehead. "Don't they have phones on Komodo Island? Or e-mail?"

Mattie thought quickly. "Well, it's pretty primitive..."

"Mattie." Her dad walked to her side, engulfing her in a huge hug.

"We are so glad you're safe. Your mom has been crazed with worry!"

"And you haven't, Steve?" Mom asked. "He even hired a private detective."

"Who turned out to be utterly useless."

Mattie couldn't believe her parents were in the same room! After all the years of conflict, the tears, and hung-up calls.

"So are you two...?" she asked.

"Your dad's been staying here while we searched." Mom seemed almost embarrassed. "I assume you're going back East, Steve?"

"Not unless you want me to," Dad said simply.

From the look that Mom gave him, Mattie had a feeling he'd be West Coast from now on!

She plopped down on the couch, the one with the floral print.

"Mom, Dad, I have *so much* to tell you."

"Never mind that," Mom said sternly. "Have you been eating okay?"

"Oh yes," Mattie laughed. "Filet mignon and rack of lamb. And this crazy strudel called *ludenhosen...*"

"You've missed so much school. We need to talk about your future."

Mom put her hands on hips, looking much like Mattie remembered.

"It's going to be awesome!" she yelled. "I'm going to be a zoologist, and I'm going to compete in crew—as a coxswain! And I want to take up fencing, and also riding again—"

Mom actually smiled, something that Mattie could barely recall.

"Well, this trip did you good. You seem to have a new lease on life."

"Not *seem*, Mom! I do!"

Mattie bounced up and went to her, smothering her with a hug.

"Oh Mom, how I missed you! I'll never be snarky to you again!"

She pulled back and saw Mom arch her eyebrows at Dad. Then Mom threw back her head and *laughed!* It was a glorious sound, almost better than Miss Fang's triangle or the call of Praeses to battle.

Mattie buried herself in Mom's arms as if she were a newborn. Which, in some ways, she was.

Mattie returned to Pico Pico and, like the MAD, had to repeat her prior year. This didn't really bother her since the subjects all seemed new now that she was paying attention.

She didn't hang with Lupe or Lana, and was able to ignore Peter, but *not* David Wang. Shortly after she came back, she saw him in the hall, juggling a few books.

"Hi, David!" she called cheerily. "Still got straight As in everything?"

David cringed, expecting to be made fun of. "Uh, yes."

"Good for you," Mattie told him. "You know, I understand the pressure you're under. I'm sure it isn't easy."

He nodded slowly. "Thanks."

"You're going to make one kickass particle physicist!"

David smiled. "I appreciate the support."

She lifted her hand, and they exchanged a vibrant high five.

"You rock, David!" Mattie crowed, before swinging into her math class.

One morning two months later, Mattie was walking to the bus. She thought she might surprise Mom tonight by making a gourmet omelet.

After a few more steps, she had a strange feeling, like she was being followed. She thought that she heard footfalls behind her, which only sounded when she moved, but stopped whenever she did. Probably some little kids pulling a prank.

Sternly, she wheeled, prepared to deliver a lecture.

She actually stifled a scream as she saw the source of the sounds—there was Artorius, crouched low to the ground, and beside him, a small brown dragon she hadn't seen in quite a while.

"Eli?" she asked, hurling her backpack aside and running forward to greet them.

About The Author

Amy Wolf is an Amazon Kindle Scout winner for her novel *The Misses Brontës' Establishment.* She has published 38 short stories in the SFF press, including *Realms of Fantasy* (2) and *Interzone* (U.K.). She is a graduate of the Clarion West Writer's program and has an honors English degree from The University of London.

She started her career working for the major Hollywood studios, including 20th Century Fox and Warner Bros. and was a Script Reader for MGM & Joe Roth.

One of three natives out of 10 million, Amy was forced from L.A. and now lives in Seattle (where it rains). She has one adult daughter currently terrorizing L.A., 2 horses, 2 dogs, and a bunny.

VISIT OUR WEBSITE
TO SEE ALL OF OUR
HIGH QUALITY BOOKS

Red Empress Publishing

http://www.redempresspublishing.com

Quality trade paperbacks, downloads, audio books, and books in foreign languages in genres such as historical, romance, mystery, and fantasy. Visit the website and bookmark it. We add new titles each month!

CPSIA information can be obtained
at www.ICGtesting.com
Printed in the USA
LVOW13s1600100517
534024LV00010B/922/P

9 780692 874516